There's no rest for the haunted.

If someone had asked Zoey Hawthorne eighteen months ago to describe her life she would have said it couldn't be better. Perfect marriage, booming business, and best of all, her son was alive. Today she's divorced, unemployed, and pissed at the universe for taking her child, a loss that's cracked her soul in half. To date, she's addicted to pain meds and anger, with no intention of turning back.

When Zoey inherits a ranch in rural Colorado from an estranged great uncle, she leaves Chicago behind to self-destruct in peace. But lightning changes her plans. Zoey is struck and left with an extrasensory gift that lets her see one more problem on her hands: vengeful spirits haunting her land. To stop the cycle of death rampant on her property, Zoey must solve a fifty-year-old mass murder while keeping her hot lover from melting her armor. She's tough enough for the task--provided she isn't killed in the process.

Books by Lorelei Buckley

Direct Strike

Published by Kensington Publishing Corporation

Direct Strike

Lorelei Buckley

LYRICAL PRESS
Kensington Publishing Corp.
www.kensingtonbooks.com

Lyrical Press books are published by
Kensington Publishing Corp. 119 West 40th Street New York, NY 10018

All Kensington titles, imprints, and distributed lines are available at special quantity discounts for bulk purchases for sales promotion, premiums, fund-raising, and educational or institutional use.

Special book excerpts or customized printings can also be created to fit specific needs. For details, write or phone the office of the Kensington Special Sales Manager:
Kensington Publishing Corp.
119 West 40th Street
New York, NY 10018
Attn. Special Sales Department. Phone: 1-800-221-2647.

Kensington and the K logo Reg. U.S. Pat. & TM Off.
Lyrical Press and the L logo are trademarks of Kensington Publishing Corp.

First Electronic Edition: June 2012
eISBN-13: 978-1-61650-367-3
eISBN-10: 1-61650-367-X

First Print Edition: MONTH YEAR
ISBN-13: 978-1-61650-851-7
ISBN-10: 1-61650-851-5

Printed in the United States of America

For Tom, and for those who inhabit the hereafter.

Acknowledgements

Thanks to Lyrical Press for getting this story in the hands of readers, with special thanks to Dianne. I'm forever grateful to the incomparable Ralph Merlino for taking the time to discuss the view through a photographer's lens. To my husband, my mother, Sandra LaPointe, Simone Dodds, Terry Kush, Yvonne Hendricks--the novel and the writer are better because of you. And to my compassionate critique partner Debra-Jupe Haney, it's always a pleasure.

Chapter 1

Zoey gasped and sprang upright, her comfortable indifference jeopardized by nightmares. She recalled vividly concession stands doused in halting yellows, Caribbean blues and circus reds, pink cotton candy and the sickening contrails of pure cane sugar.

She remembered the man in overalls, an obese guy who'd held a small white bag stuffed with popcorn. He'd tossed a kernel skyward and caught it in his mouth, and then it happened. Laughter, rickety rides and brave cackles unsparingly mutated into horrified shrills—her son's, his friend's and the muffled howls of two other people who had died that day.

Despite the madness, she'd heard the pings and tings of her camera smashing against pavement. Common with objects, not people. Not children.

The bedroom air thickened with humidity, and rolls of blue fog swelled against the windows, adding an icy hue to the row of pharmaceuticals positioned next to a deer-antler lamp on the nightstand. She'd arrived earlier and had hoped the long drive would exhaust her enough to sleep. Good fortune hated Zoey.

Her new environment exacerbated her confusion. She hadn't chosen the furniture, and the bed was too big.

Her eyes burned. She wiped wetness from her face and wished for amnesia, but the poisonous memory persisted.

From the pits of their souls, the crowd shrieked, forced to watch the tragedy like some kind of karmic punishment for collective wrongdoing or thinking. Hinges squeaked and the innocent teetered between life and death for seven minutes and two seconds.

She'd made a lucrative living as a photographer. When emotionally moved, she'd snap the picture. She'd had an impeccable sense of timing and extraordinary compassion. Her descriptive imagination and unyielding empathy were traitors. Haunted by the tiniest of details, they'd ripped her heart from her chest and ate it.

Helpless, she stood below in a mass of human shockwaves stunned by the creaking Ferris wheel bending and moaning, a destructive robot twisting its rusty wrist.

Her son's healthy flesh grew pale, his eyes bulged and his boyish fingers reached for her to save him, and she couldn't, and her mind wouldn't let go.

She would have murdered the mechanic. She'd almost murdered the machinist. Had the bolt been inserted inside the cart rather than outside, it wouldn't have gotten stuck between the exit door and the wheel, and the swinging cart would have swung back in place instead of overturning, and her son Milo and his friend Yaphet and the elderly couple from Idaho wouldn't have plunged seventy feet to their deaths.

"Stop! Why do I have to go through this?" She massaged her pulsing temples. Before bed she'd taken enough meds to anesthetize a whale. If she increased her dosage, she may not wake up. She'd often thought about the ultimate way to find peace.

Imitating a brush fire, hellish and damaging, the memory continued.

The whites of her son's eyes glowed. He grasped at invisible rope frantically trying to escape. Everything blurred. Not Milo. His fear was palpable. Back and forth the buggy swung, back and forth, back and dumped the bellowing souls like waste.

Milo's arms and legs flailed, thrashing gravity all the way down.

"Enough! I can't take anymore. Do you understand?" She grabbed the bottle of sedatives, distinguishable by height. She tossed two in her mouth and swallowed.

Milo hit a manhole cover. The thud echoed in her head. A nauseating bull's-eye, his lifeless body centered on a sewer lid. Blood outlined his hair and filled the metal grooves.

Zoey wiped tears and took a deep breath.

"Come on," she begged the drugs. "Please. Knock me out."

She hadn't said goodbye to her own child, yet everyone expected her to comfort Yaphet's parents. Didn't happen, and it wouldn't. They'd escaped gruesome imagery. As far as she was concerned, they'd won the lottery.

Milo resided within her being. He drove with her to Colorado and accompanied her when she entered their new home, an inheritance she'd claimed on his behalf. She'd do anything to bring him back. Sometimes she'd pretend he was at school or camp or sleeping at a friend's house. She'd call herself from his phone to see his number. No more radical than curing depression with a smile, tricking the brain into a state of happiness. By believing he was somehow with her, she'd deceive the universe and revive him. Illogical? Maybe not. Thoughts became things. A time existed when airplanes were outrageous, and going to the moon outright insane. She could alter reality, couldn't she?

Unreasonable mental chatter caused bouts of anxiety. She needed to be grounded.

"Where the hell is my phone?"

She scanned the night table, floor, dresser and bed for her cell in vain. Shadows consumed the room. She'd unpacked pictures of Milo but not much else. On the opposite wall, a mounted deer head studied her movements.

"What are you looking at?"

Lightning flashed. Deer eyes glistened. Her heart galloped.

Zoey flung the blankets aside and rolled out of bed. Her feet slammed against the cool hardwood, and she trimmed the furniture, patting for her phone.

Another flash illuminated a photo of Milo feeding squirrels at Lincoln Park Zoo.

His fall replayed in her mind.

"Son of a bitch! Why Milo? Why?"

She banged the stomach of a vase and knocked it to the floor along with pictures of her son. Startled by the clatter, she paused. Objects faded in and out of distinction. In a moment of clarity, she walked toward the rustic armoire. Something hard crunched underfoot. She glanced down. The frame Milo had made for Mother's Day lay snapped in half.

"Shit." She rubbed her forehead with the heel of her hand to relieve the pressure of earning the title for most wicked mother in the universe.

"One thing is all I ask. One damn thing."

She spun and bashed her knuckles on the wood. Her fingers ached. She cradled her hand, exhausted and equally frustrated. Unable to stand, she slipped into the nook between the dresser and armoire. Pressing her back to the plaster, she slid down until her ass hit bottom. A slight sailboat effect made her queasy.

Lightning cut through the darkness, allowing her to see obscure silhouettes. She closed her eyes and tilted her head against solidity, trying to remember Mitch's voice. She spoke to him almost every night, why couldn't she find his voice? Panic whirled in her stomach. She breathed in and out, slowly, inhaling, exhaling, a calming technique she'd learned the one time she had agreed to therapy. Hell with therapy.

She opened her eyes and raised her chin. The deer's neck arched toward the bed across from her cubbyhole.

She slithered up, steadied on her feet, and faced the animal head. "What do you see?"

Zoey stepped backward, closer to the footboard. The hem of her nightgown tickled her thighs, and the underside of her long hair, drenched in perspiration, caused a deep chill.

The deer seemed to gaze at something important.

"Hey, look, this isn't the best of circumstances for either one of us. You're staring. At what?"

Lightning sparked and the trophy's marbled eyes fixated on her cluttered nightstand.

Zoey rushed to the overstocked tabletop. Sidetracked by beautiful amber bottles, she maneuvered around the lamp of bones and grabbed her favorite numbing agents, the oblong pills. She took two and recapped the bottle. And there was the phone, peeking out from under a crumpled road map. Had she remembered to charge it?

Two bars and decent reception. Zoey festively punched the air. She pressed his contact button.

The phone rang.

Lightning flickered, and from somewhere behind the mountains, distant rumbles crept closer.

The phone rang again.

"Zoey?" Mitch's strong voice was akin to the uncurling thunder.

"Who else?"

"I tried calling. You didn't answer."

"I didn't hear the phone ring."

"You couldn't tell me you were leaving?"

"It was a spontaneous decision." She'd almost called him, but decided her choices weren't his business.

"You made it there okay, though, no car trouble?"

"None. Are you amazed?"

"Yes."

"It is possible, Mitch. I will prevail."

"Are you okay?"

"No." She held back tears. "Damn nightmares. I haven't slept in over a year. Three or four hours, tops. I'm exhausted."

"I know. I'm sorry."

"No, I'm sorry. You've gone on as if our son never existed."

"Knock it off, Zoey! You know that's not true."

Zoey squashed the phone to her ear and perched on the edge of the mattress. "I miss him so much."

"I know. Me too," he said, seeming to shed his fatigue. "Why don't you come home?"

"Home? What is that? We're divorced. You walked out on me."

"Living in a shrine got old. It'd be easier for both of us if you stopped lying to yourself. You left me long before I gave you my key, and you took our house with you." He paused. "And the drugs—"

"Prescription drugs."

"Abused prescription drugs. Cymbalta, Zoloft, Valium, Prozac, did I skip anything? I've said it a thousand times. I won't watch you destroy yourself."

"Pussy."

"What are you on?" he asked.

"All kinds of pills, Mitch. They're worthless. I'm still unable to function."

"Come back and get help."

"Help?" She sucked her cheeks inward, attempting to stimulate saliva. "Why are you always trying to fix me? I'm irreparable. I'm mourning. I see Milo die every night. How do you expect me to go on? I can't concentrate. I have no purpose without him. Don't you understand? My son was my world."

"I do understand, and it pisses me off. You were a wife, and a friend, a professional, an artist—you wore many nametags, and you wore them well."

"I would give it all up for him."

"You have, and where has it gotten you?"

"No! I would trade it for him, but I can't, so I'm waiting to see him. He'll return. Watch. What do you do? How do you honor our deceased son?"

"I coddle his doped-up mother on a regular basis."

"I don't need your bullshit, okay? Just listen." She reclined on her pillow. "Remember his eyes?"

"He had my eyes."

"He would have been an exceptional photographer," she said as her skin numbed.

"Sure. He would have been good at whatever he chose to do. You need to stop the drugs, Zoey."

"Why do you keep talking about me? It's about Milo, and right now I want to be here, in Milo's home, on Milo's land."

"Milo never knew that place. You'd be closer to him here. You can visit his gravesite."

"And what, stare at a headstone? He's not there. Remember his mobster impersonations?"

"'Marinara sauce? Who do I need to rough up to get a meatball?'"

"And pirates, he loved pirates." Zoey smiled.

Mitch snickered gently, and again mocked from memory. "'Take out the garbage? Arrgh, sweet merciless heaven.'"

Zoey sniffled. "Merciless heaven. Oh God, so true. He was a smart kid."

"Come back to Chicago. You have friends and family here."

Zoey glanced at the ceiling. "I can't. I belong in his house with him watching over me. I feel him."

"You're not making sense, Zoey. He didn't know your uncle and neither did you. Think. What are you on?"

"I told you, a bunch of stuff. I take whatever will destroy the film playing over and over in my head. Nothing works. I still see him get on that ride, and I still see him fall, and I can't fucking take it anymore."

"We'll find the right medication, but you have to let me help you."

"I don't need help. I need my son alive." She thumbed the Off button and tossed the phone on the floor.

It rang nonstop. She threw a pillow over the noisemaker and scooted higher in bed. She eyed the windows. A chalky mist swirled against the black backdrop of night. It reminded her of a photo shoot she'd had at the dessert factory. Vanilla ice cream and chocolate syrup spiraled in a snail shell design on a black porcelain plate. Milo had gone along and almost ruined a perfect shot with his finger. She should have let him. So many things she would have done better.

A quick crimson hue veiled the bedroom.

She watched the window for signs of another unique outburst and witnessed a spear of blood red lightning.

"Fantastic." She advanced to the glass. The next flash appeared normal. She leaned forward and examined the land. In daylight the miles of woods and mountains overwhelmed her, a fairytale bloated with a hundred shades of green, happy sunshiny sky and a mesmeric frothy river. She related to the night, to its mysteries.

Sparks of light danced on muted boulders. A bush near the driveway had tinier shrubs at its base, transforming the plant into a top hat. Beyond the rocks, a pine tree stood in front of two others, each wider than the next. A grand illusion if captured at the right angle.

Though she had no interest in resuming professional photography, she'd at least consider snapping pictures for fun. She turned for her camera, buried somewhere under a heap of clothes, and noticed her jeans. She bent over and slipped them on, straightened and glanced outside again.

To the left was a hill with a fairly steep drop, but she could see where the ground leveled at the forest's edge. Lightning flashed in shorter increments and revealed a change in the density of darkness near the tree line.

A foraging raccoon? She blinked and refocused. A coyote? A child?

A drug interaction.

She tucked a bothersome hair around her ear, rubbed her filmy eyes and pressed her face to the window. Her heart jammed. A young boy, two or three years old, sat beneath a hut of branches.

"What the…"

He had no shoes and wore tattered clothing. He appeared to be playing with rocks.

Panic surged, and she hit the glass several times. "Baby boy, don't move! I'm coming, hang on!"

Zoey rushed to the doorway, her body zinging with dread and wonder. She staggered down the stairs, passed an empty office nook, managed to miss both sofas, and poured out the front door. Cedar wafted from the deck.

Frigid air iced her arms. She massaged her skin and assessed her whereabouts. Plush forest grew on hills that bled into mountains that vanished in the smoky mist laid by a looming storm. Lightning highlighted her route. She sprinted from the porch onto the crisp lawn and headed downhill toward the woods. Immersed in darkness, she stopped and focused.

Thunder boomed. So did her heart when she spotted the boy. He seemed to be drawing abstract art in the dirt with a stick.

"Don't be scared. I'm coming!" Her long legs carried her speedily across the earth. "Stay there, honey, I'm on my way."

Somehow she'd lost sight of him. She halted. She should've seen him, but didn't.

"Don't run from me, little man. I won't hurt you."

Shivering, Zoey blanketed her arms with her hair and waited for a spear of lightning. When the ground lit, she raced the decline, tripping on a vine that threaded a spongy patch of grass. She plummeted and stopped rolling a few feet from the child.

His eyes were dreadfully sad, and he clutched handfuls of soil.

"I'm here now." She wobbled to her feet.

Slowly she entered his creation of choppy stick writings and tiny mountains of dirt, but he wasn't there. "Where did you go? Don't be afraid, baby boy. I can help you. You'll be safe with me."

Flickering spider veins spread overhead like plant roots, as odd a vision as the toddler in the woods. A crackle jumpstarted her pulse. She faced the forest and its fresh pine-scented breath, and saw the boy within reach.

"You precious little guy, what are you doing out here? It's cold and dark, and you could hurt yourself."

He held his arms up and gently bounced on his butt, urging her to lift him.

Zoey leaned forward and grabbed the baby—grabbed nothing.

"Not possible."

She looked in all directions, certain he couldn't have gone far.

Leaves rustled, and the wind hummed.

"Where are you?" She searched for his drawings and metropolis of dirt, but all proof had vanished with his body.

"No!" She confronted the wooded labyrinth. "I know what I saw! What did you do with him? Where's the kid?"

Lightning flashed incessantly. Zoey squatted and ripped at the shrubs. With scratched and blotchy fingers, she rose and kicked a tree trunk with her bare foot. "What the hell did you do with the boy? Where is he?" She tied her annoying hair in a knot. "You can't just pluck children from earth like dandelions. They're not weeds, goddamnit! Where is he?" She raised a rotted log and pitched it at the child-chomping monster she knew lived Out There.

She stepped on a stone and toppled to the ground.

"Son of a bitch." She lay on her back under evasive lightning and blunt thunder, and when she'd forced the pain from her foot, she stood.

"I know what I saw." She stammered uphill. Breathless, she paused on a spongy patch of grass and briefly eyed the malicious vine that had caused her earlier fall.

Lightning webbed the sky and tinted the blackened land with blinding white.

Zoey tasted metal. She refreshed her teeth with her tongue and saw the scorching red fist that punched her in the shoulder. Dumbfounded, she flew through the air and landed on her backside. Her head pounded, brain-splitting. She gasped at the smoke snaking off her flesh. Right before she went unconscious.

Chapter 2

"Nurse!" Zoey winced. Her right shoulder, wrapped in gauze, burned, and she might as well have chugged a bottle of lava. She massaged her neck and then canopied her delicate eyes from the harsh fluorescents. An IV dangled from her hand.

"Anyone?" She coughed and the rawness of her throat produced a tear. Her organs and bones roasted, and she lay on the nurse's button, terrified of cooking alive.

Botanical wallpaper bordered the room and sparked memories—darkness, trees, a tot in the woods with enormous brown eyes sadder than starvation. Not possible. She recoiled and blamed insomnia and drugs and incompetent medical staff for allowing her to panic.

Voices streamed the hall. One in particular drew closer to the doorway. An elderly male doctor with squinty teal eyes and a bulbous nose entered the room. He smiled and held a clipboard close to his chest.

"Good afternoon," he said, hoarse and crackly with age. "I'm Dr. Selden."

"It's about time. I need something for pain. My shoulder is killing me."

"I hadn't expected you to be so vibrant, but yes, I promise, we'll get to that. I have questions and forms for you to sign before I can administer meds." He approached the bed.

"I have questions too." Zoey clicked a green switch and the bed buzzed while elevating her upper body. "What the hell happened to me?"

"You don't remember?"

"That's why I asked."

A heavyset Asian nurse with shiny black hair, cut to her jawline, rushed in and adjusted the IV drip. "Hello," she said cheerfully. "I'm Nurse Chong. How do you feel?"

"Like shit," Zoey said.

Dr. Selden put his pen to the clipboard. "Describe the pain, is it throbbing, biting, piercing, burning…"

"I hurt all over. Was I beat with a bat? Are you going to tell me what happened?"

"You hurt all over. Can you be more descriptive?" Nurse Chong asked. "We're not mind readers."

"Neither am I," Zoey snapped. "I'm in a hospital, bandaged, and in severe fucking pain and no one will tell me why. I won't cooperate until I get answers." Talking grated her throat and she clutched her neck.

Nurse Chong shook her head. "Have some water." She filled a paper cup and then passed it to Zoey. "Careful. Don't choke."

"I'll do my best." Zoey gritted her teeth. She raised the rim to her lips and sipped. The flame in her esophagus subsided, but the pain in her shoulder drilled clear to the bone.

"Do you know if you're allergic to any medications?" Dr. Selden asked.

"That's a stupid question. Of course I know. I have no allergies whatsoever."

"Nurse Chong," Dr. Selden said, "would you please get our patient 600 milligrams of ibuprofen and Valium, 10 milligrams, to help her relax?"

The nurse rolled the IV post closer to the wall and addressed Zoey. "You're a very lucky person." Her rubber-soled shoes squeaked as she scuttled out of the room.

"What does she mean, lucky?" Zoey set her cup on the side table.

"First the necessities," he said, holding his pen tightly. "Zoey Hawthorne, is that accurate?"

"Yes."

"Birth date?"

"November sixth, 1970."

"Where were you born?"

"Chicago."

"What day is it?"

"Depends on how long I've been asleep. I moved into my uncle's house—"

"The Rayfield Ranch?"

"Yes, on Saturday. Saturday night I saw something in the woods, a large raccoon or stray dog, and today I wake up in a hospital. You tell me, what day is it?"

"Sunday, four o'clock." He scribbled for a few seconds. "Interesting. No memory loss?"

"Not that I'm aware of. But I wouldn't remember what I'd forgotten, would I?"

"I suppose not. Do you remember the accident?"

"What accident?"

"Any other loss of memory?"

"No. Not to my knowledge. I'm divorced. I'm a photographer, or was—I closed my studio last year. And that's none of your business." Her pulse raced. "What fucking accident?"

Dr. Selden retracted his ballpoint and stuck it in his breast pocket. "It appears, Ms. Hawthorne, you've been struck by lightning."

"What?"

"You have all the indications."

"You're shitting me?"

Dr. Selden shrank. "No. I'm not. I apologize for withholding information. Some folks think a lightning strike is the disciplinary action of God. I get the sense you're not one of those people. I didn't want you to feel punished."

"Too late. I've had my universal spanking and it had nothing to do with the elements. How do you know what happened to me, anyway? You weren't there."

"You have Lichtenberg figures on your back. Fern-like patterns pathognomonic of lightning strikes."

"On my back? Why is my shoulder bandaged?"

"Lightning struck your shoulder. You sustained a second-degree burn. We're not sure why Lichtenberg figures develop on other areas of the body, but they're painless and usually fade in a week or so. Factoring in weather conditions and the plum-sized occipital hematoma, I've determined it was a direct strike. Getting hit by lightning is atypical—getting hit directly and surviving is a miracle."

That was poignant enough for her to forgive the furious pain, but then the visions came, quick and streamlined—the blazing punch, soaring above ground, hitting dirt. She flinched.

"What now?" she asked, afraid of doubling up on nightmares.

"Good question." Dr. Selden walked to the window, tugged on a closed blind panel and peeked outside. The aluminum made a tinny noise like the gentle crush of a discarded beer can. "I'm not sure any of us know what to expect." He released the panel and paused, seeming to sort his thoughts. "In my forty years of practice, I've handled three lightning cases." He turned and came to her bedside, his breath smelling of bitter coffee. "I've since learned that makes me an expert."

Zoey rested her left arm on the side rail and listened intensely.

"Of the three cases, two were victims of a secondary discharge, meaning lightning ricocheted off an inanimate object and struck the individuals. Of these two victims, one man suffered immediate cardiopulmonary arrest and died. The other, a friend of a friend, was thrown twenty feet across a golf course. He sustained spinal cord injuries. He's paralyzed."

Zoey's heart stomped. "You said you've seen three cases."

"You're the third. What I'm alluding to is, under the circumstances, you're in incredible condition." He scratched his milky cheek. "Lightning ranges between twenty million and one billion volts. To put that in perspective, a police Taser has two million volts. We'll never know what voltage struck you, and granted we have further tests to run, but it appears Nurse Chong was correct. You're a very lucky woman."

"Forgive me if I don't pop open the champagne. I have a migraine, and I'm pretty certain wee little organisms are roasting marshmallows in my veins. Did Nurse Chong get lost?"

"It's imperative you try to relax. If you want my professional opinion, you're in a fragile state. Unfortunately your injuries could be extensive. Nurse Chong will be here shortly." Dr. Selden extracted his pen, and positioned to write. "So, you're a relative of Amos Rayfield?"

"Great niece."

"I didn't know Amos had family."

"His family didn't know they had an Amos. He and my grandmother were estranged."

"I see." Dr. Selden jotted, and continued, "Amos Rayfield, quintessential loner. Nevertheless, his suicide stunned me. He wasn't the type."

"To what, hang himself?" Zoey said, physically uncomfortable and too sober to discuss death. "Life kicks our asses. Either we fight back or we don't. Maybe Amos had enough bullshit, because frankly, stick a fork in me, you know?"

"As I said, he wasn't the type."

"What makes you so sure?"

Dr. Selden chuckled. "Bogeymen under the bed and monsters in the closet? They were hiding from Amos. I've known a few tough old birds in my time, but Amos was by far the toughest. It's hard to comprehend what could have driven an ornery son-of-a-gun like Amos Rayfield to end his life."

"You're an MD. You've met the Grim Reaper. He's a sneaky prick."

Dr. Selden nodded sorrowfully. "Right you are, Ms. Hawthorne."

"Where am I? I mean this place, the hospital?"

"Monroe Memorial in Telluride."

"How'd I get here?"

"Your neighbor, Kane Ballentine. He stopped by your place on his way home. It was drizzling and your door was wide open. He found you near the woods and brought you to the emergency room."

"Kind of late for an uninvited visitor."

"Yes, well, fortunately for you, Kane keeps inconsistent hours. Not uncommon for a man of his stature. He directs a long list of charity events and has real estate circling the globe." Dr. Selden lowered the clipboard. "You're new in town. He was going to leave a note on your car with his telephone number if you should have needed anything."

"That's what I'd do. Scare the crap out of a woman in the middle of the night. Where is Nurse Chong? My arm is raging."

"She's on her way," Dr. Selden insisted. "Kane Ballentine is third generation in Big Cat Canyon, and a single father to a daughter. I'd bet my savings account he meant you no harm."

"Save your bets for casinos. People can't be trusted."

"When I was a young boy…"

"Say it isn't so, Doc. You're not really going to reminisce while I suffer?"

"Would you consider yourself to be an abrasive person?"

"You wouldn't ask me that if I were a man."

His eyes popped. "I have neither the time nor the inclination to criticize my patients. The question, Ms. Hawthorne, is relevant to the incident. Lightning tends to affect temperament. Survivors are known to be volatile. I'm merely trying to determine the best course of treatment." He exhaled in apparent frustration. "Now, do you consider yourself more abrasive than usual?

"I don't know, maybe."

"Were you always—"

"What, outspoken, honest, gritty? I don't know." She quieted a moment and organized the floating jigsaw in her head. "My body hurts so bad I could vomit. My son died last year in a freak accident, and here I am a little over a year later recovering from a lightning strike. Be honest. What are the odds?"

"One in four hundred thousand."

"One in four hundred thousand. Forgive me, but I'm metaphysically frazzled, and in desperate need of a painkiller. Under the circumstances I am not being difficult."

Dr. Selden smiled. "That has yet to be determined."

Zoey wanted to wring his turkey neck, but wanted something for pain more. Angering the man with the meds could be detrimental to her health. She leaned forward, moved her long hair from the sandwich of mattress and backside, and draped the tangled strands over her gauzed shoulder. "What's next?"

"Paperwork and tests."

"What kind of tests?"

"The standards. Also an MRI, EEG, and I'd like you to have a session with a neuropsychologist. We have to check the anatomic and cognitive functioning of your brain."

"My brain? What's wrong with my brain?" she asked, stifling a screech.

"Hopefully nothing." He scribbled on his pad. "If it's any consolation, I believe you're fine."

Nurse Chong reentered with a cup and a thermometer. Without gentle precaution she swiped Zoey's forehead with the latest in medical technology. "102."

"Are you currently taking medications?" Dr. Selden asked while writing.

"Cymbalta."

"How much?"

"Ten milligrams." That was all she'd admit to.

"And you're sure you have no allergies."

"I'm allergic to pain." She licked her parched lips. "It makes me bitchy."

Nurse Chong handed her a Dixie cup of heaven.

Zoey slanted the Dixie and swallowed the pills, crumpled the cup and dropped it on the floor.

Dr. Selden and Nurse Chong glared like strict librarians. She'd seen the look in the library when her cellphone rang during story time.

"What?" Zoey reached for the cup of water on the bedside table. "I'll pick it up on my way out."

Dr. Selden's pen skidded across the paper. He muttered, "Oxacillin." He ripped a prescription sheet from a smaller pad and passed it to Nurse Chong.

"Yes, doctor." Nurse Chong leveled her shoulders and assimilated into the hectic hallway.

Dr. Selden clicked his ballpoint and put it in his pocket. "Do you have family members you'd like to call, or someone you'd like us to contact?"

Zoey pressed the button and flattened her bed. "Ha! No."

"You're sure?"

"Positive."

"Your decision," he said. "Get some sleep, and I'll check on you before shift change." Dr. Selden turned abruptly and headed into the hall.

Zoey closed her eyes and attempted to ignore various debilitating emotions she'd had for the past year. No matter how hard she'd tried to snuff her thoughts, there'd always be sprigs of memory she couldn't overlook. She wondered why her son couldn't be recuperating in a hospital bed and she resting in peace. Nothing made sense. She wiped an irritating tear. She wanted to sleep but Nurse Chong would rattle her when she returned with the antibiotics.

"How long does it take? She's got her head in her ass again."

Damn Nurse Chong.

* * * *

Zoey awoke less impassioned, her mind and body suspended in an unnatural state of calm. A familiar figure stood nearby. She rubbed the sand from her eyes and spotted the IV buried in her vein. She remembered.

"You've been asleep almost fifteen hours," Dr. Selden said. "How do you feel?"

She felt blank. "Fine, I think." She swallowed. "Did you say I slept fifteen hours?"

"Yes. You've rendered this ward speechless."

She smacked her gummy tongue against the roof of her mouth. "Why?"

"Temperature is normal, heart rate is normal." He tapped his chin with the pen. "And we've changed the dressing on your wound twice. Sunday you had three pea-sized blisters in the center of your burn. As of an hour ago, they're gone."

"My burn healed?"

"Not entirely, you still have a second-degree burn. But typically blisters take much longer to repair. Are you still in pain?"

"I don't know. I can't feel anything but a full bladder."

"I'll call a nurse."

"No." She elevated the bed. "I'm okay." Zoey inched off the mattress and stood, holding the IV post. She waited for her lightheadedness to pass and her legs to stop trembling. Her gown stuck to her back in a paste of sweat, and she pulled the material from her skin before stepping carefully toward the bathroom.

Woman in the water.

"What?" Zoey turned and faced Dr. Selden, who was engrossed in his clipboard writings.

He lifted his head and raised one eyebrow.

"Did you say something about water?"

"I haven't said anything. What did you hear?"

"Nothing." Of course, nothing. She took a step and froze. She'd slept fifteen hours without a nightmare. Was this it, she wondered, when Milo slipped into the recesses of her mind, forcing her to forget? Fear knotted in her chest. She would not forget.

She shuffled to and from the restroom without complications and crawled into bed, wincing when she twisted her bad shoulder.

Dr. Selden leaped forward, prepared for an emergency.

"I'm fine, really." She clamped the covers under her armpits, closed her eyes and willed the spasms gone.

"On a scale of one to ten, one being average and ten excruciating, how bad is the pain?" he asked.

She smiled, thinking if he knew the extent of her internal wreckage he'd realize her wounds were permanent and he'd send her home. "Eight." She turned her head toward him and stared at his squinting face. "I could use another pain pill."

"Sure." He wrote again, his pen and pad seeming like an extra set of appendages. "The nurse will bring more meds in a few minutes. What about your throat?"

"What about it?"

"Does it still hurt?"

"A little, but nothing I can't live with. La-la-la-la-la!"

"Very good," he said.

Woman in the water.

"What did you say?"

Dr. Selden offered a bewildered expression.

"You didn't just mutter something about water?"

He shook his head.

"I distinctly heard someone say something about water."

"Interesting." He paused. "Perhaps you overheard a conversation while you were asleep, and your memory is releasing it now. A type of dream echo."

"There was a discussion about water here in my room?"

"Not necessarily. You'll read about the death in the paper, so I'll go ahead and tell you. I was checking your pulse and Dr. Hicks came by to inform me we'd lost a patient. A teenage boy who'd broke his neck in the river that runs behind your house. I'm sure one of us mentioned water during the discussion."

"What was the boy doing in the river?"

"Rafting. Rafts and kayaks navigate that river all summer long. I've kayaked Coldstone many times myself. Hell of a ride. Fifteen-foot drops and sharp undercuts, definitely an adventure. Magnificent scenery too. Unfortunately, in the past few months there've been a rash of accidents and two deaths."

"The Grim Reaper never rests," she uttered. "I'm sure you're right—about the water—about your conversation carrying over."

"Hmm."

"Can I share something personal with you?" she asked.

"Why, yes."

"I haven't had a single nightmare since I've been here."

"Come again?"

"I've relived my son's death every night for over a year. Never fails. I dream it, but it's less like a dream and more like a skipping moment in time. It's damaged me, pretty much destroyed my life. And now, nothing. I'm not sure how I feel about it. To be honest it kind of fucking terrifies me. What if I forget him? And what am I supposed to do with my nights now, sleep? I don't know if I can do that guilt-free."

"I'm not sure I'm the right ears. In my line of business, we bid farewell to a patient and just as we grab a handkerchief, we're rejuvenated by a newborn. Ready or not, life goes on."

"Wow. You're not even a tiny bit helpful."

"I'll refer you to a competent psychiatrist. He's not far—"

"No thank you. I don't need a goddamn shrink, I need another Valium, or something stronger. That'd be nice."

"Funny thing about what we think we need. My second year of college…"

"I'm not an audience member, Dr. Selden. I'm a patient. Patients need meds."

"You're positive you aren't feeling abnormally short-fused or hot-tempered?"

"Yes, I probably am. I'm dealing with another inept nurse. This isn't a hospital, it's a joke. That's what it is, and she is, and you are, a motherfucking joke!"

Dr. Selden's pen danced swiftly across the pad.

"What are you writing?"

"I'm diagnosing you with volatility attributable to the lightning strike."

"You have no idea what you're talking about. I'm not volatile, and if I were, psychology isn't your area of expertise."

"Make no mistake, doctor, she's volatile," a man with a deep voice bellowed from just outside the doorframe. "Only it has nothing to do with lightning. She was mean before she got struck." He entered the room. "Ever since our son died."

Chapter 3

Her heart drummed. "What are you doing here?"

"Nice to see you too, love." Mitch approached the bed, his thick chocolate hair and rich dark eyes a jolting carbon copy of Milo. "I couldn't get a hold of you. Finally called local hospitals and sure enough. Do you know how worried I've been?" He wore the denim jacket Zoey had bought him two years ago. The Coolest Dad patch Milo ironed on the shoulder cut through her sternum like the teeth of a bread knife.

"Sorry to scare you, snookums. For your sake, let's hope lightning doesn't strike twice."

"Okay. How're you feeling?"

"Like shit. I'm sore and my shoulder's on fire, but I think I'll live." She caught herself staring at Mitch. His tall, square frame hooked her every time. In the sixteen years she'd known him, his steady voice and arresting presence hadn't waned. "Dr. Selden, this is my ex-husband, Mitch Hawthorne."

Mitch and Dr. Selden clasped palms and shook.

"How is she?" Mitch asked.

Dr. Selden eyed Zoey in a silent request for authorization to share data.

"You can tell Mitch anything. We're divorced, but he's still my anchor."

Mitch placed his hand on her forehead. "She's logical. This must be serious."

"Get away from me." She distanced her head from his touch. "What if I were dying? I could have, you know, I came close. And not two seconds ago, I told you my shoulder burns. How about some sympathy or a foot massage?"

"You want me to crack your toes, I will." He took a step back. "But your eyes are translucent green. Not a hint of brown. You're fine."

Unless someone had a mirror handy, the fact that her eyes darkened when she experienced severe pain never mattered. Her dad had noticed when she broke her foot as a girl. Mitch had noticed too when she went into labor. Her mood eyes were useless trivia no one else in the world cared about.

Mitch addressed Dr. Selden. "Sorry, doctor. Her condition?"

Dr. Selden glanced at Zoey and returned his attention to Mitch. "We have several tests before I can make an accurate diagnosis, but based on my observations, she's doing rather well."

"And volatility?"

"Common with lightning strike victims. Second-degree burn on her right shoulder and a bit hotheaded, not bad considering the numerous problems often associated with lightning victims. This includes death. I must admit, she has us all baffled."

Mitch gazed into Zoey's pupils. "It's the pills. You're like a wino falling down a flight of stairs and walking away without a scratch."

"Fuck you, Mitch. They help me and you know it. This has nothing to do with pills."

Mitch faced Dr. Selden. "She's had a difficult time dealing with our son's death. Five physicians later, she has more drugs than a pharmacy. I've been trying to convince her to cut back. As you can see, it's her Achilles' heel."

Zoey's cheeks heated. "No, you are. My supposed bad habits, my injuries, my eye color—not your business."

"It's my business when you've had a nightmare or too much liquor. It's my business when you take off and leave me to watch a house, a shrine like, what, it's gonna get ransacked? No one, not even a looter, can stomach the place. It's twisted and I don't agree with your methods of mourning and still, here I am, making sure you're okay."

"Go home, Mitch."

"Not until—"

"What? You suck the last bit of energy from me? You're a heartless vampire."

"You call me every night, sappy as a soap opera, and I'm the vampire? And don't get me started on whose chest is hollow."

"You're a jerk."

"Takes one to know one."

"Mr. Hawthorne." Dr. Selden raised his voice. "I'll have to ask you to leave. My patient needs to remain calm."

As much as she hissed and spit and snapped, she had no bite. The sudden shift in routine made her shaky and insecure. Tangled emotions made them childlike. But Mitch had tremendous strength, enough for both of them.

"It's okay," she said. "We can be puerile, since, well, it doesn't matter. I'd like him to stay. You said you don't know what to expect. I'm here in town by myself. I might need help."

"You need help all right," Mitch mumbled.

Dr. Selden shook his head. "Very well. However, I'm your physician, and I recommend rest. It's crucial. Stress harms healthy individuals, and you, Ms. Hawthorne, are in Monroe Memorial attached to an IV. You can put on the gloves when you're discharged and not before. If you're dissatisfied with my bedside manner or my advice, feel free to request another doctor. I warn you. If you choose to remain under my care you must be compliant. Is that clear?"

Zoey nodded.

A skeletal nurse breezed in the room with a nametag reading Leinfelder. She had a helmet of tight auburn curls and transparent skin. Blue veins bulged, and her uniform released a pungent mix of antiseptic and ashtray. Zoey breathed through her mouth.

Nurse Leinfelder handed two cups to Zoey. "Bet you could use these."

Zoey smiled, grateful for the pain pill and large swallow of water. She crinkled the cups. Testing her aim, she raised her healthy arm to throw one at a picture of a barn on the wall.

Nurse Leinfelder wiggled her fingers. "Give 'em here. I shouldn't have to tell you this is a hospital, not a Dumpster."

"What's with you people?" Zoey set the garbage in Nurse Leinfelder's hungry palm. "I'm not spitting or punching or dirtying bedpans. I'm bored. What am I supposed to do?"

"This is our lightning patient," Dr. Selden said, as if pardoning Zoey.

"I can appreciate the discomfort of being cooped up," Nurse Leinfelder reasoned, "and I've researched the hostile nature of lightning strike victims, but there's never a good excuse to be a litterbug. Remember that, dear." She tossed the cups in the corner garbage can. "Watch game shows or read a book like everybody else." The nurse rushed out in the same breezy way she'd entered.

Dr. Selden released a soft chuckle. "She's trying to quit smoking."

"Give me a break," Zoey said. "She's a nurse. She's supposed to be pleasant."

Dr. Selden walked toward the door. "And we make the mistake of thinking patients are supposed to be grateful."

She scratched the bridge of her nose with her middle finger. "Kind of difficult when we're overcharged and undertreated."

"You're scheduled for an MRI first thing in the morning," Dr. Selden said. "Nice meeting you, Mr. Hawthorne. I'm sure we'll speak again. Meanwhile, I have other patients I must undertreat. Get some sleep." He left.

Mitch sat on the edge of the bed next to her thighs. "You feel like crap, and your shoulder hurts. What else? What's going on inside?"

"I don't want to talk about it."

"Okay, the night you were struck, what happened?"

"You pissed me off."

"What's new? You hung up on me. Normally you answer when I call back."

"I went outside."

"At three in the morning?"

She hesitated, but the meds simplified honesty. Gradually she recalled the events. "I saw a red lightning bolt. It was blood red like a gaping wound in the sky. I wanted to take pictures."

"Really?" he asked. "So you cleaned your camera and took some photos?"

"No," she whispered. "Get ready to celebrate."

Mitch furrowed his brows.

"I had a drug-induced hallucination. I saw a little boy in the woods and ran out to save him."

"Why do you think that makes me happy?"

"You're always on me about quitting my meds. Now you have a concrete case."

He squeezed her IV-free hand. "I don't want to prove you have a drug problem, Zoey. I want you to get healthy."

Woman in the water.

"Shit." She flinched.

"What's wrong?"

"I keep hearing something about water." She clutched the fading words. "Woman, yeah, woman in the water."

"Side effect?"

"I don't know." Her eyelids were heavy. "Dr. Selden said while I slept I'd overheard a conversation he had with another MD about a kid who died while whitewater rafting behind my house. Supposedly I'm remembering bits and pieces. A dream echo."

Mitch slouched. He stared at her, not with the anger of an inconvenienced ex, but as a brokenhearted man hammered by circumstances beyond his control.

Her body weakened by the minute. She wanted to break the wall between them before she fell asleep. "There's been one major change."

"What's that?"

"I nodded out for fifteen hours and didn't have a nightmare."

Mitch straightened. "That's great, Zoey."

"Is it?"

"I don't understand," he said. "I thought the nightmares were the root of your troubles."

"No matter how toxic they were, I could count on them. They filled space. The nightmares have stopped, sure, but they've left a void. Something has to replace the dreams. I'm scared of what it will be."

Mitch smiled and released her hand. He stood and inhaled deeply and then let the air go. "I'll tell you what it'll be. No more nightmares plus sound sleep equals clear thoughts. You'll get on with your life, maybe open another studio, maybe do some traveling and freelance. We'll sort through the house, and put it on the market when you're ready. You have a chance to move forward. We'll take it one day at a time."

"Gung ho, clean the house and pick up my camera, wonderful. That hasn't been me since I lost my son."

"I lost my son too, and right after my son died, my wife vanished. The person I depended on. I've fought hard and steadfast for some sense of normalcy. You know how I finally found it?"

"Do tell."

"I remembered our son's personality, his common sense sharper than yours and mine combined. He wouldn't want us to be miserable. The pain never goes away, Zoey, but out of respect for Milo and his premature death, I look to the future. I make an effort to acknowledge the life I'm fortunate enough to live."

Tears brimmed Zoey's eyes. She blinked and wetness streamed down her neck.

"It's time. Trust me."

"I know you mean well, but don't push too hard, okay? I'm not you. I'm not ready."

"When you are, I'll be here."

"I know." It occurred to her how quickly Mitch had shown up. "Out of curiosity, what made you call hospitals?"

"Sterling had a hunch. She does that sometimes. She's usually right on."

"Sterling, of course. She's good to you, isn't she?"

"She is. Speaking of Sterling, I'm going to grab a cup of coffee and give her a call."

"Tell her I'm sorry to put her through this. I wasn't going to contact you."

"Eventually you would've, and that's fine. You didn't get injured on purpose. Besides, she's coming here. We're going to hang out for a week and take in the sights. This way we can watch you."

"What?"

"Calm down, just until you're fully recovered. No one seems to know what to anticipate with lightning. Better safe, don't you think?"

"Whatever. I really don't care where the two of you vacation. But please understand I'm not a child. I don't need you to babysit me. Go make your call. I'm tired." She shut her eyes and listened for the room to empty.

Irritation festered, but why? Mitch should be with someone willing to replenish his heart. She wasn't capable. She could barely look at him without missing Milo immeasurably. However strong their bond, they couldn't reunite without their son. The third Stooge. Why then, she wondered, even beneath a tarp of pain pills, did the name Sterling Fisk rub like steel wool? It shouldn't. Sterling was silly, calling her cat Silver and posting her flawless face on billboards.

Vain.

Bold.

Brave marketing strategy initiated by a pretty realtor. Sterling had a phony streak, but she also had spunk. She had helped Mitch sell a brownstone he'd renovated near the Steppenwolf Theatre for a staggering amount of money.

Too sluggish to go on, Zoey reconciled. Mitch the rehab genius and Sterling the trendy realtor, what a team—had to be fate, or that fucking karma.

* * * *

An entire week without a single nightmare proved a greater burden than daily blood tests, both MRIs and the unattractive electrodes squirming from her scalp like oozing brain tissue. They'd found nothing—no abnormalities or damage. The annoying dream echo finally stopped too. She should've been thrilled but instead battled a new monster, a dishonest peace. Under the calm lay a starving black hole. She felt it. An indefinable magnetic void.

She also gained a nickname: The Bride, as in *Bride of Frankenstein.*

She stood in the bathroom and angled the cabinet mirror toward the room to view Mitch. He packed a duffle bag with the clothes he'd brought her five days earlier.

"You're a true survivor," he said. "And I want you to take however long you need to recover. Your new house is damn impressive. Mountains and forest, and I took a stroll down the hill by the water. It's beautiful, Zoey. Rejuvenating. Maybe I'm wrong about Chicago. This might be the best place for you."

"I need a Q-tip," she yelled from the bathroom.

"What, why?"

"I thought I heard you say you were wrong."

"Yeah, yeah, yeah," he muttered.

Half-dressed, Zoey rubbed salve on her tender shoulder. Mitch and Dr. Selden agreed the wound looked like a star. She saw a butchered flower. She grabbed the gauze, and Mitch walked up behind her. He draped her long hair over her healthy side, his body heat persuasive and his breath loose feathers cascading along her collarbone.

She gave him the rolled bandaging. He gently wrapped gauze around her scar. His dark, depthless eyes studied her reflection. His masculine fingers tickled her skin, and because her hair only covered one breast, he'd see her nipple hardening on the other.

Affected by his intensity, she broke from his stare only to freeze on a patch of hair peeking out of his shirt. She remembered its softness. She hadn't made love since Milo passed, and susceptible body parts stirred. Unprepared for the influx of sensations and rebelling against an emotional tie, she said, "I have a riddle for you."

"Shoot."

"What does a single woman in Big Cat Canyon do for fun?"

"I give. What?"

"Whatever she wants."

Mitch finished and stepped backward. "Am I missing something?"

"Just remember I'm single now. I may have an itch I need to scratch."

"What are you trying to say?"

"I'm not talking in code. I've said what I wanted to say."

He left the bathroom and reentered with her bra.

"I can't wear that." She cocked her head toward her gauzed shoulder.

He walked out and returned with a blue cotton T-shirt. She faced him and held her arms forward. He stretched the sleeve holes and slid the shirt up her limbs, conscientious of her impaired mobility.

"Why do you hate me?" he asked while pulling the neckline over her head.

"You're the only person I don't hate. I'm in pain and cranky. I could use—"

Mitch handed her an ibuprofen and a Valium. "A nurse stopped by while you were in the shower."

"Withholding?" She swiped the pills and swallowed. "It's you who hates me."

"That's a crock." He combed and ponytailed her hair. "What do you say, Goldilocks, can we go now?"

"Yes."

In the hall halfway down the corridor, Dr. Selden stood next to the discharge desk, appearing less overpaid and more overtired. He sifted papers and chatted with a receptionist who'd spotted Zoey and mouthed, "The Bride."

Dr. Selden turned and smiled.

Zoey blurted, "A week in purgatory. At last, I'm out of here."

Dr. Selden's teal eyes gleamed. "You've restored my faith in homeostasis. The body is certainly a wondrous machine." He inspected her briefly from toes to crown. "You look radiant, ready to conquer."

Zoey wasn't interested in Dr. Selden's warmth. Memories of her son superseded the pain meds melting in her bloodstream. She'd bury herself alive to see Milo standing in the hall next to Mitch.

"Was it something I said?" Dr. Selden's squint tightened.

Mitch rubbed her back.

"No," she said. "I have flashes of my kid, and it screws with my head. A glass of wine usually helps."

"Sorry to hear that," Dr. Selden said, "but alcohol will negate the antibiotics. Your shoulder is still healing. And I'm sure you're aware pain pills and drinking aren't a safe combination. Please don't attempt to drive. Last year in April…" He droned on about a collision involving a discharged patient and an eighteen-wheeler.

Her gaze floated beyond Dr. Selden and landed on the bed of a vacant room.

Woman in the water.

The voice came from inside the room. Zoey stepped around Dr. Selden and Mitch and walked to the doorway.

Woman in the water.

Similar to the night in the woods, she noticed a change in the air's texture. Not everywhere, just a spot on the bed. A zillion tiny sheer circles meshed together and formed a lozenge shape the size of a carry-on suitcase.

Do you hear me?

"Yes," she said.

Woman in the water.

"What woman?"

Woman in the water.

"Please, explain yourself. Who are you?"

The cluster disappeared.

She blinked several times, trying to recapture the anomaly. "What woman?"

"Zoey?" Mitch said. "I could have sworn I heard you talking to yourself."

"Yeah, that was me." She laughed through her nose, making light of her mutterings. "I've got a lot on my mind. I'm trying to get it all straight."

She wondered if her hallucinations were a budding sensitivity to the drugs she counted on. Zoey turned quickly toward the hall and bumped into Dr. Selden. "Why do I feel ambushed?"

Dr. Selden offered two business cards. "I want you to have these. They're reputable therapists."

Zoey took the cards and observed each. "Shrinks? Are you kidding? I don't need these." She pushed them back at Dr. Selden. "I'm not crazy."

"Dr. Jillian Esposito has a PhD in psychology, and Dr. Douglas Doyle is a respected psychiatrist," he said, impervious to her rejection. "They're located right outside of Big Cat."

"Why are you so insistent? I'm not a nutjob."

"No," Dr. Selden said. "You're mourning. And when and if you're ready to restore your spirit, these people can help."

Mitch swiped the cards from Zoey. "I'll take them." He crossed his arms and leaned against the wall. "Might be worth looking into."

She silently reassured herself no one could force her to do anything. Her life, her disorder, her decision on how to cope.

"This room," she addressed Dr. Selden. "Who occupied it?"

"How strange," he said. "Remember the teen I spoke of who died rafting?"

Zoey nodded.

"He was here." Selden paused. "For a few hours."

"Did a female bring him in?"

"Yes, his mother. Why?"

"That damn dream echo again. You and Dr. Hicks must have discussed a woman because that's what I heard."

"Yes," he said. "She oared about ten feet away and saw his raft capsize. She tried to save him, but the undercurrent was too powerful."

Zoey couldn't seem to get enough oxygen and sidestepped farther into the hall. "We need to hit the road, Mitch. The Valium has me loopy. I have to lie down."

"Yep, let's go," Mitch said and shook Dr. Selden's hand. "Thank you for everything."

Dr. Selden smiled with special interest in Zoey. "I'll see you in a month at the clinic for your follow-up. It's all there in the bag with your prescriptions."

"Oh, goody." Zoey elbowed Mitch. "More needles and egotistical staff."

Mitch shook his head.

"Stay as long as you like," Zoey said to her courteous ex, "but I'm getting the hell out of here." She began walking backward to watch and further annoy Mitch. "See the cloud around my feet? That's smoke."

Mitch shrugged apologetically at Dr. Selden and headed with Zoey to the elevator. "Rude, that's what you are, plain and simple. You need to take a refresher course in etiquette."

"Lighten up, Mitch. You think I'm the first bitchy patient he's dealt with?"

Mitch shook his head. "You're out of control."

The door dinged open. She and Mitch stepped into the cubicle.

Two women descended with them to the lobby, a twentysomething picture-perfect black woman whose divine proportions could have earned her time in Zoey's studio and a sickly elderly woman with hopeless eyes and wispy spiderweb hair. They gabbed as if they were alone.

"She saw my turn signal and darted in front of me," the flawless woman said. "She stole my parking spot and, let me tell you, if I didn't have my nephew in the car, I would have got in her face. I would have demanded she find some other place to park her clunker."

The elderly lady snickered, showing a tiny devil's streak. "You should have. Everyone does whatever it is they want to do with no regard for their fellow man or nature or anything. People are impolite and narcissistic."

Mitch eyed Zoey as if labeling her with that description.

Zoey scratched her earlobe with her middle finger.

The old woman continued, "Last time I saw someone parked in the handicapped zone without a handicap sticker, I dumped my apple juice on their windshield."

"You did not."

"I sure did, and I'd do it again. My ankles hurt so bad that day I could have cried, and because of an illegally parked Volvo, I had to walk a quarter of a mile. Almost didn't make it."

"I don't blame you."

Zoey's pill helped her escape pointless chatter and relax somewhere semioblivious.

And then the one voice she couldn't tune out said, "I had the landline at the house connected."

"Why?"

"You never charge your cellphone. Now you don't have to worry about it."

"No, now *you* don't have to worry."

"And I stocked the house with groceries and some cough syrup in case your throat hurts. Dr. Selden said he wasn't sure if the scratchiness healed or went into remission."

"Thanks," she said.

"Picked up a box of cereal too. Corn flakes, right?"

Zoey nodded. The last breakfast she and Milo had together. Mitch was clueless.

Her and Milo's last morning together. Milo told jokes. Something about a frayed knot made him laugh so heartily, milk dribbled from his nose. Zoey reached for her camera. Milo grasped the state of his vulnerability and laughed harder, an infectious giggle she couldn't deflect.

No pill, no liquor, no environment stopped the wrenching pain in her chest. Her stomach gurgled, and her mind chanted one of many self-loathing beliefs: *wasting space, nothing more to offer. Why bother?*

The elevator doors opened, and she rushed into a corridor made sullen by dark wooden panels and portraits of scouring old men. Buttery sunlight splashed through giant windows and spotlighted the exit. She walked next to Mitch, who most likely wanted to get her home and tuck her in—keep her safe. His concern upset her because he was destined to be disappointed. She erased his expectations from her psyche. She had a plan. Maybe not tonight, or tomorrow night, but some night soon she'd sit naked in the wild, count stars and get drunk enough to eat a bottle of sedatives. She didn't belong in Colorado. She belonged with her son.

Chapter 4

Mitch had rented a Ford SUV. Zoey sat in the passenger's seat, shoeless, with her feet propped on the dashboard. She gazed out the window. In Chicago nature whispered; in Colorado it screamed, operatic and mesmerizing. She examined the anatomy of Telluride, the San Juan Mountains ribcages to the vital heart, the town pumping revenue throughout.

"Coldstone," Mitch said as they drove a modest concrete bridge over water. "Same river that runs behind your house."

"A vein."

"What?"

"Nothing." Zoey scratched off a dot of dried ketchup from the door panel. She'd rather scrape leftovers from previous passengers than risk slipping into a meaningful conversation with her ex. She didn't want to hurt him.

"Fifteen miles of boulder strewn adventure."

"River jargon?"

"Whitewater rafting," he said. "I'm going to be vacationing here, remember? I'm looking for things to do."

"Didn't you hear Dr. Selden? It's not safe. A child drowned recently."

"I know, a teenage boy. There've probably been countless deaths in that vein. We can't shut down. Life has to go on for the living."

"You get an F for subtlety."

"It wasn't a dig, Zoey." Mitch stared out the windshield, concentrating on something personal. From nowhere he said, "How's it feel to be rich?"

"I couldn't tell you. I have yet to partake in frivolous spending." Thinking about the money twisted her stomach. Everything had happened so fast. Milo's death, the call about an uncle she'd never met hanging himself, the transfer of funds—the timing—like some kind of cash compensation for the loss of her son. A sick joke.

"How much did you inherit, exactly?"

"You were there. You know how much."

"I want to hear you say it."

"Why?"

"Because you've acted as if you've inherited a bag of rusted pots and pans."

"Six million."

"Wow."

"Money wasn't a problem before Amos. I did fine. We did fine."

"We also budgeted and saved. If you invest wisely, you'll never have to worry about bills again. That's huge. Most people would cut off a toe for that luxury."

"Am I supposed to feel guilty?"

"No, but you will and you shouldn't. It's exciting. You've always wanted to put a book of images together. A coffee table hardback. Now you can." The book idea had died with her son. That person, the woman with dreams and hopes, was a sensitive topic. She intentionally switched subjects. "Do you need money? Is that what this is about?"

"No, I don't need your damn money." He shook his head. "I'd hoped there'd be a dollar amount that would make you human again, but if lightning couldn't do it…"

"Eat my ass!"

"Calm down." He glanced at her from the corner of his eye. "You got a chill pill in any of those bottles on your nightstand?"

"I don't know, do I?"

"I didn't go near your drugs." He paused. "Okay, I did, to read the labels. You're taking diuretics?"

"I am?"

"You're not. I had to prove a point."

"What do you know? I'm sitting next to a flea." She didn't give a shit if she took the wrong pills, but he wouldn't understand.

Mitch laughed emphasizing the elongated dimple carved in his right cheek, a trait Zoey always found masculine and sexy. Slightly stimulated, she turned away.

Fluffy clouds thinned across a powder blue palette, and at ground level in the side mirror, Telluride minimized. She leaned her head back and closed her eyes, enraptured by darkness.

"Your hero," Mitch said, apparently unaware she'd been sleeping.

She jerked awake and followed his finger. He pointed to an Austin stone mansion with iron gates and a freshly paved driveway.

"Kane Ballentine," he said, "the neighbor who brought you to the hospital. That's his house."

"You met him?"

"He came to visit while you were getting an MRI. He wanted to make sure you were all right."

"How thoughtful."

"It's because of him you're alive."

"Yippee. I'm thrilled. Stuck on this dingy planet and I have him to thank. Joy."

"You're warped. Where was I? He said if you needed anything not to hesitate to ask." Mitch tapped the wheel with his thumb. "He wore a Rolex. Seemed like a nice guy."

"Who the hell cares?"

"I do. Contrary to your illusions of independence, you've taken full advantage of our closeness. You've called every other day, lawn mower broke, can't find your house key, too buzzed to drive, and I've been there for you. But that's about to change. You're out here in the middle of bumfuck by yourself and, sorry to sound fatherly, but I'm glad your neighbor isn't a prick."

"The neighbor you barely know is a nice guy, and I'm warped. That's it, I'm buying a Rolex."

"While you're at it, buy a new camera and take some pictures. It relaxes you."

"I am relaxed."

"No you're not."

"I am. Pain pills, babe."

"Not the same, you're masking—"

"Let's not go there. You don't know what you're talking about, Mitch. You have your job and girlfriend and a life, and I have memories of a job, a man and a life. It sucks and I don't know how to change it, but I know without a doubt that I don't want to be pushed, bullied or manipulated into giving up the only thing getting me through the day."

"And you don't see a problem with that?"

She angled her head, moving her ponytail in front of her injured shoulder. "Of course I do, but it's where I'm at. I don't want to hear another negative comment about my bad habit. I'm not stupid. I rely on my pills too much. I know this. And when I'm ready to deal with it, you'll be the first to know."

"I worry about you."

"I know. Don't. I'll be fine."

Mitch drove up the sandy maroon road toward her house. He swung a left, parked in front of the closed garage and turned off the motor. He gazed at her face. "Have I told you today how beautiful you are?"

"No. And don't bother. I'm listening, though."

"You do, you look great. A little starved, but great."

"Starved?"

"You're too skinny. Eat something."

"You can drop a note in the suggestion box on your way out." She tore at a split fingernail.

"Now, if you were a rabbit," Mitch cocked his head at both clustered and scattered vegetation on the hilltops. "You'd have plenty to eat. Bergamot, wallflowers, wheatgrass, juniper." He smiled. "Why don't you let me pick you a salad?"

Zoey put on her shoes.

"Hey," Mitch said. "Scenic atmosphere for a photographer."

"Isn't it?" she said, relieved he'd stopped talking to her as if she were a hungry five-year-old. Her shoulder throbbed. She used her left arm to exit the vehicle. She ignored the pulse under her bandage and viewed the immense landscape. Layers of greens—emerald, lime, moss—slathered over uneven terrain gave the property incredible dimension. She couldn't see her neighbors. According to assessment records, each home had a minimum of ten acres. As much as she'd adored the city, the seclusion appealed to her dour side.

Mitch hopped out from the driver's seat and slammed the door. With the duffle bag slung around his shoulder, he said, "You can sit on the deck with a cup of tea and watch the meanderings of nature."

"Ooh, fun."

"Consider it a healthier sedative. And the house," he went on, eyeing the two-story home. "Not too shabby."

The second level was constructed of white cedar, which sat atop a base of ash brown, beige and white checkerboard bricks. Three rooftop peaks mirrored mountain tips, and scores of windows funneled natural light into every room. Not that it mattered anymore, but low electric bills came to mind.

"Oh," she said, shifting to reality, "there's a trunk in the garage. Would you bring it in some time before you leave?"

"Where is it?"

"In the bed of Amos's truck."

"What's in it?"

"I don't know. Like the truck, it came with the house. It's locked."

"A locked trunk left behind by an uncle who did himself in. Proceed with caution."

"Why?"

"Ask Pandora."

"Do you have a fucking Off button?"

Mitch bypassed the dining room entrance on the left and made his way to the cedar deck. He climbed the single stair and peered out toward the woods. "Hey, Pottymouth, where did Dr. Frankenstein resurrect you?"

She joined her ex and gazed at the grassy slope and dark forest. Minor slivers of levity were shrouded by the memory of chasing a devastating illusion, and then the fiery fist. Her stomach coiled.

"You can't see it from here," she said. "And I don't remember exactly, but I think I was ten or so feet up the hill from the tree line."

"Unbelievable," he said, scratching his chin. "I know where not to stand when it's raining."

"Tell me about it."

Mitch dug out her keys and opened the door. "Finally, home sweet home." He tossed her bag on the floor.

"Doesn't feel homey."

"A few coats of paint will warm it up."

"Maybe," she said, observing the interior she barely remembered.

Two camel-colored leather sofas faced each other, with a coffee table in between. To the left, a potbelly fireplace, dining table, kitchen counter. From where she stood, she could see the entire space. Strangely, she felt the house could see her too. The ogling deer heads, possibly, or all the windows.

"It's too open. I feel like I'm in a fucking snow globe."

Mitch chuckled. "You liked my loft."

"Your loft is half this size."

"Sell this place and come back to Chicago," he said in a salesman's tone, as if the city could cure anything.

"No. I just got here. You said this might be good for me."

"You hate it."

"Hate's a strong word." Zoey scanned the high ceilings and suddenly found it easier to breathe. "It'll take some getting used to, that's all."

Mitch met her eyes. "Okay, how can I help you acclimate?"

"Get rid of the dead animals."

"Huh?"

"The trophies." She pointed to the mounted heads. "They're gross, and they give me the creeps."

"You had to hurt their feelings, didn't you?"

"Stop it." Spending time with her ex felt better than she cared to admit. In order to break the spell, she stared at the floor.

"Where should I put them?"

She'd always been attracted to his voice. That hadn't changed. She raised her head and watched him unbutton his cuffs. "I don't care. Anywhere, as long as they're out of the house."

Mitch rolled up his sleeves. "Done. Anything else?" His deep browns swirled like hot fudge, and she wanted to swim in them.

"Stay for coffee?"

"Sure."

"I take it you know where to find everything?"

He nodded.

"I'm going up to change. Make yourself comfortable."

She ascended the stairs, thinking about their past—lazy Sunday cookouts, dirt fights in the garden, bicycle rides along Lake Michigan. She tried to discount the memories, but warmness filled her heart, forcing her to acknowledge once, not too long ago, she and Mitch had had something authentic.

She'd met Mitch during a photo shoot in Utah. He had just gutted a neighborhood of deteriorated buildings and turned a huge profit. At the time she'd worked for Curtis Greer, a journalist with a moral bone to pick. Environmentalists claimed Mitch Hawthorne planned to bulldoze a corner of the forest and erect a small shopping center. Curtis chomped at the bit to get the story, but Mitch would neither admit nor deny the accusation.

Curtis headed his article, "Ain't Mitch a Bitch!"

While Curtis conducted the interview, Zoey watched Mitch through the viewfinder. His smile was radiant and sincere, and his eyes were mindful, too mindful for money to be his motivation. Curtis grilled Mitch for a week, allowing Zoey to snap enough headshots to read Mr. Hawthorne's deceiving personality. He withheld information. Based on her interpretation of his shimmering eyes, he had surprises planned.

She'd finally confronted him. "You're not a jerk," she said. "But what I can't figure out is why you're playing this game, leading Curtis on and letting half the town think you're going to demolish a piece of heaven. Wouldn't it be easier to tell the truth?"

His vibrant laugh and watchdog expression was how she knew she'd hit the nail.

"I'm having fun," he said. "Aren't you?"

"I can think of a dozen other ways to have fun, and at least one way to have a blast."

Mitch gazed clear into her soul. "I thought you'd never ask. What time should I pick you up?"

"Depends, are we grabbing a bite to eat first?"

They made love for two days, and on the third day Mitch greeted the public with an official announcement. Six months before Zoey and Curtis had arrived, Mitch's mother passed, leaving him five hundred acres. His attorney had recently crossed the final T on clandestine paperwork, and the city learned Mitch had donated the acreage to wildlife conservationists. The forest would remain intact. Afterward he packed his bags and followed Zoey to Chicago.

Curtis renamed his article, "Mitch Madness—The Man Behind the Myth."

Zoey refocused on the present. She walked into the bedroom, noticing the walnut furniture, seaweed-colored curtains and king-size sleigh bed. Rather chic for a crotchety old man who supposedly never answered the door without a loaded rifle. She'd heard he had rabbit and raccoon carcasses draped like wet dishrags around the property. His style preference didn't reflect his primitive behavior. Nothing fit, even the suicide. Without admitting it out loud, she agreed with Dr. Selden. What eighty-year-old wealthy man hangs himself?

She inhaled, relieved Mitch had tidied her mess. Milo's pictures were in place and her luggage was put away. What were her plans, she wondered. Today, tomorrow, for the rest of her life—a busy mind made her skin itch. She went to the nightstand and swallowed a couple of her favorite oblong pills, undressed, released her hair from the tie and slipped into a long apricot-colored satin robe. After being poked, punctured and taped, the soft fabric felt kind against her skin.

Zoey headed downstairs and then paused on the bottom step to get a look around. Her main concern was the removal of the deer heads, and they were gone. She gently massaged her forehead, trying to alleviate the wavy feeling in her brain. Mitch drank coffee near the dining table. He gazed out the window, and Zoey caught herself admiring the size of his hands. She walked toward him, eyes roving for the cup of tea she suspected he had fixed.

He turned and took quick but obvious notice of her clingy robe. "Feeling better?"

"Oh yeah." She strolled into the kitchen and spotted her steamy drink next to the bottle of cough syrup near the microwave. She picked up the mug and took a sip.

"How's your shoulder?" Mitch stepped closer.

"Fine."

"And your throat?"

"Good." She sipped again and added, "How are you?"

Mitch studied her pupils with a surgeon's focus. He wordlessly accused her of popping pills.

"Yes, I took my meds," she said. "My shoulder was killing me, and now it's not. Okay?"

"I didn't say anything."

"You didn't have to." She moseyed into the dining area and stood next to the table. "Where'd you put the deer heads?"

He followed, sticky as fine cat hair. "In the garage."

"Thanks."

He crossed his arms over his chest, and receded in thought for several seconds. He finally asked, "Are you happy?"

"No."

"Why, then?"

"Why what?"

"Why the pills? The booze? Abandoning your career, your passion, if none of it helps your attitude?"

"Gee, I don't know there's this thing eating away at me. A ginormous thing. My fucking son died."

"He's my son too. Do you consider me at all in this?"

"Yeah, but you're strong and I'm weak." She slurped her tea and set the mug on the table.

"You're one of the strongest people I know, Zoey."

"Knew, Mitch, knew."

He shook his head. "Do you miss me?"

"Sometimes." She could smell his nectarous breath.

"I miss you bad." He tucked a strand of hair behind her ear, and gave a single stroke to her neck with his knuckles.

Like a pebble dropped in a pond, his touch caused pleasurable tingles throughout her entire body. "You should go." She acknowledged her toes.

"I should." He lifted her chin. "But I won't."

Her nipples hardened, and after a year of hibernation, her body awoke. Using her healthy arm, she clutched the nape of his muscular neck and smashed her lips into his. He resisted momentarily and then melted, giving in to her starving tongue. Their mouths collided, and she relished his juicy taste buds.

His powerful frame pressed against hers, and his big hands gripped her ass. Divine combination, drugs and Mitch. She breathed him in. His touch jumped from her butt to her navel, and he untied her robe and cupped her breast. He gently pinched her excited nipple.

"Oh my God," she whispered. She knocked a chair over, expecting him to follow her lead and lay her on the table.

His warm mouth devoured her lips and neck, but his body stalled.

She rubbed his brick-like bulge and her clit twitched. He growled, tickling her tonsils with the tip of his tongue. Zoey inhaled his sweet breath and alluring vapors.

Suddenly, he pulled his face from hers and distanced his body.

"What?" she asked. "Don't stop." She tugged his shirt toward the table, but he wouldn't budge.

"Zoey, wait. Wait a minute," he said with glazed eyes. He bent his knees slightly to match her height and cradled her jaw in his rugged hands.

She grasped his wrists.

"Hold on. Wait."

"What, Mitch? You said you missed me."

"I do, I do. But I have to call Sterling and tell her it's over."

A bucket of ice water would have been more humane. She backed away and covered her exposed body. "What? Why? Why would you do that?"

Mitch squinted. "Us, here, now."

"There is no us. We were going to screw, Mitch, doesn't mean anything."

Mitch's upper lip thinned. "You're a piece of work." He clutched a wad of his own hair and let go. "I cannot describe to you how fucked up I think this is."

"People have sex. It's what they do."

"Cut the horseshit. You know damn well how I feel about you, and how strongly I oppose deceit. You'd let me compromise my principles so you can get laid?"

"You started this, Mitch. You came on to me."

"I was testing the waters to see if we still had something."

"We do. It's called chemistry. We've always set the sheets on fire."

"And today I got burned."

She pointed to her injured shoulder. "No, this is a burn." She flung her arms outward. "You got rejected. And not really. I wanted sex. So you rejected me. It's time for you to leave."

He stormed through the living room and yanked open the door. "If you need me, Sterling and I will be staying in Telluride for the next week—and don't worry, this thing between you and me, this torch I've carried, it's snuffed."

SLAM!

"Whatever, Mitch. I don't need you or your dick!"

Overrun by cottonmouth, Zoey took a drink of tea. She set her cup down, inhaled and exhaled and sauntered to the sofa facing the entrance. "Your loss." Horny and high, she plopped on the cushion. Her head hit the pillow. She didn't remember falling asleep, yet when she opened her eyes, moonlight shone through the window.

Ayúdeme.

"What?" She scanned the empty rooms and motionless shadows.

Help me.

Zoey panicked. She plugged her ears and rushed upstairs to the bedroom, uncapped her meds and popped a few pills. "I dreamed something I don't remember. Another dream echo."

Help me.

Distant but close, it didn't make sense. Her pulse raced fast and strong, karate chops inside her neck. "It's only a dream," she told herself and set her hand on her pounding chest. "Too many pills and not enough sleep."

Help me, lady.

The voice was in the walls, ceilings, and floors.

Dear God, send me aid. You are it, lady.

"I'm not crazy!" She ripped off her robe and put on jeans and a black T-shirt. She stuck her feet in shoes and in the process bumped her shoulder. It pulsed with her heart.

Indistinct whispers infested her brain and she couldn't shake them.

"Shhh...."

She ran downstairs and grabbed her keys and purse. "I'm not losing my mind."

You must help.

"It's the drugs. Has to be." Zoey ran past the table and out the door leading to the garage.

Beasts attacked her legs. She kicked and blinked and wrestled with deer heads.

Do or die.

Zoey jumped in her BMW. She started the engine and hit the remote for the garage door, clutched the steering wheel and blasted the radio.

Do or die.

Above, below, within, she couldn't tell where the nonexistent voice came from.

Do or die.

Zoey wiped a tear. Her tires spit gravel, and headlights whitewashed the reddish snaky road as she sped to Anywhere Far Away.

Chapter 5

Her neighbor's house glowed like an elaborate nightlight. At some point she'd have to thank him, provided lightning, pharmaceuticals or alcohol hadn't fried her cerebral wires. Testing her sanity she cautiously turned off the radio. Tires hummed against smooth pavement uninterrupted by a voice. She sighed in relief.

Darkness cloaked the car. She slowed and focused on her location. Her eyes were heavy, but the energy of night probed something inside of her and it yawned and stretched.

Twenty minutes of instinctual driving led her to a log-structured tavern with a blinking red sign: Rock Hounds. A drink was exactly what she needed. She pulled into the driveway. Headlights washed over a row of sparkling Harleys in front and striped a collage of Cadillacs, other motorcycles and pickup trucks as she veered left into the parking lot. There was one vacancy next to a pricey black SUV. She pulled in and let the dust settle, then walked to the entrance, believing she'd found a secret hideaway.

Cold woodsy air veiled her arms, and she blanketed herself with her hair. "Hell with antibiotics," she said, yanking open the oversize door.

She met with a blast of heat, country music and an overwhelming amount of curious stares, along with a few snickers. She'd created a ripple in the social fabric—the best way to remedy mild havoc was to blend in. Zoey walked to the bar, but not without quick assessment of the environment. Polo shirts, tailored blazers and snakeskin cowboy boots trimmed the dining tables, and denim, leather vests and bandanas congregated at the pool tables. A fifties-style jukebox played in the background and dead animals lined the walls.

She stood at the maple-and-polyurethane bar and contemplated her order. The barman arrived just as she'd decided on a Long Island Iced Tea.

Stout, with thick dark facial hair and rolled flannel sleeves, he leaned forward and gazed at her throat. "Pressed for time, were ya?"

"Maybe. Why?"

"Your shirt," a man whispered from behind. "It's on backward and inside out."

She fingered her neckline. Sure enough the crisp tag hung under her thyroid. "So it is." She turned to the informative stranger, instantly captivated by his indigo eyes and strands of black, wind-tangled hair.

Taller than her by a couple inches and younger by at least ten years, he had a perfect physique, built chest, defined arms and an interestingly shaped tattoo on his right biceps.

She eyed the diamonds and tusks and face within a symbol.

"You like ink?" he said, holding a full bottle of beer.

"Not really."

"But you like mine?"

She leaned against the bar. "I do."

"Badass." He nodded.

"What is it?"

"Buddha in Om."

Zoey straightened in disbelief. "You're a Buddhist?"

"Never. Religion restrains expansion. I'm eclectic."

"And Om means?"

He seized her breath with a smile brighter than summer. "It means awake, asleep, dreaming and everything in between. Absolute consciousness and the eradication of finite thinking."

His words rolled around like marbles until they found a sinkhole. She said, "No boundaries?"

"Bingo."

"Describes me right now."

"Really?" he asked with heightened interest. "Can I buy you a drink?"

"You can buy me several."

"Are you a tequila woman?"

"No boundaries, remember?"

"Wally, get us a couple rounds of Cuervo." He pointed to the bartender. "That's Wally."

"I've gathered."

"I'm Lance." He extended his hand.

"Zoey," she said, not intending to shake.

Lance lowered his arm and studied her expression. "New in town or passing through?"

"I haven't decided yet."

Wally placed four empty shot glasses on the maple and filled each one. Lance raised his drink. "Salute."

Zoey held her tiny glass upward and toasted. She swished the fiery liquid around her mouth before swallowing and let the alcohol burn through gluey saliva. "That's better. Keep them coming."

Lance slammed his drained shot glass on the bar. "Two more rounds, Wally," he yelled.

"In a minute," Wally said from the opposite end of the bar. He handed a refined silver-haired man two mixed drinks.

The silver fox noticed Zoey and smiled. She returned the gesture. He walked to a table and sat next to a man whose face she couldn't see.

"You know him?" Lance asked.

"Nope," she said. "I'm exploring my options."

Lance laughed. "Now that I know you're strictly primal, I'll up my game." He hollered down the bar, "Put a rush on those drinks, Wally."

"You don't look like a guy who has to get drunk to perform."

"Is that an invite?"

"Doesn't matter. If it's not me, it'll be someone."

"I beg to differ. I wasn't in the mood until you denounced boundaries. That could be interesting."

"But then there's booze and too much of it might spoil an otherwise ferocious night."

Lance stepped nose to nose with Zoey and said, "Alcohol has no bearing. You'd scream my name whether I was sober or not. Guaranteed." He created a foot of space.

Zoey examined his firm torso, muscular thighs and impressive rounded zipper. For a fleeting moment his vigor and striking features frightened her—she was, after all, older, injured and abstinent for longer than she cared to admit. Tonight, though, one simple thought set her free—live life as if it were your last day on earth. In her case, it could be. So, regardless of her insecurities, if he made an advance, she wouldn't resist.

"Where're you staying?" he asked.

"In Big Cat. I inherited a house, but I haven't moved in. I'm here on a trial basis."

"You're not from Colorado, are you?"

"Chicago."

"Chicago's badass. North or South Side?"

"Go Cubs."

"Sweet. Blues bars and killer food. Crazy times in Chi-Town." His eyes were luminous.

Wally refilled their shot glasses. She and Lance finished them before Wally had a chance to walk away.

"More?" Wally asked.

"Yep," Lance confirmed. "She's living on the wild side tonight."

"And chivalrous Lance is here to help, eh?" Wally poured the booze.

"I do what I can."

Wally rushed to another customer.

Zoey snickered. "I hope you're not feeding me booze trying to get lucky. I made up my mind the minute I saw you. I'd like you to come home with me."

Lance jerked his head back slightly as if stunned. "This may be hard to believe, but tonight my alcohol purchases have nothing to do with sex. I'm celebrating."

"Birthday?"

"No. I build custom bikes and sold one I've been tinkering with for about two years. It paid off. I made a respectable amount of money."

"Congratulations."

He licked his shapely lips and narrowed his eyes. "What brings you to Rock Hounds?"

People whirred in and out of the tavern, and conversations overlapped into illogical noises. Despite the many distractions, Zoey felt alone with Lance. "Got tired of sitting home. I went for a drive and there it was, the red flashing sign. Actually, I'd hoped a drink would ease the pain."

"Sounds severe." He swigged his beer.

"It is. I was struck by lightning last week."

"Bullshit."

Zoey pulled her hair to her left side and revealed the gauze on her right shoulder. "Second-degree burn."

"Ouch."

"Doctors say I'm lucky to be alive."

"You're trying to turn me on, aren't you?" Lance asked. "Divulging your battle wound, your spar with lightning. That's fucking sexy. Super badass."

She smiled.

Lance quietly inspected her appearance. He glanced at her collar and leaned inward. "The bathroom is down the hall past the jukebox if you want to fix your shirt."

She clamped the brittle tag and ripped it off. "Not an issue. I want to be out of the entire shirt in, say, thirty minutes." She dropped the paper on the floor. "Sooner if you have the nerve."

Lance bit his bottom lip. "Hey, Wally, bring me another beer!"

"Yeah, yeah," Wally answered from the register.

Like the woman in the elevator at the hospital, Lance was blessed with divine proportions—golden ratios. Naked and surrounded by a thousand mirrors at every angle, Lance would be flawless. She hardly understood herself, her desire to devour him where he stood. Maybe Mitch had snapped a twig in the jungle and awakened a dormant tigress. Reasons were irrelevant. She wanted Lance. End of story.

Wally delivered a beer and poured more tequila in the empty shot glasses.

"You're in Big Cat, where?" Lance asked.

"The Rayfield Ranch."

"Never heard of it."

"I have," Wally slanted over the bar. "Amos Rayfield's place."

Zoey nodded. "I'm his great niece."

"Sorry for your loss," Wally said. "What a way to go."

"I'm in the cold," Lance said.

Wally dealt with Lance. "Amos hanged himself."

"Damn," Lance said before he swigged. "That's kind of distressing."

"Not necessarily. I didn't know him," Zoey said.

Wally continued, "He used to come in here once a month and drink. Didn't read or watch TV, just sat there drinkin'."

"Did you ever talk to him?" Zoey asked.

"Occasionally," Wally said. "Never 'bout anything important, the weather, hunting, shit like that. About a week before he died, he came in and drank a six-pack. That's a lot for Amos. I asked him how things were going, and he had this blank look on his face. He said he wouldn't survive." Wally reduced to a whisper, "He said someone was trying to kill him."

Zoey's stomach twisted. "Who?"

Wally straightened. "He wouldn't say. He was pale and weak-lookin'. Hell, he was scared. Seven days later they found him hanging from a beam in his garage."

"You're full of shit," Lance said.

"Not this time," Wally said. "Gave me the willies."

"Was he senile?" Zoey asked.

"Can't be sure. He was a strange man. A hermit." Wally paused. "Hey, you're that gal that was struck by lightning."

"How'd you know?" she asked.

Wally shrugged. "News travels fast in a small town."

"Yeah, I'm the gal."

"Nutty." Wally shook his head. He eyed her. "You doin' okay?"

"So far so good."

"We underestimate our reliance on a sound environment. We're fools." He slammed his palm on the counter and then dissolved into the bustle.

Lance gazed at Zoey. "Murder and mayhem. My dream woman."

Zoey twirled a strand of hair near her breast. "What do you say we go back to my house and lose our minds?"

He grinned. "Let's go."

At the other end of the bar, Wally served the classy silver-haired man she'd noticed earlier.

"Would you rather go home with him?" Lance asked.

"You tell me."

"No. You wouldn't."

"Are you sure?"

"Positive." He swigged.

She feasted on his youthful energy and the glint in his indigo eyes. She imagined burying her fingers in his black hair, the thin ropes obviously spun by a sensual witch. Zoey swallowed her last shot, her body tingling with urgency and her brain a succession of X-rated blurs.

"Come on," she said. "My vocal cords need a workout."

Lance put a fifty-dollar bill and his unfinished beer on the bar. He strode to the pool table near the jukebox—his ass completely grabbable—and snatched a leather jacket hanging on a nearby hook. He yelled to a few apparent friends, two of whom held pool sticks, "Don't wait up."

A Goliath-sized biker with tattoo sleeves and shaggy blond hair threw his hand over his mouth. "Lance got lucky. Imagine that."

"Suck it, Tank," Lance responded with a cocky smile. He returned to Zoey and handed her his coat. "Wear this."

"I'm not cold," she said, thinking something about the man he'd called Tank wasn't normal.

"You will be," Lance said.

She put on the jacket and zipped up. She almost pulled her hair out from underneath but Lance suggested she'd be warmer if she left it.

As they passed the bar, Lance said, "Thanks a lot, Wally."

"Yeah," Wally answered. "Take her easy!"

Zoey wandered outside and stopped, awed by the immediate transition to silence. She could see a thin curl of breath under the moon's golden aura.

"Aren't you cold?" she asked.

Lance approached and groped her for his keys. "I can handle it. Let's seal this deal." He placed his hand behind her head and put his lips to hers, his kiss strong and his tongue deadly. He consumed her mouth, and the contact made her insane.

She tore away. "What are we waiting for? Let's do it, right here, right now." She grabbed the waist of his jeans and fidgeted for the button. "We'll go in the woods."

"Whoa." He spun out of her grasp. "I'm in no rush. I plan to spread you out and make love to every inch of you." Lance proceeded to an iguana-green Fat Boy.

"Nice bike," Zoey said.

"Thanks. This one's my favorite. First hog I paid for in full." He patted the rear seat. "Hop on." He straddled the motorcycle and stuck the keys in the ignition.

Excessively stimulated, her body hurt. She and pain had a permanent relationship. She crawled up behind, leaned into Lance's backside, and wrapped her arms around his midsection.

"Big Cat Canyon, right?" he asked.

"Know where it is?"

"Yeah." He revved the motorcycle and rolled forward. The muffler reverberated, and the headlight spliced the night like a Jedi sword leading the way to victory.

"I'll tug your shirt when it's time to turn," she said.

The bike hiccupped and sped ahead. She jolted backward and muscled herself closer to Lance. She clung to him. A fierce gust ripped at her cheeks, kept her alert. She rested her chin on his shoulder blade, periodically ducking to block her eyes from the wind.

It didn't seem far enough, but Lance yelled over the rumbling, "We're here. Which way?"

Two huge boulders marked the access to Big Cat's residential section.

"Right, and when you see a sandy red road, turn right again," she hollered. "Follow that road to the house."

Lance accelerated and effortlessly found Rayfield Ranch. He parked in front of the opened garage and cut the engine. He held the bike steady while she climbed off.

"We alone?" he asked.

"Why? Are you planning on murdering me?"

He snickered. "No, man, the truck." Lance pointed to the tailgate of Amos's forest green Dodge.

Zoey planted her feet on the grass and wiped tears from her eyes. "That was my uncle's."

"Oh," he said while dismounting the Harley. "Nice place. You must be loaded."

"I've got a little spending money. Uncle Amos had a hefty bank account." Zoey staggered through the garage and hesitated before entering the house. "I'm not giving you a dime."

Lance laughed as he neared her side. "If I charged, I'd have to lower my standards. Not happening. I'm too selective." He lifted her long hair from under the coat and let it fall over her arms.

"You've never had an ugly one-night stand?"

"Not since I was sixteen."

"But you've thought about it?" She gently slapped his chest.

"About an ugly one-nighter?"

"No." Zoey tsked. "Becoming a gigolo."

"It's not my thing. Why are we having this conversation?" Lance folded his arms.

"Be honest," she said.

"Other people have thought about it."

"Lusty older women…"

"Mostly." He tugged the jacket hem.

"I'm a lusty older woman, and I'm not paying."

"You'll want to when I'm finished with you." He glued his front to hers and licked her mouth.

She scraped his saliva from her lips with her teeth. "You're a tasty little morsel, aren't you?"

"There's nothing little about me." He reached around her hip and turned the doorknob.

They spilled into the dining room and landed on the floor. She winced, unsure of what ached more, her shoulder or her clit. He moved smooth as magic and remarkably, however brief, she had a will to live.

He arched his spine upward and unzipped her coat. His eyes were piercing, and his nostrils flared. "You want me?"

"If you have to ask, I must be doing something wrong." She slithered out of the leather, flung it somewhere and then ripped at his T-shirt. He helped, and the shirt sailed over the table.

She savored his salty chest and kissed up his neck to his edible lips. She pecked and sucked and nibbled. "Mm."

Lance separated from her and untied his boots. He took them off and tossed them across the room. Without pause he unbuttoned his jeans.

She removed her pants while she watched the denim slide down his legs. She felt like a moonstruck werewolf speaking predator, grunting and groaning, pawing at his taught limbs and chiseled chest—drooling at sight of his long, hard dick as perfect as the rest of his parts.

He pressed his naked flesh to hers and stuck a finger inside her, and she pushed him in deeper. Fluids released and her soul screamed. His head inched downward, and he meticulously lapped her juice.

Overcome with chills she gasped, hands finally buried in his matted suede hair. "I can't," she whispered. "I can't take this anymore. It's been too long."

Lance lifted his head and offered a sympathetic expression. He gazed into her eyes and walked upward on his hands, then thrust into her and pumped and pumped. His soft pubic hairs tangled with hers, and he fit as if he belonged.

"Holy shit!" She locked him in with her legs and hoisted her hips. Gliding repetitiously she faded in and out of reality, her sexual appetite bottomless.

Lance thoughtfully pushed himself as far inside as she'd accept. "Damn, you're tight."

Zoey rolled and flipped him over, rode him fast and slow, maneuvered her body to nourish her famished G-spot. She lifted her ass to better feel his length enter and exit her walls. Multiple orgasms shattered whatever identity she'd retained from her previous self. She watched him, his face twisted in bliss, and despite their age difference, her scars—C-section and burn—and her so-called volatile temperament, she felt desirable.

And reckless.

And unchained.

She let him have her in every way, every position, and in exchange, she had him. She couldn't care less what he'd think of her in the morning. He tasted sweeter than organic honey, and his everlasting hardness and determination to please brought her higher than pills and booze combined. She would do it again in a heartbeat.

At some point, Lance carried her upstairs and they finished round four in bed.

Lance lay on his side, propped on his left elbow facing Zoey. "Fucking you is my new favorite diversion."

"Better than collecting coins or stamps," she said groggily.

He smiled.

Through the window opal-colored clouds marbled across an ashen sky, and the sun threatened to rise above the treetops.

She stared at the corner of his lips and followed the contours of his right arm across his spiritual tattoo, over his small, perfect nipples and down to his tight abdomen. For him, she'd resume photography. She imagined his nude body in black and white against a white backdrop.

He extended his arm and lined her C-section with his finger. "How many kids do you have?"

"None," she said.

Lance raised his head and glanced at the photos of Milo on the dresser as if they'd previously sparked his curiosity. "Who's he?"

She knocked his hand away from her belly and covered her scar with the sheet. "My son."

"But—"

"He died last year."

"Shit. I'm sorry."

She didn't realize a tear had trickled down her cheek until Lance smeared it with his thumb.

"I am. I'm sorry. My foot visits my mouth once in a while."

"It's okay," she said. "How could you know?"

Lance gazed at the pinkish shredded flower etched in her shoulder. "We should wrap that."

Her sweat-sopped bandage had fallen off an hour ago, and her buzz had escaped in the same pool of perspiration.

"It'll be fine," she said, too exhausted to rummage for the gauze. She grabbed a bottle of pills and poured a couple in her mouth.

"What are you taking?" he asked.

"Valium. I'm in pain."

"Valium isn't the best thing for pain, but okay. Are you sharing?" Lance opened wide.

She aimed at a silver filling and tossed him a couple, like fish to a seal, relieved he'd rather join her than the typical nitpicking. She watched his Adam's apple dunk and rise, and his skilled tongue moisten his lips.

"We'll have to exchange numbers," she said. "In case you'd like to do this again."

"Oh, I want to do this again," he said. "ASAP." He gently touched her prematurely aged shoulder and spoke carefully. "What was it like getting struck by lightning?"

"I'm not sure." Fatigue guided her into thought. "I remember feeling like I'd been punched by fire. After that, nothing. I woke up in the hospital and, from what I understand, I dodged brain damage, paralysis and death."

"Unreal." He seemed to mull things over. "You have a mission. You're supposed to be here."

"What?"

"You were spared. Why?"

"I got lucky for a change."

"Last night, too, four times."

"I'll give you that."

He focused on the wrinkles of her scar and tickled a trail to her breast with his forefinger. He outlined her areola and rolled his fingertip along her nipple. She lifted the sheet over her breasts and closed her eyes.

Lance laid his arm across her chest. Within seconds he was motionless.

* * * *

Sirens bellowed. An ear-popping noise jolted her awake. She jumped to her feet when she understood the hideous sound was the doorbell. She moved slower than usual, a symptom of too many chemicals, not enough rest and her naked wrestling match with Lance. Her apricot robe lay rippled on the floor. She threw it on and left her sleepy lover rolling about under the sheets.

The awful duck-bell quacked, and she weaved around the crooked sofa, tipped coffee table, come towel and phone receiver. She stopped before answering the door and combed her fingers through her hair.

She turned the knob and wheezed.

Three squad cars, a fire truck and an ambulance parked on the maroon road, and a crew of cops, firemen and paramedics rushed up and down the hill. An old-timer with childish freckles flashed a badge, and behind him in the front yard stood Mitch and his too-short-for-him girlfriend, Sterling.

"I'm Detective Grady," the cop said. "Zoey Hawthorne, I presume?"

"Yes."

"You're okay?" His forehead creased.

"I'm fine, why? What's going on?"

Mitch blazed up the deck, his face devilishly crimson and his eyes packed with fury. "I'll tell you what. We found your unlocked car in the parking lot of Rock Hounds tavern, and your purse and house keys in the front seat."

"Holy shit. How did you find Rock Hounds?" she asked.

"You can't miss it, Zoey. It's off the main highway."

"I didn't know. It was dark," she said, holding the neck of her robe closed.

"Would it make a difference? What the hell happened?"

"I got a ride home. I didn't realize—I'm sorry if I worried you." She eyed Mitch. His anxiety made her nervous.

Shirtless, in a towel-skirt and smelling of unruly pheromones, Lance emerged. He craned around her shoulder and eyed her hectic front yard. "That's what I call a clusterfuck." His bloodshot blues widened. "What's up?"

Mitch's eyes raged, but his body remained composed.

"I'm sorry, Mitch," she said, referring to Lance.

"You're an adult. You can do what you want with whom you want. Scratching an itch, right?" he said and she could see him swallowing knots. When he'd contemplated having a relationship with Sterling, he discussed it with Zoey. This wasn't fair.

She turned away from the fight inside Mitch, and spoke to Lance. "They found my car at Rock Hounds."

"Oh, she's cool. I brought her home on my bike." He withdrew into the house.

Lance wasn't the only blistering reminder of their severed marriage. Sterling waited nearby in her Western-themed outfit complete with cobalt blue boots and a cowboy hat. Her whitish blond hair turned heads while her double-D breasts broke necks. No matter how hard Zoey tried to overlook her, Sterling Fisk glowed like neon.

Mitch slowly closed his eyes and reopened them with a renewed vivacity.

Detective Grady went on, "There's something you should know, Ms. Hawthorne. The cars and lights, all the ruckus." He cocked his head toward the busyness. "A couple hours ago a young girl flipped her kayak. She cracked her head." He glanced down at the deck and up again. "She didn't survive."

Zoey's legs weakened. She leaned against the doorframe. "Today, now? You're telling me a girl died in my backyard while I slept?"

Detective Grady nodded.

"How old was she?"

"Twelve."

"What about a helmet. Why wasn't she wearing one?"

"We found the helmet. Not a dent on it. Her folks said the current ripped it off."

Blood drained from Zoey's face. "This is so fucked! I lost my son last year. I know how it feels. How are her parents? Did anyone ask? Does anyone care?"

The detective recoiled. "Sure, they're emotional, irrational, upset. It's to be expected."

"To be expected—you think?"

"Calm down, Zoey." Mitch removed his invisible armor. "This isn't about us."

She couldn't bear to look at Milo's features in her ex right now. "Go away, Mitch. I'm fine. You see." She stepped forward.

"I see," Mitch said.

Detective Grady interrupted them. "The accident is under investigation. We'll be on the premises for a few hours." He turned toward the stair, paused, and swiveled in Zoey's direction. "In the future you might want to lock your car and take your personal effects with you."

Zoey slammed the door. Not enough sleep left cracks large enough for memories to creep forward. One year Milo hit a homerun and laughed and ate pizza. The next year he was dead. Zoey's lips quivered.

Are you listening?

"What? No. Stop." Zoey rushed into the kitchen for water.

Lance stood at the sink rinsing a pear, bare feet and chest, with his blue jeans unbuttoned. "Check it out. My pants were in the potbelly stove."

"Get out of my way," she said, desperate to cleanse the heartache and whatever else lurked. She shoved his body from the faucet and splashed lukewarm water on her face. She cupped her hands and drank.

Help me.

She smothered her ears.

"What's going on?" Lance asked.

Listen.

"No!" she said. "I hear someone. I don't know who it is, but it's a voice and it's talked to me before and it won't stop."

Lance returned to the sink. "It's okay," he said sweetly, and turned off the faucet. "What's it saying?"

"Fuck you. I hear it. It's real."

"I believe you," he said.

"No, you don't. You think I'm crazy. Leave me alone. Just go. Get out of here."

"Don't do this, Zoey. I believe you." He clutched her arms to keep her still, but she squirmed from his hold.

Help me, lady.

Zoey turned and paced looking for the voice. "Who's there? Who's talking to me?"

Are you listening?

"No. Shut up." Zoey yelled at nothing and everything.

Lance stepped backward as if she were a ticking bomb. "What the fuck, Zoey? What should I do?"

Help me.

Streams of tears flowed. She ran through the living room to the stairs, set on a mouthful of pills.

Lance breathed down her neck. "Zoey, tell me what to do and I'll do it."

The front door flung open and Mitch ran in. Sterling followed.

Do or die.

Zoey collapsed on the first step and cried in her hands, grateful her hair concealed her breakdown. "Shut up!"

A set of arms scooped her from the floor, carried her upstairs and laid her in bed. She opened her eyes, and Mitch wiped tears from her cheeks with the corner of the sheet.

"You need help, Zoey," he said tenderly while stroking her scalp with his knuckles. "Milo's death ruptured a piece of you, but I promise it's fixable. Let me call the psychiatrist Dr. Selden recommended. I'll be there with you, and for you, or not. Whatever you want."

Zoey nodded, eager to mute the voice and absolve herself from anything perplexing. "Get rid of Lance for me, will you?" She sniffled.

"Gladly." He read the label on one of her prescriptions and uncapped the bottle. "Never thought I'd say this, but take a pill." He handed her a Valium and stood. "You get why I have to remove these, don't you?" He plucked her medications from the night table.

Zoey nodded.

"Try to sleep. I'll be back soon." Mitch left with her beloved meds.

Zoey closed her eyes, breathed deeply, in and out.

You cannot avoid me.

She stuffed her head under the pillow.

Do not deny my demand. You must help me.

"One plus one is two. Two plus two is four. Four plus four is…"

Acknowledge me.

Suddenly, like a slamming tomb, everything hushed. Zoey slowly settled in the sound of her own breath, terrified to move and make noise, afraid she'd stir the voice, or Mitch.

Chapter 6

After her tepid shower, Zoey rubbed antibacterial ointment on her unsightly scar. Her tendons and muscles hurt, but she rolled her shoulder frontward and backward, pleased with her increasing mobility. She crawled into loose-fitting jeans and a black linen blouse, and paused in front of the window. The sunset cast brilliant pomegranate whiskers across the sky.

A glass of water, two ibuprofen and a Valium were on the nightstand, prescribed by Dr. Selden. She gulped her meds and at last managed to braid her own hair. Before she went downstairs, she chose not to think about her embarrassing tantrum.

The house was so quiet her cough echoed. She walked to the kitchen. Sterling sat at the dining table, engrossed in a crossword puzzle. Her cowboy hat hung on a chair post and her wispy blond hair lit the room similar to a bouquet of daisies. She chewed the end of a pencil.

"Inevitable," Sterling said.

"What?" Zoey turned on the flame under the teapot.

"Ten letter word for karma."

"Hell with karma," Zoey said, setting a teabag in a mug. "She and I don't get along. Where's Mitch?"

"Detective Grady gave him a ride to the tavern to pick up your car. He had other errands too, and calls to make. He's been gone all afternoon."

"Why didn't you go with him?" Zoey asked, banging a bowl on the counter next to the unopened cough syrup.

"I stayed behind and cleaned your pigsty."

Zoey realized she had been able to walk without tripping on a tipped piece of furniture. "Thanks."

"Besides," Sterling said, "Mitch wanted me here in case you needed something."

"In case I go into hysterics again?" She poured corn flakes and opened the fridge for milk.

"No." Sterling drummed her French-manicured nails on the table. "In case you needed help with your hair or a tissue to cry in or someone to run Lance off if he should come back."

"Shit. Lance," Zoey muttered, remorseful.

"Mitch gave strict orders to keep that punk away from you. He doesn't trust him, said he's too young to have a reliable conscience."

"What's he think Lance is going to do?"

Sterling shrugged.

"Mitch has to stay out of my affairs," Zoey said as she carried her meal to the dining room. She sat in the chair opposite Sterling and ate.

Sterling rolled her crossword magazine into a cylinder and with one eye spied Zoey through the hole. "Don't you think he's tried?" Though apparently a victim of boredom, she had a soothing voice. "Every time he distances himself from you, attempts to rebuild his life, plans a vacation, you coincidentally have to be rescued." She removed the magazine from her eye.

"What are you smoking?" Zoey dropped her spoon.

Sterling rose. Her striking blond hair and giant breasts competed for attention. "I'm not telling you anything you don't already know. What about the gas-station incident? We were on our way to Michigan for a long, romantic weekend."

"That's ridiculous. I had to pee for an hour. Do you think I intentionally picked the gas station that was being robbed? Do you think I planned to be held hostage?"

"No, not consciously."

"Not anything."

"Our lives are physical manifestations of our subconscious thoughts," Sterling said.

"Bite me. Nowhere in my mind knowingly or otherwise am I partial to gun-slinging thugs. I had to flirt with a guy who had four tattooed teardrops on his cheek. Do you know what that symbolizes?"

"Yes, Zoey. We've heard it all before. And you were scared, and you had to discuss it with someone you trusted, and of course that person is Mitch."

Zoey recalled various other details of the robbery and cringed.

Sterling continued, "What about the flat tires and the plumbing and the late-night calls after a bad dream?"

"And the lightning strike?" Zoey stood, and towered over Sterling. "Mitch and I had a son who died a horrible death. The gas station, the plumbing and flat tires, the nightmares and lightning, it's all clumped together and amounts to one messed up—I don't know—clusterfuck. It is what it is. Mitch and I have known each other for sixteen years, and yes, he's the only person I can talk to who truly knows me. I don't have to waste time explaining myself." She lifted her bowl and took her unfinished cereal to the sink. "Personally I think you're selfish. If you disagree, I recommend less romantic getaways and more introspection. What kind of year did you have? Did you lose a child? Did your basement flood while your deceased son's clothes were on the floor? Did you have to make out with a parasite to keep your wallet? Did you get hit by fucking lightning?"

Sterling shook her head. "No, and I don't pretend to understand. But do you ever see a blessing, however small?"

"Not yet, princess, I'm working on it." Zoey stomped through the dining room and plopped on the sofa. "Frankly, if my boyfriend jumped every time his ex called, I'd leave him. So, Sterling Fisk, why haven't you dumped Mitch?"

Sterling stepped slowly into the living room, seeming physically affected by Zoey's zinger. She sat on the other sofa facing Zoey, coffee table between them. "To be honest, I should leave him. But there's a lot to love. He's kind, thoughtful, handsome, funny, loyal and he listens to what I have to say. He wants my opinion. A successful middle-aged man who prefers an intelligent woman with life experience over a twentysomething girl who strokes his ego with childish giggles is virtually nonexistent. Then again, you wouldn't know. You've only dipped a toe in the dating scene. It's rough for women our age. A guy like Mitch is worth the wait."

"I'm well aware of Mitch's qualities. So what exactly are you waiting for?"

"For him to get over you. He deserves to be happy. I want him, and you don't. Let him move on."

The kettle whistled. Simultaneously Zoey's pharmaceuticals took effect.

"You're flushed," Sterling said. "Stay put. I'll get your tea." She walked to the kitchen and clanked a few items. "What do you take in it?" she yelled.

"A teaspoon of honey, hold the spit," Zoey responded before concluding Sterling honorable enough not to hack in her Earl Grey. She was nice, a martyr when it came to Mitch. Good for him, she thought. Good for them.

Sterling returned and set the hot drink in front of Zoey on the coffee table. She resituated on the unoccupied couch.

"It's Milo," Zoey said.

"What's Milo?" Sterling sat still as a mannequin, ladylike and pretty.

"Mitch thinks by helping me he's honoring the memory of our son."

"If only that were true."

"It is. You've never mourned a child. That kind of sorrow wears many disguises. On Mitch it's a Batman mask, dark and wounded, but elusive because he claims he's fine. Deep down he's hurting. I'm his occasional damsel in distress. I help restore his sense of purpose. I can't change who he is and neither can you. And me, well, I'm having trouble controlling myself these days. I'm sleeping with strangers and leaving breadcrumbs the size of BMWs."

"Yes." Sterling laughed. "However, a girl can't be expected to think of everything when the stranger is jaw-dropping gorgeous."

"You're too kind, but tequila and Valium had something to do with it. Anyway I can't promise to stop calling Mitch. It's what I do. My addictive personality is no secret. But maybe one day I'll call and unexpectedly he won't come. I'll get the hint, and it'll be a huge leap forward for all of us."

"Devil's advocate here. If you were one-hundred-percent certain Mitch loved you and it wasn't about Milo, would you want him back?"

Zoey hadn't seriously thought about it and wouldn't start now. "No." She leaned forward, allowing her braid to fall over her left shoulder. "What about the accident in the river? The victim and her family?"

"Nothing profound to report. Police and firemen packed up a few hours ago. They said they couldn't close Coldstone but they'd issue a public warning to be aware of a dangerous undercurrent near the Rayfield Ranch."

"Figures," Zoey muttered.

"What?"

"Of course I would have a deathtrap in my backyard. I'm cursed."

"Why do you insist on belittling yourself? It's a state river. It's not your fault."

"What about Lance?" Zoey probed. "What did Mitch say to him?"

"That was interesting. Mitch told Lance to get out, but believe me, Lance didn't want to go. He repeatedly asked how you were, and Mitch wouldn't answer. I felt awful. Lance seemed genuinely concerned. He and Mitch eventually went outside. I don't know what they discussed, but fifteen minutes later, Lance raced away on his motorcycle. Before he walked out with Mitch, he said something I'd nearly forgotten. He said, 'Tell Zoey I believe her.' Does that mean something to you?"

Immature mumbo jumbo. He believed what? That she heard a voice, thus making her a lunatic? "No, means nothing." She took a swallow of tea.

Without comment, Sterling rose. She motioned through the house in a fashion resembling a suspicious pirate searching for valuables. "What do you think of your new home? Do you like it?"

"I'm not crazy about all the windows, or Amos's decor. It's cold."

"Do you ever get frightened here?" Sterling's gaze roved dreamily.

"Yes. I've been afraid. Not because of anything external. It's my imagination, my brain on drugs. Why do you ask?"

"I've always appreciated your straightforward nature. No one has to guess what's on your mind. I'll be honest too. I get hunches about things." Sterling stroked the furniture and walls as if petting a dog. She crouched and placed both palms on the floor. "This house has complex energy."

"What?"

Sterling straightened and smiled. "Don't get defensive. And don't get weirded out. Please. I know it's hard to comprehend, but some say I'm psychic or clairvoyant."

"You are high." Zoey studied the five-foot Barbie doll. She used to wonder what Mitch saw in Sterling—she seemed too perfect, uninteresting. But there they were, the cracks hidden in the etched glass, the intriguing defects.

Sterling opened the door to the garage, ducked her head in, and popped back into the dining room. "That's where your uncle committed suicide?"

"Yes," Zoey said, surprisingly enthralled.

"But *he's* not the problem," Sterling said, returning to the sofas. "There's something very angry—infuriated—here."

"And that's the problem?"

"I'm not sure. Something terrible happened in this house, and if I were you, I wouldn't stay."

"What? Come on. Why should I believe you?" Zoey asked, frustrated she'd let Sterling interfere with her buzz.

Sterling sat on the couch and eyed Zoey. She clasped her fluttery claws and set her hands in her lap. "There's a strong presence here, and it confuses me because it's protective yet extremely destructive."

"What are you trying to do, Sterling?"

Sterling appeared to explore an indiscernible world. "I've never sensed anything like this, usually a presence is heavy and ominous or light and benign, but this entity is unique. It's kind but seeks revenge. "

"What entity? It's you and me, and nothing else. Hello? Hello, hello? See? Nothing."

Sterling's focus returned to earth and she stared at Zoey. "What did Lance mean when he said he believed you?"

"None of your business." Zoey pulled her knees to her chest, feet on the couch.

"Okay, then who were you yelling at? Do you remember shouting 'shut up' right before Mitch carried you upstairs?"

"Why are you doing this to me? You know I'm on meds, and I'm sure Mitch told you they've been vandalizing my head. I've agreed to see a shrink."

"I'm not accusing you of being crazy, I swear to you. I think there's more to it." She paused and said, "*Help me.* Sound familiar?"

Zoey's stomach plummeted. "Impossible. How..."

"I heard it too."

Zoey set her soles on the floor and studied Sterling's lips to avoid misunderstandings.

"Only once," Sterling went on, "but I suspected it was more aggressive with you. Every so often I tap into noises inaudible to the average person. I think that's what you're going through. I think you're clairaudient."

"Clair-what?"

"Clairaudient. It means *clear hearing.* It's the ability to hear what others can't—human and animal spirits, music, whatever resonates in bordering dimensions."

"I'm hearing all right—a lot of metaphysical crap."

"I don't want to overwhelm you, but let's consider a few facts. Sound is invisible, interpreted through vibrations. The number of vibrations per second is called a frequency, and frequencies are measured in hertz—one hertz is one vibration per second. Do you follow?"

"No."

"A healthy young human being hears at a frequency of about twenty to twenty-thousand hertz."

"Human as opposed to extraterrestrials?"

"No, Zoey, as opposed to other animals of the feathered, furry, scaled, four-legged breed."

Zoey sipped her tea. "This can't be true, but go on."

"Most animals hear infrasound and ultrasound. These are frequencies too low or high for the human ear. Take bats. They can hear a frequency as high as one hundred thousand hertz. Rather significant when compared to our measly numbers. Cats, dogs, whales, elephants, dolphins, they're all able to detect frequencies inaudible to humans."

"What does this have to do with me?"

"Sound is registered in the brain. When a person is capable of extraordinary hearing, there's an area in the brain, an area of receptor sites that are, for whatever reason, opened. Similar to other species of animals, you have cross-capabilities. I'm suggesting a region of your brain has matured."

"Let's say I'm wrong and you're not a complete crackpot. What I've heard is a voice, sometimes mellow, sometimes threatening, but always determined. You call it clairaudient. Am I honestly supposed to believe I'm hearing someone in another dimension?"

Sterling smiled. "Yes. The only dividing factor of a dimension is frequencies. Everything physical and nonphysical has a vibration. A radio for instance is a physical component transmitting nonphysical messages. Both the object and the sound waves have a measurement. The fact that you're listening to FM90 doesn't mean FM107 is imaginary. It only means you haven't turned the knob far enough."

"Supposedly I have. That's what you're saying, right?"

"Right."

"We're not close friends or family. How do you know this about me?"

"I don't—well, not absolutely. I'm only weighing what I've seen and heard with what I sense. And I sense you have a useful gift."

"Now you lost me. How in the hell can voices in my head be considered useful?"

"Not fabricated voices, Zoey, spirits. Nowadays we don't question what we see as much as what we hear. Mediums like the internet, cinema, TV, local and world news stretched our eye-brain axis. Most of us have seen remarkable if not unbelievable things. But we're still in the Dark Ages because if someone mentions otherworldly voices, the energy fizzes." Sterling crossed her legs. "Clear hearing is rare, and because there isn't a show on cable about attuned listeners, the challenge is greater. The clairaudiently gifted must convince themselves they aren't insane. However, no one fits in a predesigned cookie cutter, and trying can make us feel crazy. For those who refuse to acknowledge their individuality, the internal argument can get endless—and scary. But if we're open-minded and brave, clairaudience enhances the hearer in unpredictable and exciting ways."

"You sound as if you're trying to sell me a timeshare in Florida. I don't see how voices in my head can enhance my life."

"Lots of dead guys roaming around Vegas."

"Little Miss Sunshine cheats? I don't believe it."

"I do. Sometimes. But I donate my winnings to charity."

"Other than someone to play blackjack with, what do they want?"

"Sometimes messages from the other side offer closure, or warnings—don't drive, don't fly, don't eat the birthday cake—and sometimes it's the spirits who need closure. They seek until they find a conduit, and unfortunately, they can be extremely forceful."

Zoey clasped her head, unable to mentally file the influx of information. Irritated, she stood and rushed into the kitchen. She ripped open the cough syrup and guzzled it half-gone, hoping for enough alcohol to intensify the effects of the Valium. Has to be nonsense, she thought, but how could Sterling have guessed what she'd heard verbatim?

She licked the sticky from her lips and entered the dining room, where she could see Sterling perched on the sofa. "Say this garbage is real—what if I don't want it? How do I make it stop?"

"A more disciplined person can block whatever it is they don't want to hear, but I've never known anyone to eradicate it. Were you clairaudient as a child?"

"No. It's the drugs. I'm telling you, when I quit the pills the voices will stop."

"Mitch says you've been abusing pharmaceuticals since Milo died—over a year ago. When did you first notice clear hearing?" Sterling asked in a counseling tone.

"I don't know when it started." But she considered the question, and remembered. "In the hospital, I heard 'woman in the water,' and Dr. Selden said he and a colleague had a discussion in my room while I'd slept about a teenage boy dying in the undercurrent behind my house. The kid's mother watched him drown. Dr. Selden assured me my brain was simply regurgitating what I'd perceived in my sleep."

"Maybe he's right."

Zoey sped into the living room and stared at Sterling. "Am I special or aren't I?"

Sterling laughed. "You most definitely are."

"Don't be a bitch. You know what I mean."

"I do, and there's no reason to get hostile. I'm saying it's possible in that particular instance…"

Sterling's rambling faded in the wake of a literally shocking epiphany. The timing—the hospital—the first voice Zoey had heard. She set her hand on her hopping heart. "Lightning," she mumbled. "My so-called gift started following the lightning strike."

"Are you sure?" Sterling asked with owl eyes.

"Yes." Zoey reentered the kitchen, trancelike. She took another swig of cough medicine and quietly examined the string of events.

Blondie emerged behind her, holding out her munchkin hand.

Zoey relinquished the medicine. "You're not going to tell Mitch I'm chugging cough syrup, are you?"

"No," she said, and took a swig. "Lightning? That's incredible."

"It's horrifying. What else did lightning do to me? Do I have a third kidney?"

"Don't be silly. You've had extensive tests, and you're fine."

"Seriously? I'm hearing dead people and I'm fine?"

Sterling nodded reluctantly.

They passed the cough syrup back and forth until it was gone, and made their way to the dining table. The women sat hushed in the artistry of twilight smearing ivory above the trees.

Zoey broke the silence. "Does Mitch know you're psychic?"

"I think he suspects something peculiar, but he can't put his finger on it. We've never discussed it. I'm not sure he'd believe me."

"I'll convince him."

"That's not necessary. He relates to the businesswoman in me, the sexy pit-bull, not the mystical gypsy. And that's fine. I don't admit my ability to everyone. I felt morally obligated because of the danger I sensed."

"What should I do?"

"I can't advise you, Zoey. A spirit from the other side has contacted you for help. It's up to you to decide whether or not you'll listen. It's risky, the whole process. I don't think it's safe."

"Perfect. I'm staying."

Someone knuckled the door. Zoey and Sterling jumped inches off their seats.

Mitch walked in carrying a pizza box.

"You scared the shit out of us," Zoey said.

He chuckled. "Telling ghost stories?" He shut the door.

"Oh great," Zoey said. "ESP is contagious."

"Huh?" he asked.

"Nothing."

Sterling winked.

Mitch tugged Zoey's braid. "How're you feeling?"

"Peachy."

"How about you?" He addressed Sterling. "Were you able to nap?"

"No," she said, "but I'm okay. Second wind."

"Great." He set the pizza on the table and flung open the box lid. "Half spinach and half pepperoni."

"We were supposed to have dinner in Telluride," Sterling said.

"Yes, but..." He hesitated briefly and eyed Zoey. "Don't go ballistic. I called the psychiatrist Dr. Selden recommended."

"Are you out of your head?" Zoey snapped.

"You don't have to do anything you don't want to do. But we talked about this, didn't we?"

Before the voices were real, she thought. On the other hand, she had a long list of unresolved problems to sort through, including a four-bedroom shrine in Chicago. She nodded.

Mitch walked into the kitchen and returned with three plates. "Dr. Doyle. Nice guy. I briefed him on some of the things you've been dealing with—insomnia, nightmares, addiction—and don't take this the wrong way, but he doesn't think you should be alone. Not until he's had an opportunity to evaluate you."

"Just because I rely heavily on meds doesn't mean I'm addicted. And I can make my own appointments, Mitch. I'm an adult."

"An adult who couldn't walk up the stairs this afternoon," he said. "I think we all know how hard losing Milo has been for you, and we're in agreement you're having a strange drug interaction. It happens. Let us camp here tonight, and tomorrow he'll have some answers for us. Besides, your guest room is nicer than our hotel."

"Tomorrow?" Her stomach curdled.

"Yeah, in the morning." Mitch doled out pizza slices.

"What about clothes?" Sterling said.

"I stopped at the hotel. We have a suitcase in the car."

"I don't want to impose," Sterling said. "Zoey, do you mind if we stay tonight? We won't be any trouble."

"You can stay." Zoey folded a slice. "Mitch has to sleep outside."

"Couple of things before I pitch a tent. Your car is in the garage, and where did you say that trunk was you wanted me to bring in?"

"In the bed of Amos's truck."

Mitch walked to the adjoining garage door and exited. Within seconds he returned with the big black antique and set it down in the living room. "I'll pop the lock later. By the way, that truck's in pretty good condition. What do you plan to do with it?"

"I don't know. Do you want it?"

"I have an employee who needs a car."

"Sure. Take it."

"I'll call him tonight and let him know."

Zoey anticipated a dispute over her percolating question. She didn't want to care, but couldn't help herself. "What did you say to Lance?"

"Who?"

"You know damn well who I'm talking about. What did you say to him?"

"You asked me to get rid of him, and I did." Mitch slid out a chair and sat. "I accused him of being a gold digger."

Zoey swallowed a softball. "What! He's not."

"He might be."

"He has his own money."

"You have more."

"He has a Buddhist tattoo."

"Don't be naive. He's the type, Zoey."

"What else did you say to him?"

Her ex wouldn't speak.

"Mitch?" Zoey persisted.

"He was stubborn. He didn't want to go. I reminded him he was a one-night stand not worth blood on my fist. Bar trash. A punk."

Zoey shook her head. "You're an asshole."

"No, I'm not. When you sober up you'll know why I did what I did and you'll thank me."

"Enlighten me. Why did you feel the need to run your mouth?" Zoey asked.

"You're a fine one."

"Mitch," Sterling said, and that seemed to do the trick.

Mitch grunted, and resumed a level tone. "I don't think you're making rational decisions right now. I'm protecting you."

"Who's protecting me from you?"

"Me," Sterling said. "That's enough, Mitch, really. Zoey's still recovering from a lightning strike."

"By the way," Mitch poked. "Does Lance shave yet? How old is he?"

"Why don't you go chew on a tire or something?" Zoey said, tossing her half-eaten pizza slice on her plate.

"Am I invisible?" Sterling asked.

"No, babe, I'm sorry." Mitch withdrew like a scolded pet.

"Maybe we should all get some much-needed shut-eye and start over in the morning," Sterling offered.

Mitch nodded and smiled warmly at his tactful girlfriend.

Zoey stood and strayed to the staircase. "Best idea yet. I'm going to bed."

"I'll check on you in an hour," Mitch announced.

She didn't respond. At that moment she longed to hide in the sheets she and Lance had christened and pretend the rest of the day had been just another bad dream.

* * * *

Wind beat on the glass. Zoey rose from bed, her white T-shirt damp with sweat. The night flickered on and off—lightning. Her body tingled, strangely rhythmic with the voltage. She hesitated, afraid of the scattered bolts, and then, slowly, she advanced to the window. Clouds slithered across the horizon.

Down the hill at the tree line, a shadow wandered in circles.

"The boy."

Under the sky's whipping strobe, she watched the toddler take shape, his pudgy little hands and naked feet. He called for someone. Zoey closed her eyes and listened. Nothing. Impulsively, she opened the window and leaned out as far as she could. The air smelled humid and green, a divine terrarium.

Still unable to hear what the child was saying, she asked, "Are you lost?"

An unexpected gust formed and grew stronger by the second. She extended her neck and let the invigorating wind blast her face.

Momma.

"What?"

Momma.

Zoey's heart melted. She gazed at the baby boy searching for his mother.

Momma.

Another figure appeared near the child. The vision seemed more a memory than a current event. Whoever it was held a large ax. The weapon gleamed under fits of lightning. Zoey strained to identify the person, but wasn't sure whether to look at the tree line or close her eyes and retrieve information from her *matured* brain.

Momma. The child plopped on his butt and sobbed.

A streak of lightning touched the ground. Silver glinted above the boy's head.

"No!" Zoey's guts scrambled. She raced through the house and out onto the deck. Lightning flashed and she ducked.

A second blinding bolt dared her to save the child. She sprinted off the deck and treaded cold blades of grass, hard stones and brittle pine needles. She reached the memorable spongy area of grass, tasted metal, and continued running downhill.

The boy sat, confused and lost. He frowned, his face soaked in tears. Above him, the ax hovered.

"No!" Zoey's throat prickled.

With pitiless force, the weapon impaled the toddler's head. He screamed.

Blood splattered.

The ax came down a second time, slicing his skull. Lying on the lawn, the child whimpered, trapped somewhere between life and death. Bone and brain drenched in red, his fingers wiggled slightly, and the ax hit again and again and again.

"God, why?" Zoey bent forward and vomited.

She heard a swish in the lawn behind her, a rattlesnake, a bobcat, she didn't give a shit. Death would be a huge favor. She rubbed her forehead, trying to erase the images, but the incident remained vivid. She wept and puked.

The footsteps were Mitch's. "What are you doing out here?" he asked, wiping his eyes. Velvety dark outside, he hadn't noticed her chucked dinner. "You okay?"

"There was a child sitting by the trees." She panted. "He was killed. Brutally."

Mitch glanced at the flashing sky and cringed. "Come on, let's go in."

"Right there." She pointed to the murder scene, hoping to wake up. "He was there, and someone chopped him to pieces."

Mitch scanned the yard. He squatted and stroked her cheek. "There's no child. You had a nightmare."

Zoey smeared her tears with her wrist. Spurts of light illuminated the placid forest and unstained foliage. "The night I was struck, I saw a boy. I told you that, do you remember?"

"Yes."

"I saw him again tonight."

"There's no boy, Zoey," he said softly.

Zoey had heard the boy calling for his momma. She tried to communicate. Sterling hadn't said anything about soul-crushing images. Clairaudience was a joke, a lie. Zoey wanted nothing more to do with it. Drug-induced hallucinations were at least treatable.

Mitch helped Zoey to her feet, and she cried for a moment in the crook of his neck. After a deep breath, they turned and headed to the house.

"You need to tell Dr. Doyle what you saw," Mitch said. "I think he can help you."

"Where's your girlfriend?"

"Inside, why?"

"Doesn't concern you." Zoey darted through the doorway and into the living room.

Sterling waited near the sofa, snuggled in her cotton robe, observably worried.

Zoey confronted the paranormal parasite. "Wrong, Sterling. I'm not gifted, I'm insane. Do you understand? I need help. You have to stop feeding me bullshit that makes sense out of voices and children getting murdered."

"Murdered?" Sterling said. "What did you see?"

"A vision I never want to see again." Zoey rushed to the stairs. "Bring my fucking pills, Mitch. All of them." She stomped upstairs, sick of life and death and everything in between.

"You're seeing a vision that's important," Sterling yelled. "Don't disregard your talent. It's rare. I told you something terrible happened here. A spirit or spirits want your help. They're not going away, Zoey."

"Shut up!" Zoey went in her bedroom and slammed the door. Mouth soured, she went straight to the bathroom and brushed her teeth.

Mitch entered with water and meds. "What's going on with you and Sterling? What did she say to you?"

Zoey neared the bed. "Sterling's not who you think she is."

He set the glass on the nightstand and dumped a couple Valium in her pleading palm. Then he walked to the window, shut and locked it.

Zoey popped her sedatives and sniffled. "Make her explain her true self. Ask her to tell you what she told me."

"What is it?" He approached Zoey.

"None of your business," Zoey said. "I can't take much more of this."

"That makes two of us. We'll figure it out. We have to."

"I'm sorry about everything." She stared into his sensible eyes. "I've been grieving, but whatever is happening to me now is entirely different. I'm scared shitless."

"I'm here."

"Why?"

"Glutton for punishment." He stepped into the hallway.

Zoey closed the door on Mitch and his drama.

She lay in bed, unable to sleep. She sat up and unbraided her hair, then inhaled Lance's aroma from the sheets. Not even memories of Lance's perfection erased the toddler's bloodbath. She needed more Valium and a few ibuprofen. When she couldn't hear a sound, she sneaked into the hall and crept downstairs to scrounge for meds. Her inner guide told her she wasn't an addict. Anyone in her position would do the same thing.

She rummaged through kitchen cabinets and drawers, but knowing Mitch he'd have her pills in his suitcase or on his person. Control freak. Antsy, she went into the living room to flick on the tube. Her uncle's trunk sat next to the coffee table. Digging through it would be the perfect project to help occupy her mind.

Silently she hoisted the heavy trunk up the stairs. The corner of it bumped her shoulder and she nearly screamed. Inhaling through her teeth, she waited for the blistering pain to subside. She proceeded. The strong mildew odor suggested the trunk had been stored a long time. Final step and her feet touched the landing.

"What the hell are you doing now?" Mitch hollered from the shadows.

Zoey squealed and dropped the trunk.

"Ahh! Son-of-a-bitch!" Mitch hunched over and grabbed his foot.

"Mitch. I'm so sorry." She switched on the hall light. "You scared me."

"Obviously." He winced.

"I couldn't sleep. I thought I'd try busting the lock."

"I see that." He groaned and peeked at his puffy purple toes. "Crap. It's broken."

She set her hand on her forehead. "I'm really sorry." She eyed him. "Why'd you sneak up on me anyway? I mean, if what I was doing was so damn obvious, why did you have to ask?"

He grimaced and grabbed Zoey's arm. "I was scared too. You could have been sleepwalking or seeing children. These days there could have been a million reasons why you were up and walking around."

Zoey helped him balance on his good foot.

Sterling ran into the hall. "What on earth happened?" She rushed to Mitch's other side.

"I broke his foot," Zoey said.

Sterling looked mortified.

"It was an accident," Mitch said as he placed his hand on Sterling's shoulder and used her petite frame as a cane. "I heard noises and yelled. I frightened her. She dropped that old box on my foot."

"We have to go to the emergency room," Sterling said.

"It'll wait 'til morning. We'll take Zoey to Dr. Doyle's and you can drive me from there."

"Mitch," Sterling said, "we need to get your foot X-rayed. It's broken."

"And it'll be broken tomorrow."

"Sterling's right," Zoey said. "You should go to the hospital."

"What?" Mitch sniped. "You can't be alone while we're here, and you want us to leave?"

"I was fine," she said.

"This time. You're unpredictable. As soon as you stop seeing the boy and hearing voices and agree to help me clean the house in Chicago, I'll leave you alone."

"You had to squeeze the house in didn't you? You're crippled. Do you really want to fight?"

Mitch growled.

The three of them hobbled into the lavender-scented guest bedroom. Not her doing. There had been jars of potpourri on the dressers when she arrived.

Zoey helped Sterling get Mitch into bed, and propped his swollen foot on a pillow. "I am sorry, Mitch. I feel terrible."

"Don't beat yourself up. You didn't do it on purpose," he said.

According to Sterling's theory, their lives were physical manifestations of their subconscious thoughts. If that were true, Mitch had gotten off easy.

"Can I trust you to stop wandering around and go to bed?" Mitch asked, all tucked in.

"Yes." She modeled a curt smile and left, stopping in the hall to push the trunk against the wall. Her injury throbbed. She lifted the shoulder of her T-shirt and blew cool breath on her scar.

Rock Hounds.

She ignored nothing and hurried to her bedroom.

Rock Hounds.

"Subconsciously I want a drink."

Rock Hounds.

"Subconsciously I want a drink really bad." She closed the door.

Rock Hounds.

"Subconsciously I want Lance."

Rock Hounds.

"La-la-la-la-la-la-la!" She crawled into bed.

Rock Hounds.

Zoey cut through the intricate web tangling her mind. How had she strayed so far beyond health and reality? Her thirsty alter ego finally silenced. Zoey drifted off thinking about Dr. Doyle and a size six straitjacket.

Chapter 7

Bright, sunny day and the trio piled into Mitch's rental. Sterling drove, Mitch yelled on his cellphone at a flooring company, and Zoey sat in the back with her eyes shut, pretending to be anywhere but en route to a padded room. She even went so far as to imagine a less stressful destination with someone else driving. Sterling sat like an elderly woman crammed as close to the steering wheel as humanly possible. Zoey could do without another crazy image inking her brain.

She thought of her son. She remembered the last time she'd brought Milo to school. He bounced around in the back seat, bopping his head to whatever played on his iPod. She wished she had asked him what it was he enjoyed so much. Instead she'd tapped his knee and told him to turn down the volume.

"Mitch," Zoey said. "My shoulder hurts. I need a pain pill."

He turned. "You've had two. You're nervous, that's all."

"I'm not an adolescent. Contrary to your perception of me, I'm capable of telling the difference between pain and nerves. It's definitely pain."

Mitch huffed. "You can't pop a pill every time something makes you uncomfortable. Don't you want the hallucinations to stop?"

"Has nothing to do with pills," Sterling blurted.

"Yes it does," Zoey said. "And there's a cure."

"Cure for ghosts? Cure for clairaudience?" Sterling asked.

"You're relentless," Zoey said. "But you'll have to loosen your jaws on this one. I'm not buying it."

"You know the truth," Sterling went on. "You're a chicken."

"I'm not afraid of a drug interaction. You should be afraid, though. Your superior intuition is out of order. Dr. Doyle will prove I'm unstable, and then what, almighty oracle?"

"You ladies care to fill me in?" Mitch asked.

Zoey and Sterling simultaneously exclaimed, "No!"

He held his palms up in surrender. "I'm not about to challenge two of you." His gaze met Zoey's. "Before I get my head bit off again, I want to remind you Dr. Doyle has to impress you, not the reverse. If you don't like him, we'll find another specialist."

Overwhelmed by fears and failures, Zoey reclined, searching for a miniscule sense of tranquility. Wanton brain cells led her directly to Lance, his muscular body, round firm butt and perfect fit. She shook her head, wondering when she'd become so immature. And then she sighed, not really caring.

The SUV rolled into a parking lot trimmed with red brick buildings, each hooded in matching triangular rooftops. Sterling parked near the entrance, next to a black Escalade.

"Thanks for the ride," Zoey said as she exited the car and slammed the door. She hung her purse on her uninjured shoulder.

Mitch lowered his window. "You'll be fine. Dr. Doyle seemed like a real nice guy."

"Yeah, that's what you've said, over and over."

"I want it to sink in. He's not the enemy."

Zoey nodded, unconvinced.

"We're going to Monroe Memorial," Mitch added. "Sterling will be back in an hour to pick you up. If for whatever reason you need to leave early, call. Try to give it a chance, though, okay?"

Zoey's self-appointed caretakers made her palms sweat, the way they watched her enter the office. She wasn't a teenager. Then again, she'd admit she wasn't exactly stable either. She'd thought nothing could be worse than reliving her son's death nightly. Faceless voices and bloodbath visions came close. And her controlling ex and his dual-personality girlfriend weren't scary on their own, not really. But they'd certainly intensified her already weird experiences.

Depending on one's mood, the boxy waiting room colored in heavy earth tones could soothe or smother. Plush burgundy leather furniture lined the walls, and an attractive older man sat in a chair by a brass lamp, reading *Gold Rush* magazine.

He'd raised his head and stood abruptly. "Zoey Hawthorne?"

"Yes?"

"I'm Kane Ballentine, your neighbor. I brought you to the hospital the night you were struck by lightning." He extended his hand to shake.

She obliged. Used to be she'd analyze a person's bone structure first, their photogenic qualities. Lately, however, she went straight for the eyes, and his bewitchingly complemented his short silver hair and dazzling belt buckle.

"It's nice to finally meet you. Lightning. Crazy, isn't it?" she asked.

He laughed politely. His smile outshone every toothpaste model she'd ever photographed. "If it's any consolation," he said, "I'm not unscathed by the episode. I did some research on lightning. Golfing in the rain is a habit I've since quit."

"Sorry to put a damper on your game."

"Don't give it a second thought. Now when it storms, I paint. It's much safer. I'm hoping to have a smiley face completed by Christmas."

She snickered until she noticed the bulletproof glass shielding a Wicked Witch of the West clone.

Kane whispered, "She's not as grumpy as she looks, and the glass? One certifiable ruins it for the bunch."

"Nice to know I'm not alone."

Kane tilted his head, seeming unable to make sense of her comment.

"I must be crazy. I'm standing in a shrink's office."

"I've had my session, and my daughter will be out any minute."

"Oops."

"No, no, you're fine. We've heard the rumors. I'm sure a few crazies help Dr. Doyle pay the rent. I'm not one of them. I'm here because I needed an intelligent listener. Glorified confidant, that's what they are. The whole process is awkward. I've been coming here six months, and I haven't forgotten the feeling of inadequacy that walked with me through that door. If not for my daughter, I wouldn't have come. I'd be drunk in a ditch somewhere."

"Is he effective? Dr. Doyle, is he helping?"

"Absolutely. I've stopped overworking, and my daughter is back in her own bed—no more nightmares. Bottom line is, if she's happy, I'm happy." He paused. "My wife was killed in a car accident. I lost my best friend and Kendall lost her mother. It's been tough, but yes, Dr. Doyle is pulling us through it."

As many times as she'd resented people uttering those empty words, she'd said, "I'm sorry for your loss." She quickly compensated for her shallow acknowledgment. "My son died last year, and I'm still mad at the universe. Scratch that. I'm pissed."

"Then you're in the right hands." His silver eyes narrowed. "How old was your son?"

"Ten."

"Kendall's age." He looked as if his digestive juices went through a blender. "I am deeply, deeply sorry. No parent should ever have to endure the loss of a child."

"I couldn't agree more. I'd do anything to take his place."

Kane nodded.

Zoey couldn't tolerate the heavy conversation. "I should check in."

"By all means." Kane stepped aside. "If the cons of psychiatry intimidate you, I'll be sitting right there." He pointed to the chair with a magazine on the cushion. "I could present a few pros."

"I'll keep that in mind." Zoey turned and forced herself to confront the Wicked Witch, whom she discovered was Mrs. Doyle and, as Kane had implied, very gracious.

Following a brief and uninformative chat about the thick glass, Mrs. Doyle handed Zoey several forms and a pen. "Fill these out, only the lines that are X'd and Dr. Doyle will be with you shortly."

Zoey sat across from Kane, who'd hid behind a magazine. She focused on X's, and as she crossed the final T on the last questionnaire, a compact man with strict gray hair, cow eyes and small lips opened a door adjacent to a private hall.

He released a young girl, presumably Kendall, and she hurried to her father. She had big green eyes and her dad's charisma—she didn't hesitate to smile at Zoey. Kane could have been Kendall's grandfather, an observation Zoey didn't dwell on.

Kendall clutched a book with the passion of a drowning person hanging on to a life raft.

"*No Such Thing,*" Zoey read aloud, "by Skye Harper. My son loved that book."

Kendall gave the cover a glance.

"Kendall, honey," Kane said. "This is Zoey Hawthorne, the lady who moved into the Rayfield Ranch."

"The lady who was hit by lightning?"

"Guilty," Zoey interjected.

"Did it hurt?" Kendall's angelic face conveyed a touch of fear.

"Not at all," Zoey said. "I wouldn't have known I'd been struck by lightning if the doctor didn't tell me."

"Are you okay?"

"I have a small scar on my shoulder, but it's not too ugly."

"Can I see it?"

"Not now, honey," Kane said. "Ms. Hawthorne is here to talk with Dr. Doyle."

"About the lightning?" Kendall asked.

"That and some other things." Zoey said.

The girl peeked again at the cover of her book and went on, "Who's your son's favorite character?"

Kane contorted his face, apparently unsure of how to explain Zoey's son had died.

Zoey glanced at the screaming primary colors on the book cover. "My son liked Chaz."

"Me too," Kendall squealed happily. "Chaz isn't afraid of anything."

Zoey agreed. "And he's supersmart. Don't you think?"

"Yeah. They couldn't have sailed anywhere if Chaz didn't staple tablecloths together. And I like that Chaz likes bugs. A bug doesn't know it's bothering anybody. It's just living its life and then some crybaby annihilates him."

Kane stood. "Here's where I correct you if I may," he said to Kendall. "Having killed more than one or even two bugs, I'm displeased by your accusation." He playfully cleared his throat. "I am not a crybaby."

Kendall giggled. "No, Dad, you're not."

"Good." Kane smiled. "Now I think we need to let Zoey keep her appointment with Dr. Doyle."

Kendall's head lowered.

"I'm fine," Zoey assured. "Just need to vent, you know?"

Kendall nodded.

"Hey, kiddo," Kane said. "Why don't you wait in the car?" He handed her the keys. "I'll be right behind you."

"Okay, Daddy." Kendall addressed Zoey. "Dr. Doyle is really nice. You'll like him."

Zoey rose. "I appreciate the input."

Kendall pushed open the door and headed outside.

"She's a cute girl," Zoey said.

"She's my reason for living." Kane grinned, and several quiet seconds passed. "I hope this isn't too forward, but would you like to have lunch sometime?"

Her stomach roped.

"Not a date. Just neighbors getting better acquainted."

Her thinking blurred and various body parts perspired. She'd gotten messy, her life, her mental health. She wasn't interested in putting forth effort pretending to forgive the universe for taking her son.

"The support groups I've tried don't work for me. No one seems to understand why I want to fistfight the idiots who give me cross looks for mentioning my deceased wife's name. They think her name is a sand trap. They think by saying it I'm going to sink into irreversible depression. I love the way her name sounds. Tess Ballentine. I'll never forget."

"Milo Hawthorne."

Kane gazed compassionately into her eyes.

She agreed to lunch and wrote her cell number on a blank corner of her family history sheet. She ripped the paper and passed it to him.

"We'll talk soon." He cocked his head toward the door as if to remind her of Kendall. "I hope I'm not rude, running out so fast."

"Not at all. Children keep us busy."

"It was a pleasure." He smiled and rushed outside.

When the time came, she could always tell Kane she had the flu. She submitted her forms, and the idea of clairaudience trickled through her mind—batshit crazy, that's what she was, and she'd rather have a few strong drinks than talk to the doctor. She tiptoed toward the exit.

The door that had previously burped out Kendall creaked open.

"Zoey Hawthorne?"

"Yes."

Zoey turned and eyed the rigid man. He held a file, and if she were to photograph him, the picture would tell the tale of a person who lived by textbook laws.

"Shall we?" he asked as he moved aside, offering her plenty of entrance room. He'd released a daydreamy sigh, and she wondered if she had misinterpreted him.

She passed the expensive counselor slowly, his forehead barely reaching her chin, and noticed several floor-length pictures lining the hall. By the time she entered his office, stuffed with oversize furniture and bookcases, she'd diagnosed him correctly this time. He had an inferiority complex. Everyone on the planet had cracks, but like Sterling and Dr. Doyle, some concealed them better.

About five feet from his desk were two giant chairs. He stood between the seats and hand-modeled the one on the right. "Sit down, please."

She walked guardedly and sat with her purse in her lap.

"I'm Dr. Doyle." He lowered into the partnering chair. "Mitch Hawthorne is your ex-husband, is that correct?"

Zoey nodded.

"He explained some of what you've been experiencing. I'd like you to tell me in your own words. What do you think you've been experiencing?"

Think? She cringed.

"Ms. Hawthorne, I implore you to speak freely. I can't assist you adequately without full comprehension of your circumstances." He scooted farther into the chair. "Let me initiate. Your husband, excuse me, your ex-husband said you'd lost your son a little over a year ago. Is that why you're here?"

Her attention turned to the halogen desk lamp, and then a fake rubber tree near the window.

"Ms. Hawthorne?" he nagged.

"What was the question?"

"Are you here to expedite recovery from the loss of a loved one?"

"I think so, to some extent." She fiddled with the snap on her purse. "I'm out of my comfort zone. I'm a nervous wreck inside. I can't seem to focus on a reason. All I feel is the urge to run."

"Confronting your fears is part of the procedure. If you weren't tense, I'd be concerned. Are you here to resolve inner turmoil regarding your divorce?"

"What? No."

"Mr. Hawthorne said you had nightmares. Is that why you're here?"

"I haven't had a bad dream since I was struck by lightning."

"Ah, so that's why you're here, to understand why out of approximately seven billion people, lightning hit you?"

"No, but when you put it that way…"

He bent his elbow and set it on the arm of his chair. His jaw melted in his palm. "I've scored zero. Why don't you try again? Give it some thought and tell me, Ms. Hawthorne, why are you here?"

"Well, Dr. Doyle, initially I wanted to discuss the young boy I saw get bludgeoned to death in the woods."

Dr. Doyle lifted his head from his hand and widened his eyes.

"But if you were to ask Mitch, he'd say I needed to be here because I take too many pills. He's right, I do. And if my love of pharmaceuticals is why I saw the boy die, I'll stop. Then there are the voices. I'm hearing things, weird things that don't make sense. And yes, I miss Mitch sometimes, the way we were. Fuck. He'd be happy if I'd dismantle the shrine I've made out of our home in Chicago. But really, I think I'm here because I want my son back. He's why I take the pills. Not him, he was beautiful, but the pain. It hurt me more than I can ever verbalize."

"Of course," he said and shifted in his chair. "Who did you see get bludgeoned in the woods?"

"Mitch's girlfriend, Sterling, boy, she's an interesting character, anyway, she seems to think I saw a spirit."

"A spectral being?"

"Yes, a ghost." She picked at a snap on her purse.

"And this ghost was bludgeoned?" Dr. Doyle scratched his temple.

"Yes. But maybe it wasn't a ghost. I'm crossing my fingers, hoping I was hallucinating. And I'd settle for a slight nervous breakdown."

"I wouldn't go that far." He reclined, and Zoey got the impression he was showing her how to relax.

"All of a sudden I'm a damn motormouth. What's your secret?"

"It's my understated charm. Now, let's start with your son. Can you tell me what happened?"

"Stupid question. I was there and relived it in my dreams every night since. I can tell you what I smelled—popcorn. The man next to me just bought a bag. I can still smell the fake butter." She paused to keep tears at bay. "The look of fear on the face of a child who's about to die eats through your soul like turpentine to paint."

Dr. Doyle set the file he'd been holding on the table. "I know this is very difficult for you. I admire your strength. But do you mind starting from the beginning?"

She'd never have described herself as strong. Her constant desire to escape reality made her a weakling. Yet a strange internal phenomenon had occurred. Dr. Doyle had uttered a compliment. He probably didn't realize how much it meant, he just remarked, but his sincerity put a dent in her faux-steel wall.

"Sixteen months ago I picked up my son and his friend Yaphet from Yaphet's grandparents' house. They had a farm in the country, and the boys spent spring break there." She smiled. "The kids had a blast. They rode horses, went fishing, milked cows, drove tractors—they were miserable when I showed up. It's ridiculous, but I felt guilty for dragging them away from their fun. Driving home we spotted a county fair. It had the largest Ferris wheel we'd ever seen and the boys went nuts and begged me to stop. If only I'd have said no." Tears welled.

"Continue."

Zoey inhaled and exhaled a shaky breath. "That's it. It was the first ride they went on and the last. Their buggy broke, and the boys and an elderly couple on their way home from a road trip to Nashville fell to their deaths."

"I'm sorry. You've suffered a great loss. Is that all you'd like to share today?"

"Hell no, I've come this far, I might as well keep going. I have a lot of baggage. It's fucking heavy." She wiped her eyes. "My son landed smack on a manhole cover, and his blood dripped into the sewer. Shitty, right? Rats drank my baby's blood."

"Perhaps, but—"

"I'm not finished."

Dr. Doyle bowed his head, urging her to carry on.

"I used to pretend it wasn't a sewer, but another world, and his blood somehow helped a doctor or professor or prophet. Why else would he have landed there? I'd create stories about the people in that sewer. Before bed I'd imagine fantastic uses for Milo's blood. Pathetic, and I knew it, and knowing made it worse."

Dr. Doyle handed her a tissue from a box on the floor. "Coping mechanisms," he said. "Short term, they help us survive tragedies."

"Afterward I had nightmares—every night. Not even nightmares but graphic replays of the accident. That's when I started to go crazy with the meds. I needed sleep. I needed to forget for a while. I was desperate."

"Did you fill the forms out honestly?"

"Yes."

"Then I have a list of what you're taking?"

"Yes."

"Continue."

"On the way here I thought about the day Milo cranked his iPod. About how I made him lower the volume, and how I wish I would have talked to him about the song he liked. Why don't we do that, Dr. Doyle? Why don't we take time to truly connect with the ones we love?"

"Good question and one we cannot answer in an hour. What about the nightmares..."

"Lightning healed the dreams."

"Elaborate assumption."

"It's true. That night I woke up from a routine nightmare and took enough pills to sedate a rhinoceros. Fog swirled outside, real pretty, and lightning flashed—red lightning. I was a photographer for twenty years, and I never saw anything like it, brilliant red bleeding through slits in the sky. Thinking about it now, the drugs may have had something to do with it. Anyway, I walked to the window to get a better look. That's when I saw the little boy in the woods for the first time. I ran out to save him, but when I got there he was gone. I remember having a tantrum, and it was shortly after, as I walked back to the house, that lightning hit me—a direct strike to the right shoulder. The nightmares were replaced with voices, and I still see the boy in the woods."

"Voices?"

"Yeah, the boy I see is a young Hispanic child, maybe two or three years old. The voices don't make sense. Not really. I hear things like 'woman in the water,' 'do or die' and 'help me.'"

"How do the voices make you feel?"

"Fuck. I know there's no boy. I'm aware the voices are in my head. And that's even scarier."

"Why?" Dr. Doyle's eyes probed like a creepy scientist needling a Monarch butterfly.

"Proves I'm insane. I don't want to die in a padded cell. And if by some chance they're real, they're expecting something from me and I can't deliver."

"What do you think they expect?"

"I think I'm supposed to help the boy. He calls for his mother before he's murdered, and I'm supposed to help him. How, though?"

"Is he real or is he a figment of your imagination?"

"When I see him he's as real as my hand. In retrospect, my mind hasn't been clear, not for a while, maybe my brain is playing tricks. I'm sure it is."

"I understand." Dr. Doyle leaned forward, leather chair squeaking under him. He lifted her file and opened it, then read from a sheet of paper. "What about the lightning, Zoey? May I call you Zoey?"

She nodded.

"Getting struck by lightning is atypical. Oftentimes life-altering. What is your interpretation? Do you think you were selected by God or a higher power for one reason or another, or was it a random accident? Coincidental?"

"Don't be absurd. It was an accident," she snapped and paused in thought, slowing her final response to a wistful tone. "There was a moment in the hospital when the accident seemed meaningful. After all, I'd survived the assault of a killer, a remarkable killer with ties to the universe. It's kind of profound, don't you think?"

"I do," he said, moving on to the next question as if she'd revealed nothing. "After your son's death, did you experience physical illness?"

Dr. Doyle threw a pebble in another box—psychological hopscotch. Zoey had to mentally adjust to his fast pace.

"Yes," she said. "I puked every day. I had to carry a roll of toilet paper everywhere I went. I shit like a horse that lived on prunes. It was disgusting."

"You had mentioned pain, referring to emotional pain, is that correct?"

"Emotional and physical. It was too much. I couldn't handle it."

"And you're handling it now?"

"Other than the burn on my shoulder, my body doesn't hurt anymore, but my heart aches and I still can't believe my son is gone."

He made a few notes and continued. "You've recently relocated from where?"

"Chicago. Six months after Milo died, my husband and I separated. Three months later we divorced. Three months after that, Milo inherited my great uncle's estate. It automatically transferred to me."

"Why did you get divorced?" He arched an eyebrow.

"Mitch said he couldn't live in a shrine."

"A shrine?"

"I'm doing my best."

"You're doing fine."

Zoey caught herself hugging her purse, and it gave her a sense of security. Suddenly she understood why Kendall held her books so tightly. "Our home in Chicago is unlivable. Pictures of Milo, his clothes, shoes, toys, occupy every inch of space. Maybe if I didn't relive his death every night, I wouldn't have expressed my sorrow in that way. I tried to get help. I saw six different doctors and each wrote me a prescription for something, Cymbalta, Valium, Darvocet, Demerol, Prozac—they're on the list."

"Ever contemplate suicide?"

"Yes."

"Why?"

"Because I had nothing to live for." She shrugged.

"And now you do?"

"Not exactly. But recently I met someone in a bar and we had sex, phenomenal sex, and it completely changed my perspective—I don't feel so out-of-body anymore." A strand of loose hair tickled her cheek and she tucked it behind her ear.

"Interesting." He rifled through more of her paperwork and took a few minutes to read. "You've passed all of your medical exams. No indicated brain damage, white blood cells are normal, lipids normal, normal motor skills."

"Okay…"

"Says here you're volatile. Do you think you're volatile?"

"No—just pissed off every day of the week."

"You've built a place of worship in honor of your son. When you think about your home transforming into a place of worship, how does it make you feel?"

"Mitch hates it. But the house stays. I'm not touching it."

"Then you haven't progressed."

"I'm not here to discuss my fucking house. It's not the problem. It's there, not bothering anyone."

"Your former husband may disagree."

"So what. I'm sure at some point in our sixteen years together, something he did bothered me. Payback."

"I have more questions. Are you up for it?"

"Sure. But let's stay focused on the actual problem. Not the shrine."

"I'll make vigorous effort. How many siblings do you have?"

"None."

Dr. Doyle jotted her answers on one of the sheets of paper. "Are you ambitious?"

"I don't know. I used to be."

"Do you socialize?"

"With the human race, are you fucking kidding?"

"No," he said while writing. "Are your parents still alive?"

"Yes."

"How would you describe them?"

"Unnatural. They're too forgiving."

"When was the last time you had intercourse?"

"What does that have to do with anything?"

"How long after meeting the individual who returned you to your body did you have sex?"

"Same night."

"Do you consider yourself promiscuous?"

"I don't know. I hadn't had intercourse since my son died, and then I met Lance and had the best night of my life. So if the question is, do I enjoy sex? Yes, very much."

"Is that a scenario you would repeat?"

"Seven days a week."

Doctor Doyle closed her file, scooted to the edge of his seat and stood. "Ms. Hawthorne," he said while pacing from his desk to the chair. "Here are my thoughts."

Zoey surprised herself by giving a damn.

"I'd like to see you twice a month. I'd like to see you once a week, but routine questioning would daunt you into canceling appointments. So twice a month is my recommendation—it's doable. If an emergency should arise, you'll have access to my cell and landline. I'm available anytime. Our top priority is to reduce your prescriptions. Over time, you should eliminate all but the Cymbalta. It's the best drug for your condition."

"What condition?"

"Besides Dr. Selden noting volatility, which I'm in agreement with, you're having hallucinations associated with complicated bereavement, or abnormal grieving."

"Abnormal grieving? Who would be arrogant enough to tell people how to grieve?"

His eyebrows furrowed. "A psychiatric board of highly qualified doctors who, combined, have over a century of experience. They've devised a set of criteria that describes your case, hallucinations, long-term depression, marital breakdown, antisocial behavior, drug abuse, promiscuity—even the fact that you're here. You're not in total denial. You recognize your grief as a disabling emotion which indicates to me your healing process has already begun."

"How do you know I shouldn't be fitted for a straitjacket?"

"Simple. You have no family history of schizophrenia or mental disorders. Prior to losing your son, you had no symptoms of visions or voices. Your son died in an unforeseeable accident and logically you understand. But the subconscious mind is a labyrinth comprised of memories, ideas and stimuli, and somehow you've obtained an inflated amount of guilt. You couldn't save your son, Ms. Hawthorne. You've invented another boy to save—the child in the woods."

She inhaled the largest whiff of relief she'd had since she counted her newborn's fingers and toes. "What about the voices?"

"Auditory hallucinations caused by drug interactions interrelated to complicated bereavement. What you hear is nonsensical, and therefore you cannot save the child. There isn't enough information. You weren't aware the buggy was faulty. You lacked the information necessary to save your son. You're creating a guilt-based pattern."

Zoey recalled hearing a voice in the hospital room of the boy who'd died while rafting. And news of the young girl who'd met her end in the river had also triggered voices. She couldn't save those children either. "Another boy to save," she muttered. "How do I shut them off, the voices and visions?"

"That's the true challenge. I'm certain the drugs are exacerbating your symptoms. Suffice it to say we cannot rid the symptoms without ridding the cause. But—" He pointed a finger at the ceiling. "—drugs are not the cause, are they? Severe, prolonged mourning is. If we manage your grief—in other words, if you make peace with the idea that your son's death was not your fault. You'll find it easier to accept his passing and eliminate the drugs. The voices and scary images will disappear."

Zoey rose. "Are you telling me the voices and visions won't stop until I'm off the pills? Because realistically, I'm not ready to quit, not entirely."

"You don't have to, not yet. Now that you're aware of the origin, I think you can better control the hallucinations. However, you cannot expect a full recovery unless you address your addictions. Be it drugs, grief, sex."

Zoey huffed. "Where do I start?"

He scurried to his desk, jotted something down on a small piece of powder blue paper and handed it to her. "Follow these instructions."

She observed his writing, his drug protocol, dosages and discards. She read aloud, "Valium, ten milligrams before bed, and decrease Cymbalta to twenty milligrams, twice daily."

"Doable, do you agree?"

"Actually, Dr. Doyle, I haven't taken Cymbalta in a while. I've been on ibuprofen for pain. And Valium to sleep."

"Well, given the set of circumstances I believe are drug related, it may or may not be helpful to continue taking them. I almost feel, if you've omitted your antidepressant without major side effects, that's terrific, one less hurdle to jump. But if you find you're struggling, if the voices don't stop, please, take the recommended dosage. Consider hot tubs and saunas, and plenty of liquids too. You might experience mild flu-like symptoms. I want you to sweat. But keep hydrated. This isn't Chicago. We're at a much higher altitude."

"What are you saying? You're a psychiatrist; you don't want me to omit drugs."

"I want to you to be well with or without pharmaceuticals. Unemployment doesn't concern me. There is no patient shortage. Plenty of fruitcakes."

Zoey carefully observed the doctor.

"You heard correctly. It's true." He lifted his chin and gazed into her eyes. "How tall are you?"

"Five-ten."

"Ever play basketball?"

"No."

"You get that a lot?"

"Yes," she said. "Imagine everyone assuming since you're closer to the ground you collect rocks."

"Exceptional," he said.

"Do you?"

"Do I what?"

"Collect rocks?" she asked.

"No. Might I remind you a friendly attitude is essential to healing?"

"There's nothing wrong with my attitude. No offense, but I have to run."

"Running is acceptable as long as you stop and get my patient support card from Mrs. Doyle. You can call any hour of the day. I look forward to facilitating you through this difficult yet manageable process. See you in two weeks?"

"I'll think about it."

"If you schedule an appointment and can't make it, I expect twenty-four-hour notice or you'll be charged a cancellation fee on top of the service fee."

"Got it," Zoey said.

They shook hands and she exited, stalling at the receptionist's desk to write a check. Emotionally drained and awkwardly sober, she stepped outside and stood in the warm sunlight for five minutes before Sterling pulled up to the curb.

Zoey opened the passenger door. "Psychic powers at work?"

"No, I was parked under the tree in the shade, doing a crossword."

"How's Mitch?" Zoey got in and slammed the door.

"Second and third metatarsal bones are fractured. I'm going to take you home and go back to the hospital. Will you be all right for an hour or two by yourself?"

"I'm not a child."

"I didn't mean to imply you were incompetent. I'm talking about being alone with ghosts."

"Give it up, Sterling. Dr. Doyle explained everything. I'm not clairaudient. I'm an abnormal griever."

Sterling shook her head.

Zoey continued, "I'm a classic case. Everything, the voices, the so-called apparitions and even Lance are all symptoms of complicated bereavement intensified by drugs."

"Dr. Doyle put your symptoms in a box and tied it with a sparkly red bow. I wouldn't expect anything less from a conventional psychiatrist."

"He wants to wean me off the pills—bam!—unconventional."

"I'm not convinced. I've heard a snippet of something otherworldly in that house and what I feel there isn't static. It's lively. I'm not wrong about these things."

"What color am I thinking of?"

"Yellow."

"Fine. Again."

"Purple."

"Lucky guesses. One more."

"Lance," Sterling said.

"Maybe you're a freak of nature, but I'm not. I'm going to deal with my son's death, lay off the pills, and all of this head-spinning bullshit will be over. I have something real to fight, and I think I can beat it."

"I'm happy for you. You've made tremendous progress. But the spirits in and around that house are real too, and if you stay there and attempt to ignore them, they may harm you."

"You know what? I'm done with this conversation." Zoey turned on the radio and increased the volume. Drums and guitar kept her yapping driver quiet.

They arrived at the Rayfield Ranch, and Sterling parked next to the deck. "We'll be back as soon as we can. Keep your cell with you or stay near the landline. Mitch will probably call."

"He needs a shorter leash." Zoey hopped out of the SUV.

"I wish." Sterling gazed at the house and released a ferocious sigh. "Zoey, why don't you come with me? We'll pick up Mitch and eat an early dinner in town."

"No, ma'am. I'm not in the mood for Mitch. I'm going to rummage through the guest bedroom and see if I can't find the Cymbalta. I've been off them, maybe that's the problem. Anyway, Dr. Doyle said that was the best medication for my symptoms. Then hopefully I can relax and put some thought into other things, like resuming photography."

"I can't convince you to come along?"

"No. Drive careful." Zoey hip-bumped the door closed.

It took a few moments, as if Sterling considered how else she might persuade Zoey, but soon the silver bumper vanished in a column of dust.

Zoey walked up the single stair of the deck and examined her land with more awareness. The mountain peaks were sharp, and the scent of greenery wafted crisp and clean. Not a new lease on life, but at last she saw the sanctuary Mitch had raved about.

She entered the house, set her purse on the sofa and drank a glass of water. She walked upstairs and unsuccessfully snooped around for her pills. With a nap in mind, she passed the old trunk in the hallway and noticed the lock lying on the floor. Mitch must have picked the keyhole sometime that morning. Excited, she knelt and opened the creaky lid.

The heaviness belonged to the trunk, not the items inside. A thin layer of black and white photos covered the bottom. She lifted a stack. Most were outdoor shots of mountains and hills and various angles of a nineteen-fifty-something Chevy. There were a few of the Rayfield Ranch too, before Amos added the deck and second level.

She found a picture of three men in what was probably a cave. The tall lanky guy was no doubt her great uncle in his younger years, and the other two men she'd never seen. Her uncle stood in the back, behind a camera tripod. To his left a stocky man with a deep cleft in his chin crouched against a wall, and to her uncle's right, a bulkier fellow sat with his arm on his knee. They wore hardhats and smug expressions.

She spotted a manila envelope wedged in the corner of the trunk. Raising the envelope, she noted a weighty object inside and tore the seal. She dumped a sterling silver money clip with an intricate knot design in her palm. While twirling it she noticed a letter L engraved on the back. Double-checking the envelope, she found another photo.

"Ooh," she said as she reached for the picture. "What do we have here?"

A Hispanic family posed before a forest. Six adult men, four adult women, two teenage boys, three adolescent girls and one toddler—the child Dr. Doyle said she'd invented to save.

Zoey gasped. "He's real." She dropped the picture and the saddest eyes in the cosmos stared into her soul.

Rock Hounds.

"What?"

Rock Hounds.

Her body trembled with fear.

Rock Hounds.

"Right," she said. "I'm on my way."

Chapter 8

She sped to the tavern with no idea what she'd do when she arrived, her mind swaying somewhere between "holy shit" and "this can't be happening." As she whirred past trees hooped in sunrays, she decided to start with a drink or three and move forward from a more relaxed vantage point. It didn't take her long to get there. Just as Mitch had declared, the building stood slightly off the main highway. Her heart forgot to beat when Lance's Harley came into view.

"Shit," she said, parking next to his bike. "Doesn't he have chrome to polish?" She took a deep breath and got out of her car.

The hopping evening hangout she'd remembered crawled at noon. Only six patrons drank, mumbling and dragging, as if under water. Two burly guys cracked peanuts at a table next to a window. At the far end of the bar, a couple of wrinkled skinny men hung over their chairs, cackling at whatever conversation they'd whispered between them, and Lance and his abnormally large buddy Tank played pool.

Lance aimed at a stripe and paused when he sighted Zoey.

"Well, well," he said, "The flaxen-haired maiden graces us with her presence. Wally, set her up with whatever she wants, on me." He sank the eleven.

"Motherfucker." Tank stomped his foot.

"Calm down," Lance said as he hunched over the table for another hit. "It's not the first time I've kicked your ass in pool, and it won't be the last."

"True dat." Tank swigged beer from a glass mug.

Zoey noticed Tank's eyes, yellowish, almost feline. She didn't want to stare.

She ignored Lance's blazing eyes too, and all of his perfections taunting her the way chocolate cake might tempt a weak dieter. If lightning truly had left her with the unique gift of hearing the dead, then perhaps it also fueled her sexual desire. Why else would she want to lick Lance from top to bottom in a public establishment?

She walked to the bar, surprised to see Wally. "Don't you sleep?"

"Not today," Wally said. "Day barman called in sick." He wiped his hands on a towel. "Welcome back. What can I do you for?"

"I'm not sure," she said, thinking of how to phrase her illogical questions.

"If you're not sure, then I'm useless." He turned, and Zoey grabbed his upper arm.

"No, wait," she said. "This is going to sound really crazy."

"Try me," Wally said.

She stopped chewing the inside of her cheek. "I've been having recurring dreams and in them a man tells me to come here."

"Here?" Wally twisted his eyebrows. "What man?"

"Doesn't matter, I never see his face. But he tells me to come here to Rock Hounds. In fact, that's all he says, Rock Hounds."

"Why do you care? It's just a dream."

"A recurring dream, sleeping, naps, pretty much every time I close my eyes, the dream directs me here. It's annoying. What do you think it means?"

Wally laughed. "How the hell should I know?"

Zoey searched the place for some sign of why the spirit wanted her in the musty old tavern. She observed the glistening bottles of booze, the cash register, and Wally eyeing her as if she'd slapped herself between sentences.

"You said you knew my uncle?" Zoey pried.

"No, I said he used to drink here."

"You thought someone wanted to kill him?"

Wally leaned forward. "No, *he* thought someone wanted to kill him."

"Did he ever mention hearing voices or seeing ghosts?"

"You need a drink." He turned and grabbed the Cuervo from the shelf and filled a shot glass.

She downed it. "So he never said anything about his house being haunted?"

"Are you serious?"

"Yes." She pointed to her shot glass.

Wally poured more Cuervo, put the bottle back and clutched an empty beer mug that suddenly appeared on the bar to her left. He headed to the tap.

Lance shadowed her periphery.

Zoey placed her hand above her navel to ease the blizzard whipping around in her stomach. The indefinable grip Lance had on her was a language only her body understood. She forced an apology. "I'm sorry about what happened."

"No harm done."

"Don't be an asshole. I'm making amends. I'm going through a lot of shit right now, but I want you to know I had a great time, and I'm sorry we didn't end on a better note. That's all. I've said what I had to say."

Wally returned with Lance's beer.

Lance took a few gulps and set his mug down. His eyes slimmed. "I can't figure you out. First you show up wearing your shirt on backward, set on getting me in the sack. I bite and it's badass, but then you go berserk on me in the morning. Now you're asking Wally about ghosts. Are you one spoke short of a rim or what?"

"The shrink said I'm fine, but I disagree." She drank her shot.

Lance smiled. "You're trying to take the easy way out. A crazy person can get away with just about anything." He looked at Wally. "Do you think she's crazy?"

Wally scratched his beard. "Crazy as a monkey on roller skates or a good mystery novel. I'm hooked. I want to know what happens next."

"Awe, shucks, Wally," she said. "Glad I entertain you, but I'm losing sleep."

"She was telling me about her dreams," Wally said. "Someone wants her to come to Rock Hounds."

"Your subconscious is leading you to me. I'm touched." Lance set his palm over his heart.

"As irresistible as you are," she said, "that's not it."

"You say you're having dreams about Rock Hounds?" one of the skinny guys yelled down the bar.

"Uh, yeah!" Zoey massaged the back of her neck.

"Are you dreaming about the tavern or about rock hounds?" Skinny asked.

"What's the difference?"

A deep voice from behind offered, "The tavern is where you get alcohol. Rock hounds drink alcohol."

She turned and addressed the two fellows cracking nuts at the table. "What?"

The man with a handlebar mustache crushed a peanut and very daintily picked out the legume. "Rock hounds are what they called prospectors. This is an old mining community."

His peanut-crushing partner swiveled in his chair, adding, "'Specially up in Big Cat."

"That's where I live." Zoey spun toward Wally, pointing to her shot glass. She readdressed the two at the table. "So maybe my dreams are about prospectors, not the bar?"

"Maybe," Skinny interjected.

"Why'd you want to know if Amos thought his house was haunted?" Wally asked.

"I heard footsteps. Could've been a squirrel on the roof."

"It's probably haunted," Skinny said.

"Is Amos in your dreams?" Wally asked.

"No," she said.

"Amos Rayfield?" the mustached peanut lover asked.

"Yep," Wally said.

Zoey turned in every direction, following the conversation.

"He hanged himself!" Skinny said.

"Yeah, in the garage. So?" Zoey asked.

"So maybe he's haunting the place," Skinny countered.

"No, it's not him," Zoey said.

"Barbiturates," Lance mumbled.

Tank released a single chuckle.

"You're a prick," Zoey said to Lance. "And no it's not the pills. I'll admit," she announced to the others, "I appreciate a buzz. It makes the trials of life easier to cope with. Smoothes the edges, you know?"

The room nodded in agreement.

"Can I trust you guys?" she asked.

Cooperative grunts implied she could.

"I'm not really here because of a dream."

Silence.

"The night I was struck by lightning, I saw a boy in the woods."

"You were struck by lightning?" Skinny asked.

"Yes."

"I knew a guy who was struck by lightning in the thigh," mustached peanut man said. "He can't drink a beer with dignity anymore. He drools."

"Anyway." Zoey tried to stay on track. "I thought seeing the boy was, well, due to a drug interaction."

Sympathetic grunts folded into one another.

"But lo and behold I found a picture of the boy in an old trunk at the ranch. He wasn't a dream, and I didn't hallucinate. At some point the child existed in the flesh. And now I'm hearing 'Rock Hounds.' What do you have to say about that?"

"There's the cause of the footsteps. It's the boy," Skinny said.

Lance studied Zoey.

Zoey quietly skimmed over the incoming information. "So, Big Cat is an old mining community?"

"Yep," Skinny said. "Started in 1859 and a hundred years later the place was scraped clean. Regulations got stiff and taxes went sky high. There ain't been no activity in Big Cat since about 1955. Tell you what, I've seen ghosts up on 'nem mountains and in the woods. Prolly prospectors who've died of hunger, thirst and disappointments. If you ask me, that whole town is haunted."

"No one asked you," Wally blurted. "I have to draw the line somewhere."

Zoey stepped to the table where the mustached man ate peanuts. "What about you? Do you think Big Cat Canyon is haunted?"

He broke open a shell. "I think money corrupts, and lots of money kills. It was rough times then, people traveled a long way with big hopes. Men worked their fingers bloody and went days without sleep. Their minds weren't right. I think history like that can haunt a place. But I also think Big Cat hasn't suffered too much. It's a wealthy community. If folks get scared, they can hire a bodyguard. Better yet, they can leave town and spend a month in Vail."

"I inherited Rayfield Ranch and a nice sum of money." Zoey gazed out the window and the sun blanketed her front. "Not sure I belong here, but I don't know where to go. Maybe when the smoke clears, I'll visit Italy."

"Shit," peanut lover said, "I've never been out of the States. Plenty to see in the USA. I'm an American. I'm right where I belong."

"Give me another shot, Wally," Zoey said.

Lance crossed his arms. "I'm curious. You say you found a picture of the boy you've been seeing in the woods. Are sure you've never seen the kid before and recreated him. I don't know, maybe while you were drunk or high?"

"Positive." She drank, feeling slightly tipsy. "It's an old picture. I think from the fifties. How could I have seen him prior to the photo?"

"Newspaper, online?"

"Nope."

"Magazine, television?"

"No. I've never seen this boy. But I've seen his ghost in the woods and the picture proves it. I still don't know what I'm supposed to do."

"Ghosts and voices?" Wally asked. "That's some predicament."

"It is, because the boy was murdered. But what would he have to do with mining? He was only two or three years old."

"A little boy was murdered?" Tank asked as his odd pupils dilated.

Zoey nodded.

Skinny blurted, "How in the world did you see that?"

"I told you he's a ghost. I don't know how I saw him or his demise. Same way you see ghosts in the mountains. This whole thing is bizarre and hearing them is something else entirely. My ex-husband's girlfriend thinks I'm clairaudient."

"What?" Wally asked.

"It's the ability to hear voices in other dimensions."

Silence.

Tank said, "Go on."

"So I heard this child calling for his momma—"

"The boy in the woods?" Wally asked.

"Yes. I listened and watched and he was bludgeoned to death. I think I'm supposed to help him..." She huffed. "Or, I don't know, I'm supposed to do something, but what? He's already dead."

"You're in a pickle," Wally said.

"Sure are," Skinny agreed.

Lance's face softened, and despite her compelling mission, she had to turn away to calm her hormonal urges.

"We're on the same page then?" she asked. "We think rock hounds isn't the tavern, but miners?"

They nodded in consensus.

"What do I do?"

"You keep asking us," Skinny said. He swigged from a brown beer bottle and set it down on the bar. "Ask whoever sent ya here."

"Yeah," she said. "Why not? If I can hear it, maybe it can hear me." She approached Lance. "Thanks for the drinks." She turned and hurried to the door.

"Keep us posted," Wally said.

"You bet."

"Wait up." Lance followed. "Where're you going?"

"Home, first to call my psychiatrist and demand a refund, and when I've convinced him to retire, I'm going to hang up and start a conversation with a ghost."

"Need help?"

"With?"

"Either, or."

Drawn to the waves in his thick black mane, she said, "Absolutely."

Stepping out of dim light and into daylight burned Zoey's eyes, and she stopped to focus.

Lance walked leisurely and put his face inches from hers. "For the record," he said. "I'm not after your money."

"I know."

"So we summon the dead, and then what?"

"We'll think of something," she said.

"You promise not to throw me out in the morning?"

"I make no promises. Take a chance."

"My pleasure."

"Cornflakes and coffee is what's for breakfast and will be available as soon as you open the box and pour the food in your bowl."

"I don't have a problem with that."

"Good answer." She gestured her car. "Want to ride with me?"

"A cage on a beautiful day like today? No way."

She inhaled fresh afternoon air. "I understand."

* * * *

She pulled into the garage, and Lance parked next to Mitch's SUV. She thanked serendipity for leading her to alcohol. Sober, the Mitch-Lance reunion would have been unbearable.

Lance turned off the ignition, dismounted his motorcycle, and stared at her ex's rental car, seeming perplexed.

Zoey got out of her car and playfully bumped into her recruited lover. "Don't worry," she said. "I'll take care of him."

On the deck, at the door, Zoey paused.

"Having second thoughts?" Lance said.

"No."

"He's your ex," Lance said. "Why do you give him so much control?"

"I don't know... Sixteen years together... He looks like our son... I won't let him sell our home... Guilt? Pick one." She turned the knob and entered the living room with Lance.

Mitch sat next to Sterling on the sofa, his plastic cast propped on the coffee table and his cellphone in hand. He and Sterling went into visible shock when they spotted Lance.

"For Christ's sake!" Mitch lowered his wounded foot and stood at light speed. "Where the hell did you go?" he asked Zoey and eyed Lance. "And why are you here?" His glare darted back to Zoey. "Why is he here? We've been worried. Why didn't you leave a note? Or call?"

Lorelei Buckley

She exhaled agitation. "You won't ask one question at a time because you don't want answers. You want to talk at me, not to me."

"I'm upset." Mitch lowered his tone. "What's he doing here?"

Lance smiled. "The house is haunted. I'm helping her communicate with the dead."

Zoey addressed Sterling. "I think you're right. There's a spirit here, and I can hear him."

Mitch squinted.

Zoey went on, "Mitch popped the lock on the trunk and I—"

"No, I didn't," he said.

With an expression, Zoey asked Sterling if she'd unlocked the trunk. Sterling shook her head.

"There you go," Zoey sliced the air with a presenter's hand. "A ghost."

"Cut it out," Mitch said. "You're drunk. I can smell the alcohol."

"I had a few shots, no big deal. I'm one-hundred-percent coherent. And for your information, Dr. Doyle wants me to lower dosages, not stop altogether. Leave my pills on the coffee table."

"Done." Mitch raked his fingers through his hair.

Lance tiptoed around Zoey and Mitch, and sat next to Sterling on the sofa.

Sterling urged, "Finish what you were saying. The trunk?"

"Somehow it miraculously unlocked," Zoey said, "and inside was a pile of old photos. There was an envelope too, with a money clip and an old picture of a group of people. Here's where it gets crazy. One of the people in that photo is the boy I've been seeing in the woods. The same child Dr. Doyle claimed I'd invented to save."

Sterling jumped to her feet. "No!"

"Yes."

"Where is it? Let me take a look. I want to feel for information."

"What kind of information?" Mitch asked.

"Mitch," Sterling said gently, "I sense things. Energy, and—"

"Colors," Zoey said. "Go ahead, think of a color."

"No, don't," Sterling said. "I'm trying to tell you there's more to my hunches. Some might describe me as highly intuitive and others would swear I'm psychic or a channeler or clairvoyant. I prefer the term sensitive."

Mitch froze as if the earth had cracked beneath him. It had.

Sterling had more to say. "Zoey and I have determined the lightning affected her in extraordinary ways. She's not only seeing ghosts very vividly but hearing them. It's called clairaudience."

Lance smiled proudly.

Mitch raised his arms and chin and yelled, "For fucks sake, what's going on?" He stared at Sterling as if she'd stepped out of her skin and then gave Zoey a scorching look. "We need to talk."

"Fine." Zoey hurried to the staircase. "After I get the picture for Sterling." She raced upstairs, grabbed the photo and returned to the trio. She handed the evidence to her ghost-tracking partner. "The boy is in the bottom row, the youngest child."

Lance stood and viewed the image over Sterling's shortness. "Are you scared?" he asked Zoey.

"Terrified."

Mitch reached in the duffle bag near the sofa and withdrew two prescription bottles. He slammed them on the coffee table and zeroed in on Zoey. "Outside."

On her way to the door, Zoey addressed Sterling. "Obviously I have no idea whose voice I'm hearing, but I think that picture is the answer. Stroke it, hold it, kiss it, chant, I don't care what you do. Just help me understand what the spirit wants."

Sterling remained focused on the picture.

Mitch rubbed his forehead and took a long deep breath. His casted foot thudded against the floor as he followed Zoey out to the deck.

Gaining a glimpse of the forest, Zoey noted leaves dazzling like emeralds in the sunlight, and a brilliant topaz blue sky. Coldstone River swooshed in the background, audibly beautiful and daringly violent.

Zoey faced Mitch. "Look, I know we seem like a couple of dippy chicks closing in on a naked pillow fight, but what we're telling you is the truth. Your girlfriend is psychic, this house is haunted and ever since lightning hit me I've been hearing a ghost, or ghosts." She paused briefly. "It started in the hospital with 'woman in the water,' and here at the house I've heard 'do or die,' 'help me,' and 'rock hounds.'"

"Horseshit. There's another explanation—has to be."

"Okay, let's say there's a million ways to spin this thing. For your information, Sterling and I heard the same thing on the same day. How?"

"Coincidence." He exhaled. "You hallucinated, and she's sensitive. She picked up on your thoughts."

"You are so damn stubborn!" She shook her head. "Why is it you can believe Sterling's sensitive, but you can't believe the lightning gave me a gift?"

"It's absurd."

"What about the boy in the woods? I saw him prior to finding the photo. I saw someone murder him. Explain that, Sherlock."

"I don't know," he said, blatantly perturbed. "Maybe you've seen him before. You don't remember. How could you? You're a pharmaceutical junkie."

With a decent amount of strength, she smacked his scruffy cheek.

Mitch held his reddened jaw, eyes glassy and voice subdued. "I deserved that. I'm sorry."

Zoey studied the man she'd once loved with her entire being, evaluated his confusion and wounds as apparent as the mountains. "This isn't about ghosts, is it?"

Mitch stood quiet, but his sorrowful gaze conveyed the depth of his pain.

"We can't go back," she said. "We're not the same people who fell in love. We're not even the same people we were yesterday."

"I miss you so much it hurts," he said softly. "I miss our family. I miss helping Milo with his homework." A tear streamed. "Shooting hoops, playing video games, fishing. I miss you and your camera capturing everything from stress to love to curiosity. You're an amazing photographer, Zoey. Don't give it up."

She wanted to hold him, but didn't. "I'm speechless. I thought you were putting the past behind you, graceful as a butterfly. I was jealous."

"It's the hardest thing I've ever done."

"Well, you had Sterling. She made it easier."

"Let's be clear, Zoey. You dismissed me. I wanted to talk with you more than anything. I wanted to help each other through the pain, and you shut me out. Do you know what that was like for me? My whole world came to an end. My son, my wife, my home—gone in a blink. I didn't go looking for a relationship, but when I met Sterling I had an instant ear. She's been tremendously supportive."

"I know. I'm happy. I am."

"I realize we're over. I know Milo's gone." He wiped his eyes and sniffled. "Sneaks up on me sometimes. Must be all the changes."

"Changes?" she asked.

"You and Sterling. She took her mask off, and you put one on, and you're both telling me things that go bump in the night aren't my imagination."

"No one's wearing clown makeup. I didn't want to believe it either. I didn't like what I saw, and I still don't know what I'm supposed to do with the images. I'm not Nancy Drew. I'm a woman who doesn't typically give a shit, and I'd like to pop my antidepressants in peace. But that's not happening." Zoey's shoulder tingled and she breathed the annoyance away.

"Okay, suppose it's true. You don't have to stay. You don't have to do anything."

"Sterling told me it would be dangerous to stay. She said there's tremendous rage here."

Mitch smiled. "Like attracts like."

Zoey shrugged.

"I have to backtrack, though." His dark brown eyes penetrated her shield. "Do you love me even a little?"

Zoey licked her lips and glanced at the horizon, searching for the right words. Not sure she'd found them, she answered with what came to mind. "You're in my heart, forever. What we had was the most amazing thing anyone could hope for, and I'm grateful I had the chance to experience it. But there's a part of me that hates it too. If not for you and me there wouldn't have been a Milo and he wouldn't have died. It was a tragic death." She huffed, questioning her rant. "I don't know who I am anymore. But I'm positive I'm in transition and incapable of going backward. Sterling is mad crazy in love with you. Don't take her for granted."

"I don't mean to. Maybe I'm not ready."

Zoey crossed her arms. "She's willing to wait."

The door ripped open, and Zoey and Mitch jolted.

Lance stood in the frame. "Get in here. Sterling hit the floor."

"Speak human, will you?" Mitch asked.

"She fainted," Lance said.

Zoey and Mitch zoomed past him through the doorway and froze. Sterling lay on the hardwood, anemic-looking and sweaty.

Mitch knelt next to her and lifted her lifeless head. He put his finger under her nose, and then on the pulse of her neck.

Lance stood close. "She was staring at the picture, and it was insane, she started trembling and muttering 'family' and 'rock hounds.' She repeated it a bunch of times and then fainted like a fucking ragdoll. She just collapsed."

Mitch gently slapped Sterling's cheek. "Sterling, honey, wake up."

"Something's here," Zoey said.

"How do you figure?" Lance asked, scanning the room.

"I can feel its breath against my ear. It's hot and smells like rotten meat."

Chapter 9

Pellet-sized chills grew on Zoey's skin. "Get Sterling out of here."

Mitch crinkled his eyebrows as he packed Sterling in his arms. He teetered to his feet. "I'm taking her to the ER."

"She doesn't need a doctor, Mitch, she needs to get the hell out of this house," Zoey said, smoothing goose bumps on her arms. "Feed her fresh air, water and placid energy and she'll bounce right back."

"Placid energy?"

"Yeah," Zoey insisted while setting his car keys and Sterling's handbag on Sterling's stomach. "Think flute music, a gentle breeze, a fawn nibbling berries. Be creative."

Mitch turned toward the door. "Can't be aspirin or chicken soup," he mumbled over his clomping medical boot. "Has to be stardust and sleeping fawns."

Sterling's limbs hung like damp stockings.

Zoey ran ahead with his duffle bag and threw it in the back seat. Returning, she crossed paths with Mitch on the deck. "She'll be okay. I promise."

"Don't be a heroine. If this house is haunted and some enraged destructive spirit wants revenge, you shouldn't be here either."

"Like attracts like, remember? Take her to the hotel. Let her rest."

"Our suitcase is in the house."

"I'll bring it by later. Sterling needs to distance from this place like ten minutes ago."

Mitch shook his head as he carried his overwhelmed girlfriend to the SUV. He made her comfortable, and minutes later drove down the red dusty road.

Lance shut the door quickly, seeming slightly jacked up on adrenaline. "How do you know she'll be all right?"

"I don't." Zoey brushed her hand along the furniture and walls. "Sterling senses energy through touch. It's not working for me."

"This has reality TV written all over it."

"Not in a million years." She picked up the photo from the floor. "What do I say? Where do I start?"

Lance examined the ceiling. "Hello? Anyone here?"

Zoey waited a few hopeful seconds, but nothing happened.

"Do you still smell rotten meat?" he asked.

"Yes." She inspected the photo again, the sad-eyed boy and his—

"Sterling said family." Zoey handed the picture to Lance. "What do you make of this?"

Lance looked. "Migrant workers, maybe *braceros*?"

"You're not helping."

"*Braceros* were people transported from Mexico—some legal, some not—to work on farms. Mostly in Texas and southern California."

"I've read the paperwork. The only animal that ever lived on this property was Amos Rayfield."

A loud clunk echoed from the second floor hall. Zoey and Lance made eye contact before walking together toward the stairs.

"Hello?" Zoey said, inching up the steps. "You can talk to me now. I'm listening."

Familia.

Zoey stopped. "I heard something—*familia*. Family," she said. "Whose family?"

Familia.

Another nerve-rattling sound in the hall had her racing to the trunk. The picture of three men in hardhats lay on the lid.

Lance caught up. He reached over and grabbed the print. "Here's your rock hounds."

"What?"

"They're wearing hardhats, and it looks like they're crouched in a mine shaft. Rock hounds."

"That's my great uncle." She pointed to the man standing in the back. "I don't know the other two. Would *braceros* come this far north?"

"Why not? When you're broke you'll go anywhere. Especially if you have kids, and I count six."

"Farming, though?"

"Mining."

"I haven't seen anything even remotely close to a mining shaft on this land. Three kids died in the river. Policemen, firemen and paramedics scoured the grounds. No one's mentioned an old mine."

"Doesn't prove anything. The mine could have been anywhere."

Zoey knelt and opened the trunk. She held a wad of pictures and flipped through them, searching for a hint. The antique money clip glistened. She put the photos down and lifted the clip.

"Here." She gave the bill holder to Lance. "This was in an envelope with the picture of the supposed *braceros*. It has an L engraved on the back. You should take it."

Lance kneeled next to her, seeming flattered but hesitant. "An heirloom should stay in your family."

"It's initialed with an L, and my uncle's name was Amos. I think it belonged to someone in the photo. I have no use for it—L for Lance—makes perfect sense."

Lance stuffed it in his pocket and spread all the photos on the floor. "We have a picture of the boy you see, and evidence suggesting your uncle and two other men were rock hounds. What else do we know?"

"I saw someone murder the boy in the woods," Zoey said. "In my darkest hours I couldn't have imagined a more heinous act. Was it real? I'm not sure. Pain pills and rebellion make for a trippy ride sometimes." She exhaled. "Damn it, Lance, I'm trying to focus, I am. But this thing is too big for me because the only absolute right now is that I want a strong drink, pain pills, and you inside of me. Am I screwed or what?"

"Not yet." Lance chuckled. "Seriously." His grin faded. "Old habits, especially old fun habits, are hard to break. You're used to shutting down your emotions. This must bother you. Give yourself time. And be realistic— we're talking about tormented spirits, psychics and clairaudience. Surreal madness in its rawest form—shit'd make a nun hit the bottle."

"Okay, then. Let's take a few Valium and do what we do best. We'll talk to ghosts afterward."

"That's the easier option. Stay with me a minute longer and when we're done, I'll carry your sweet ass into the bedroom and spin your head."

"An offer I can't refuse."

Lance stood and in the process swiped the photo of three men in hardhats. He directed the image outward. "Rock hounds! Am I right?"

Zoey rose, intrigued by Lance's outburst.

"You see," he said, turning circularly, showing the picture to the ethereal dweller. "We want to help, but we need confirmation. Are these tools your rock hounds?"

Zoey stood next to Lance, shoulder to shoulder.

"Come on," he said. "Stop dicking us around!"

An ice-cold wind slapped Zoey's back clear to her spine. "Holy shit."

"I felt it too. We're not alone. Still smell like dead cow?"

Zoey nodded. She let her hair loose to blanket her arms and yelled, "What good is my gift if you won't use it? Talk to me."

Another arctic gust blew through her, and she looked to Lance, whose lips had turned blue.

"Fuck," he said, shivering. "Can it hurt us?"

"I think so," she said, unable to find warmth. "It's threatened me, but we're useless to it wounded or dead."

Rock hounds.

"Is Lance right?" Zoey hollered eagerly.

Rock hounds.

Her heart fisted her chest. "I'm listening."

"To a ghost?"

"Yes," she said to Lance and readdressed the invisible. "What about rock hounds?"

A whitish blur appeared near the staircase. It moved like a child's helium balloon.

Lance's eyes were as big as camera lenses. "I can't hear voices, but I'm seeing—"

"An apparition," Zoey whispered in shock.

Several nervous breaths later, the apparition flew down the stairway. It reminded Zoey of photos she'd snapped at a shutter speed of 1/8 of a second, similar to the one she'd taken of Milo on his skateboard to give the impression he was zooming across the ground.

Sheer milky streaks smeared down the stairs, and Zoey raced after the apparition, skipping steps to keep up. She'd landed in the living room, and Lance banged into her backside, apparently just as intrigued.

"There it goes!" Lance pointed at the ghostly spectacle as it entered the dining room and penetrated the door leading to the garage.

Zoey followed. She opened the door and stood on the concrete next to her car's bumper. When she'd parked, she'd left the garage door open. The entity hadn't flown outside. She felt it in her bones. Something watched them.

"Where'd it go?" Lance asked.

Zoey scanned the deer heads, her filthy BMW and bug-splattered windshield. She eyed Amos's empty Dodge. "I don't know."

"Here, Ghost, come on, don't waste our time."

"Let's not antagonize something capable of making ice cubes of our organs."

He nodded and glanced over her shoulder. "There it is!"

Zoey spun and swallowed a lump. The transparent smudge hovered at the far end of the garage. Seconds later it darted into an empty wood cabinet, vanishing the way an episodic daydream might.

Lance lunged forward, trying to grab the entity. He laughed as his boots hit the floor. "Did you see that? Your house is haunted and that ghost isn't bashful. Totally badass."

Zoey's pulse ticked like a pencil tapper on crack. "If you recall, our Casper wasn't all that friendly."

"No, it wasn't," Lance said. "But you're right. We're helpless if we're dead."

"And dead if we're helpless?"

Lance fell silent long enough to scratch his chin. "Possibly."

"I wouldn't blame you if you left."

"We're all doomed anyway. Death by ghost is at least original."

Zoey shook her head. "Are we being courageous or stupid?"

"The bigger the risk, the greater the adventure." Lance grinned.

"Spoken like a true biker cliche."

"What's your excuse?" he asked.

"Nothing better to do, I guess." She paused. "The smell is gone. We can go in now." Zoey walked through the dining room, past the potbelly stove, and into the living room. She plopped on the sofa. "All of this excitement, this insanity, children dying in the river and a spirit talking to me from the other side, I should be meditating or seeking spiritual advice or checking myself into a mental health facility and all I want to do is take you upstairs and tear off your clothes. Doesn't make sense, does it?"

"Sure it does," he said as he sat on the coffee table facing her. "Sex relieves stress, and in my brief involvement with ghosts, I've already deemed hauntings and basically anything in the supernatural category as the number two cause of adrenal fatigue. The crash, you know? After the excitement." He combed his fingers through her hair.

"Okay. What's the number one cause?"

"Unintentional celibacy."

"Right." She stood. "Let's get to it."

Lance rose.

Zoey took a step and the landline rang. She glanced at the ID and answered. "Mitch?"

"Yeah, it's me. Your cell isn't charged, is it?"

Zoey dug her dead cellphone from her purse. "No."

"Takes less than a minute to plug it in. What if there's an emergency and you're not home? What if you're in a bind and you need to reach me?"

"I'll cross that shitpile when I come to it."

"Nice. Anyway, I wanted to let you know Sterling came to, and she's fine."

"Great. Where are you?"

"The hotel. I'm on the balcony, and she's lying down. She's afraid for you. She says you don't know what you're getting yourself into."

"And she does?"

"Not really. She says she senses terror and sees you running for your life. She doesn't think you'll survive."

"Wow. That's drastic. Do you believe her?"

Mitch grunted. "I don't know what to believe. Uncharted territory isn't the half of it. My mind won't wrap itself around even a corner of paranormal possibilities."

"Then what I'm about to tell you will be especially difficult," she said. "We saw a ghost. It led us to the garage and then it vanished."

Mitch didn't say a word.

"Nothing?"

"Why did it lead you to the garage?"

She thought a moment, surprised by the quality of the question. "I don't know. Other than Amos ending his life with a noose and the soccer-ball-sized orb, nothing seemed blatantly irregular. Maybe the garage was a convenient escape route."

"It looked like a soccer ball?"

"More like four deflated soccer balls. It was about two feet wide and two feet tall, and transparent like a puff of steam or large splotch of white watercolor paint."

"And you're not scared?"

"No." She decided to sit again and made herself comfortable.

"I'm not either. I can't believe it. Any of it."

Zoey leaned forward and rested her elbows on her knees. "I'm sorry for you."

"Why?"

"Your girlfriend and ex-wife have more than just you in common, and it's important. It must be. Your world is changing, and there's nothing you can do about it. I'm not sure how I would have reacted if I were the sober, nonsuicidal, logical one. I was losing my mind anyway, so what the hell difference does all this make? Maybe that's the key, Mitch. Let go of the handrails and jump in. Open a new set of eyes. Accept a fresh perspective."

"Easy for you to say. Your new eyes are compliments of the lightning strike."

"First of all, my new eyes started developing before the lightning. I was outside trying to save the boy in the woods, remember? Why was the ghost visible to me, why was I struck by lightning? You know why?" She stood and circled the coffee table. "Because I have nothing to lose. I'm already broken. I'm not afraid to step in the ring and fight the fight, no matter how silly or bizarre."

"You're wound tighter than a drum. Let's change the subject. How's your shoulder?"

Zoey snapped out of her nervous walk and huffed. "Stings. How's your foot?"

"Swollen."

"We'll bring your suitcase by later."

"We?"

"Lance and I." She pulled her hair to one side.

"Lance, huh? Do you like him or is this a cougar thing? That's what they call it, right, cougar?"

"Don't insult me. Wouldn't matter how old he was, look at him. Any woman would welcome him in her bed."

"If you're trying to hurt my feelings, you've succeeded."

"Then we're even." This is normally when she'd throw the phone at the wall. Something kept her on—the real possibility of death.

Quiet.

"Don't worry about delivering our luggage," he said. "Sterling and I will pick it up. It's time to leave Colorado. I'm not ready for this— paranormal gal pals, sticky one-night stands, bogeymen. I'm a basic man with basic needs and I'm okay with that."

Zoey smiled. "You're solid, Mitch. You'll come around."

"I know you've let go of the handrails and all, but do me a favor?"

"Anything."

"If you stub your toe and your boyfriend doesn't notice your eyes changing color, get rid of him."

"It won't bother me either way." She made a seat of the sofa arm.

"Just trust me on this. You've graduated from a pain pill to a penis. Lance is nothing more than a drug. Wasn't it you who once said 'if a man overlooks a woman's subtleties, he's already failed her'?"

"Sounds like a bad romance novel."

"They sell like hotcakes for a reason." He laughed lightly.

"You've never failed me, Mitch. I, on the other hand—"

"Stop right there. We're getting off this hamster wheel. You need to quit beating yourself up, and I need to let go of the past. You couldn't help what happened to our son, and our dissolving marriage was part of the ugly process. I'm not completely there yet, but in time I'll be a better ex, and a better man for Sterling."

"She's a lucky woman."

"Not quite, but thanks." He hesitated. "Think about Chicago. Think about when we might transfer items to a storage unit and list the house."

He had to go there. "I'll leave your suitcase on the deck. Chances are I'll be upstairs overdosing on penis." Zoey hung up and stared at Lance, whose twisted expression implied he'd heard her last comment.

"Damn," Lance said. "*My* penis, I hope."

"Works for me." She rose.

"Where's your cellphone cord?"

"On the counter by the sink, why?"

Lance took her cell into the kitchen and, she presumed, plugged it in. He returned with a broad, bewitching smile. "Ready?"

Zoey found the medicine bottles Mitch had deserted. She unscrewed the lid of the Valium and popped a couple.

Lance held out his hand.

She dumped three pills into her palm and fed him one at a time. With each visit to his mouth, he sucked the tips of her forefinger and thumb. Then he noiselessly drifted to the staircase and ascended the steps. "Are you coming?"

"I will be," she said as she trailed him. "Wait for me," she added when she'd reached the landing.

Zoey rushed into the guestroom and threw whatever she could locate belonging to Mitch and Sterling into the expandable upright. Mitch nagged too much. Nag. Nag. Nag. She carried the bag downstairs and wheeled it to the deck. Hardly able to maintain a polite thought, she hurried back to Lance.

He'd taken off his shirt.

She moved slowly to his front and caressed his firm chest, allowing her fingertips time to identify his beautiful slabs of muscle, tight skin, navel. She lowered her hand, and then grabbed his healthy bulge. He grew. She remembered his relentless hard-on and delicious flavor, and the world and beyond vanished.

He stared into her eyes and the energy alone produced heat. Holding her gaze, he unbuttoned his jeans. She nudged his arm to the side and took over lowering the zipper to its natural end. Locked into his pupils, she wrapped her fingers around his champion dick, acknowledging the weight of blood.

"You're exquisite," she whispered.

Lance stepped closer and sunk his fingertips in her hair, his breath an unfair entity baiting her mouth. He tightened his grip near her scalp, leaned forward and kissed her with force. Chills trickled along her flesh, erected her nipples.

His throbbing cock and saliva sweet as fruit drove her crazy. She slapped her free hand behind his head and pushed her mouth against his. Tongues crashed and entwined, famished and restless. He broke away and ushered her to the bed, tore at her garments, freeing her body and weeding her mind.

Her eyelids opened a crack and clothes soared overhead like flags of surrender. Even her thoughts were volatile because she imagined him in every orifice and the idea of pain revved her adrenaline.

On the mattress he gnawed her neck, suckled her breasts and licked her stomach. Before long he'd wrenched between her inner thighs and nibbled. Each bite tickled and dots of wetness cooled in the air.

"You're fucking perfect," she said, digging her claws in his hair. She twirled a few strands and then directed his head just below her pubic bone.

He separated her feminine lips and ate the tender inside. She moaned. While his mouth made love to her clit, he fingered her, in and out, and she nearly screamed.

"I want your cock inside of me."

He raised his head. "When I'm through eating." He continued to lap her swollen clit.

She squealed and numbed when she climaxed. The stinging feeling in her shoulder disappeared too.

"I can eat you all day," he said.

Once wasn't enough—ecstasy made her hungrier. She yanked him upward by his hair. "Don't be stingy. I want the rest."

He inserted his fantastic penis and no amount of pills could go where he'd gone. He gyrated like an artist, careful and thoughtful.

She cried. He licked her tears.

For hours they ravaged one another, on the bed, the floor, in the hallway and finished downstairs near the coffee table.

Lance had her breathing heavily and sedatives wrapped her in satin. On a blanket she'd dragged off the bed, she lay next to her proficient young lover, her breasts, scars and bony limbs shadowed by dusk. She watched his chest rise and fall.

"What are you looking at?" he asked with a twinkle in his eyes.

"Your body contracting and expanding as you breathe."

"Badass."

"It is, isn't it?"

"What?"

"Contraction and expansion—tragedies reverting us to seedlings, folding us up until we marvel again. On and on. Never ends unless we die, so I thought. And then I heard a voice from another realm."

Lance concentrated. "If we're done, no hang ups, no regrets, the universe reabsorbs us like water. Apparently if we're not, we're spit out and left...where?"

"Here, but vibrating at a different frequency, or something like that. Sterling compared frequencies to radio stations…"

"Ah yeah. That's cool. What about life itself? I'm leaning toward a series of projections and reflections. I think I know, therefore I project my ideas, which in turn reflect back and reinforce my beliefs. Tricky shit. A belief is the mortar in whatever we create. Shapes our entire fucking existence." Lance yawned. Even after insane sex, his exhale smelled sweet.

"And Sterling and other psychics? Are their visions predetermined or are they building a reality based on a belief system?"

"Either premise stems from a belief. Both possibilities are true."

Zoey stroked the sole of his foot with her toes. "Heaven and hell?"

"Mortar."

"Where does mortar develop?"

"Home, school, society."

"Shit, Lance." She shook a strand of hair off her face. "Why do I feel like I'm talking to a teenager on LSD? Your theories are too simplistic."

Lance drummed his fingers on his sternum. "The universe *is* simple. *Shih shih wu ia.* Essentially means 'between all things and all events the universe has no boundaries.'"

"Boundaries. We talked about this, didn't we? Refresh my memory."

"Rock Hounds. My ink."

"So the universe has no boundaries and that means what to you?"

"Without boundaries the world is seamless. Or could be. The human race sodomizes simplicity. Screw the forest; we dissect it into trees, sticks, leaves, whatever. We miss the significance of its interconnectedness to the rest of the world as a whole. I dig your eyes, but they wouldn't be as striking without your face. The radio imagery is badass, though—frequencies, not boundaries." He nodded. "I get it."

"Look what I brought home," Zoey teased, "a curious little pup. Can I keep him?"

"Suck it, Hawthorne."

Zoey laughed. "I have, and it was divine."

Lance grinned.

"So," Zoey said, "you obviously dabble in philosophy. What else, or dare I ask?"

"What specifically do you want to know?"

"Well, why is a good-looking young man like you boning a forty-year-old? If it's a numbers thing, you can have two twenty-year-olds and double your pleasure."

"Get over it. I'm thirteen years younger—not a big deal. And I'm not boning any forty-year-old, I'm boning a fucking savage, and I like it…a lot."

Remembering how his lips had sent her to paradise, she watched him talk.

"Threesomes, orgies—been there, done that. Not my thing. Detail is too important to me."

"Details have seams, don't they?"

"Details and contrasts are the whole."

She was determined to outsmart him. "Okay, then, an orgy is the same as one on one."

"Could be, but people are too complex—no female I've been with sees my hand on her knee as a good time. She wants my mouth on her puss. Even with everything I own buried or busy, someone ends up whining."

"I'd have thought you'd have enough to go around."

"I've got more than enough. I'm a one-woman man." He rolled and propped himself up with his left arm, his spiritual tattoo visible as he moved more hair from her temple. "You want me to bring a friend next time?"

"What makes you think there'll be a next time?" she said, noticing a chill in the air.

"You like me."

She shrugged.

"I definitely like you," he said, tracing her C-section scar and stopping to play with her pubic hair. "You're passionate, and we're compatible in bed. One night together and I couldn't stop thinking about you. When you threw me out, I wanted to come back, beat your ex and toss you over my shoulder. I would have taken you home with me. I haven't felt that way since high school when I beat Anthony Sardinia for Rosie White only to have her despise me."

"Poor Lance."

Lance removed his fingers from Zoey's pubic hair. "Whatever. Rosie was sorry. She tried to reconcile a month later. By that time I was sunk deep in Jennifer Reed and loving every minute of it."

"Nice to see you don't hold a grudge."

"No grudge, but Rosie can suck it too."

Zoey grabbed a sofa pillow and stuffed it under her neck. "Okay, Romeo, when you're not riding your hog and detailing women, what're you doing?"

"Riding women and detailing hogs."

"What?"

"We talked about this too."

She silently rehashed their earliest conversation. "You build motorcycles?"

Lance nodded. "That and repair Harleys. Remember the big guy I played pool with?"

"Yeah, Tank."

"He's a force. Loyal too. Fuck with me and you'll have a Tank up your ass. We've been through our share of shit. The night I met you, we'd just delivered a pearl white and chrome chopper with a drag race engine to some famous ski expert. It's a badass bike."

"Delivered? You're not from the area?"

"Nah, Denver. I like it here, though."

"When are you leaving?" Zoey drew small spirals on Lance's chest with her finger.

"I've decided to stick around a while. You don't mind do you?" He grabbed her flirty hand, seeming to hold it ransom until she answered him.

"Depends."

"On?"

"I'm not interested in a relationship."

He let go of her. "Every interaction with someone is a form of relationship. You're relating to me right now."

She sat, her hair draping her back. "Seamless universe, really? I'm tired. Do you have to turn everything I say into a discussion?"

"Details make the world go round."

"You and your details. That's opposite what you preach. Either you're interconnected or separate, which is it?"

"A hog is badass but the details make it special. They become part of the description—the whole. No separation. One cool chopper. Get it?"

She smacked the floor and vibrated her wounded shoulder. A couple deep breaths and the throbbing pain subsided. "You are so full of shit. No, you know what, you're young. You don't have it figured out yet."

"And you do?"

She gazed at him, his mouthwatering body and delectable features. "Maybe we should do less talking and more—"

"Boning?" Lance sat too, and stared into her eyes. "Suit yourself. Your loss if you don't get to know me."

"I know enough."

"Cool. I'm not forcing the issue. We'll preoccupy our mouths with oral sex and bubble gum."

"You're a babe, a studling, and life has yet to kick your ass proper."

Lance shot to his feet—coppery bare skin wooing her femininity—and rushed up the stairs.

"You know what I know?" he yelled. "You hear voices, your house is a paranormal playground and grief drives you. You're a perpetual bitch because you don't give a shit. You intermittently reengage in life, but you're insecure. You think something terrible is going to happen, so fuck it." He walked down the stairs slower than he went up, concealed in blue jeans and a T-shirt.

She listened, for the most part, but couldn't help wanting to turn back time. She preferred him next to her, naked, tickling her breasts the way he always did after sex.

"You have two scars, one from giving birth and one on your shoulder, and if you haven't noticed the scar on your shoulder never scabbed, and it's getting lighter. And that's another thing. Surviving a lightning strike—major curve ball. Guarantee you were mad as a kicked rattlesnake. And now you're here in a house your ex-husband's freaky girlfriend keeps telling you to get out of, and you won't because you have a death wish. Don't get me wrong, I'll die fighting for something I believe in too, but I'd rather not."

The cocky Adonis gathered his belongings—socks, wallet, steel-toed boots. Her heart thumped hard, afraid he'd leave, and then harder scared of giving a shit.

Lance continued, "You're a dichotomy, addicted to sedatives and adrenaline. Addicted to boning." He stopped as if considering his last comment a reflection. "I'm all about a good time. But if you want me to play dumb, I can't. I'll get drunk with you, pop your lame kiddy drugs and keep a hard-on as long as you need it, but don't talk down to me. I'm not thick in the head."

"Lance," she said. "You're not stupid. I only meant you're young, and—"

He walked to her and squatted. "Don't think because of my age you have me pegged. You don't." He gently twisted her hair around his wrist and let it fall over her crinkled shoulder.

Zoey kneeled, eye level, and gazed into his hypnotic pupils. "Here's what I know." She set her hands on his thighs. "You're not just another pretty face. You're artistic, in and out of the sack, and like me, you're prone to verbal diarrhea."

He smiled and shook his head. "You're fucking wicked."

She pushed her lips to his and forced her tongue into his mouth. He reciprocated. Through her nostrils she inhaled his summery breath. Their fiery kiss had a powerful charge. She adored and feared him. The possibility of developing something psychologically intimate curdled her stomach. She receded and rested her butt on her feet.

Lance undressed, a beautiful shadow dancing in dusk. He wandered behind her and braced his naked front against her backside, skin warm and soothing. He let a whisper wash down her neck. "Mellow out, Hawthorne. We can be lovers and friends. This doesn't have to get messy."

She lay down. He stretched out next to her, resting his chin on her scalp.

They'd moved the coffee table and lay between the sofas. Lance breathed on the brink of snoring, and she contemplated her uncle's suicide and possible connection to the ghost child's death. She wondered if Amos simply couldn't live with what he'd done and finally proved his remorse with a noose, or had he been innocent? *Family*? Whose family? Questions streamed through her mind, useless as exposed rolls of film, and always led to the most puzzling—what would possess someone to bludgeon a toddler?

"Hey," Lance said, startling her blank. "You and Sterling heard *family*. You think the ghost is talking about your great uncle, or its family?"

"I was just— Forget it."

Lance exhaled strong, she assumed, preparing for his REM plunge. "The picture's old. Amos is dead. The other dudes might be dust too. If not, Death is banging on their door."

"Probably." Zoey's eyes wanted to close. "Let's finish this conversation in the morning."

"Yep," he mumbled.

Her cellphone rang, jerking her from a peaceful lull. She sat, smacking her lips, trying to ascertain where the noise came from—purse, kitchen, under a piece of clothing somewhere?

Lance opened an eye. "That your phone?"

"Yeah. I can't find it."

He chuckled. "You looked?"

"No. Whoever it is will call back." She decided to crawl under the blanket they'd slept on.

Lance joined her and they snuggled beneath the cover.

Evil is alive.

Zoey sprang up. "What?"

Lance rose with wide eyes. "What, what?"

Evil is alive.

"It's talking to me," she said.

Evil is alive.

"I'm listening," Zoey hollered.

Evil is alive.

"You're not giving me enough information. Can you tell me more?"

The voice spoke like a second heartbeat, louder and faster, booming in her chest and ears, rattling her bones. *Evil is alive—Evil is alive—Evil is alive.*

Lance lowered his brows as if trying to interpret Zoey's expression.

Evil is alive—Evil is alive—Evil is alive.

Pressure clamped under her neck, and she gasped for air—uttered through inward wheezing, "I can't breathe." Zoey tried to inhale but her throat closed. She gurgled and yanked at the nothingness strangling her—like a lucid dream, she saw a silvery weapon hit the toddler. Blood sprayed. The child wailed.

Lance jumped to his feet and lifted Zoey parallel to him. He stood behind her, performing the Heimlich maneuver. "Come on," he said while clenching beneath her ribcage. "Cough it up!"

Panic weakened her limbs, and she relied on Lance to hold her upright. "Not—huhg." She tried to tell him she wasn't choking. Unable to talk or mime murder, she'd die dry heaving in Lance's arms.

"Fuck, stay with me, Hawthorne," Lance yelled. "What the hell is happening?" He winded her repeatedly.

Glowing speckles discolored the atmosphere—spots floated aimlessly and collided like intoxicated fairies. Clinging to consciousness, she inhaled once more and air rushed into her lungs. She breathed in and out, slowly and deeply, in and out, oxygen, lustrous and smelling like God.

"I can breathe," Zoey said, panting.

Lance released her midsection.

"Holy shit," she said. "I can breathe." She balanced on her feet and stroked her neck, grateful. She focused on regaining strength. Feeling cold and preyed upon, she cautiously walked to the staircase and headed up to her room for clothing.

"Where're you going?" Lance asked. "What happened?" He followed her up the steps and into the bedroom. "Talk to me."

She threw on jeans and a baggy blouse.

"Zoey." Lance grabbed her arm.

Zoey froze. "Whoever did this."

"Did what?"

"Tried to strangle me."

Lance released her. "If that shit was intentional, Sterling is right. We can't stay here."

Zoey inhaled and exhaled a few more times, allowing her pulse to relax. "Whoever tried to kill me is related to the boy in the woods. When the ghost says family, it's referring to the slaughtered child."

Lance's indigo eyes looked less like liquid and more like stones. "Someone told you this stuff?"

"Not exactly." Still piecing the violent attack together, and the image she saw, Zoey sat on the edge of the mattress. "My son fell from a Ferris wheel. A misplaced screw caused the buggy to tilt upside down. At first I couldn't believe it. I heard him scream and watched him teeter but I couldn't—wouldn't—believe he was going to fall. When he hit the pavement, I went berserk, hitting, pushing, punching everyone in my way to get to the man who operated the ride, and when I finally reached him, I went for his neck. I tried to strangle him."

"You didn't kill the boy in the woods. Why would the spirit come after you?"

"And the machine operator at the carnival didn't kill my son. Ten guys put the Ferris wheel together, and he wasn't one of them." She paused, struggling to articulate emotions. "When whatever it was cut off my airway, familiar feelings rushed through me—heartache, rage, revenge, but they weren't mine. It's hard to explain."

"Try," Lance said, clearly mystified.

"I don't know if I can. Say each of us lost someone at war. You'd sympathize with me, and I with you, but we'd be capable of separating the grief. You'd feel my sorrow, but the sorrow of your own loss would outweigh mine. That's what I felt, desperate sadness, heavy and significant, but different from my own."

Lance nodded and moved catlike across the floor. He sat beside her on the bed, wrapping his bottom half with the rumpled sheet.

"I'm sorry about your son. I understand you better now."

"No, you don't."

Lance shook his head and wisely changed the subject. "The ghost you hear lost its child and took its anger out on you?"

"I think so."

"According to your visions, the child was murdered. How do you think the ghost in the house died?"

"I don't know."

"Can you sleep here knowing a ghost, an invisible being, can't control its rage?"

Zoey wasn't sure.

"Why don't you move out? Come to my place in Denver. Stay as long as you want. I have a spacious house with a Jacuzzi and a badass ferret that sleeps in a Kleenex box. If you ask him nicely, he'll pass you a tissue. No shit. You'd like him. His name is Chaos."

A ball of fury spiraled in the pit of her stomach and grew as she breathed. She couldn't change history and save her son or the mysterious toddler, but maybe she could ease the anguished entity. Profound grief was hell on earth, trapped in that same hell for eternity was unimaginable.

"I'm not going anywhere," she said. "I may have a death wish, I'll give you that. But right now it isn't about me. I'm told Evil is alive, and I believe this evil had something to do with the murdered boy. For obvious reasons, I'm compelled to stay and destroy it."

Chapter 10

For three days Zoey hadn't heard anything but Lance and a busy landline—Mitch, Sterling, doctors, none of whom she cared to talk to. She started to believe her gift, like the scar on her shoulder, had grown lighter or diluted with time. She'd just dedicated herself to the cause and then poof, the voice went away. This made her ears hot.

Lance had picked up one change of clothes from the hotel. He should have packed more. In his travels he'd purchased a laptop. He booted it in the office nook and searched for information on Amos Rayfield and the Rayfield Ranch. The only things circulating the internet were articles regarding his hanging and a blog by a guy who suggested Amos hadn't done it soon enough. Apparently the Asian blogger had literally bumped into Amos outside a grocery store, setting off an avalanche of racial slurs. Clearly, no one missed Amos.

Despite irritation, profuse sweating and headaches, Zoey managed to decrease her pill intake, but felt she owed her success to Lance and his penis. The more sex she had, the less she thought about Milo and Amos and ghosts.

Another morning and Zoey awoke pleasantly with Lance's breath warming the nape of her neck and his finger wiggling inside her. She avoided interpreting her abstract dreams and lost herself in his touch. He pulled her close and, from behind, pushed his erection into her moistened puss. He pumped slow and easy, deep and deeper, until she'd reached that final overall tingle.

She sighed, releasing an unexpected deluge of apprehension.

Afterward he followed her into the shower and lathered her like an explorer of the human frame, starting at her toes. With his eyes closed, he announced the location of his hands. "Heels, calves, knees, thighs, ass, hips." He swirled soap over every fleshy crevice. "Sweet meat, scar, navel, ribs, breasts, nipples, yum, nipples, fingers, arms, elbows, shoulder, lightning's wrath, throat, lips." Lance opened his eyes, leaned in and ended his expedition with a kiss. "This house is clean."

Words that conjured a visceral sense of unfinished business... The shrine in Chicago? Evil at large? Or was it confusion, what to do, where to go, who to be?

"Shit," she blurted and rinsed off.

She stepped out from under the water flow and dried herself. She rubbed ointment on her disappearing wound and wandered into the bedroom, where she slipped on jeans and an airy top. As she combed her wet, tousled hair, Lance walked up behind her, already dressed in yesterday's slightly wrinkled denim.

His smile made everything else appear shabby. "Hey, Hawthorne."

"Morning."

"Tea?"

"Yeah, thanks."

"Not a problem." He headed downstairs.

She patted the puffiness under her eyes with her fingertips and jerked at the sound of a shattering dish.

"You okay?" she yelled.

"Yeah! Butter fingers, heh. Where's the broom?"

"In the garage!"

She kissed Milo's picture and heard the downstairs door creak open, but she didn't hear it creak closed.

"Lance?" she hollered.

Dead silence.

"Hello? Answer me, Lance."

Strangulation?

Her blood iced. She shoved her feet in her shoes and descended the stairs. Nervous heart battered her chest. She rushed through the untidy house to the dining room. "Lance?"

"I'm in here," he said. "You'll never believe what I found."

Zoey exhaled fear and entered the garage. "I thought you were in trouble. You wigged me out."

"You were worried about me," he said while investigating a long narrow compartment in the wall.

"I'm over it." She approached him.

The shelf that had previously hung over the opening lay on the floor near Lance's feet, and he'd relocated the deer heads to the opposite side of the garage, by Amos's truck.

"What is this?"

"I couldn't get to the broom." He pointed to the animal heads. "Trophies were in the way. I bent over to move them and knocked the piece of shit shelf off the wall." He shut and reopened the slim panel, revealing tiny slits cleverly hidden by the shelving unit. "This is where the ghost went, remember?"

Zoey nodded.

"They're rifles. Just about everyone in Colorado has one, especially a crotchety prick like your uncle. No surprise. So why'd he hide them?"

"I don't know. Lots of eccentric old people stash their prized possessions."

"Sure," Lance said with a hint of frustration. "But lots of eccentric old dudes don't hang themselves, or live in a house with a spirit seeking revenge. Too bad you can't hear inanimate objects. I guarantee these guns have a story to tell."

Zoey gently touched the barrel of the firearm. She coiled her fingers around the cold, hard metal. It felt indifferent and cruel. Gravity led her to the trigger. Her heart thumped.

A muffled conversation gained distinction as the volume increased. Suddenly she stood in the dining room next to a mahogany federal-style dining table. She poured lemonade in a glass, her hands manly and darker beyond the gloves of dirt.

"Quench your thirst yet?" a tall, thin man asked, reeking of booze. He leaned against the counter. He wore acorn-colored slacks and a shirt buttoned clear to his Adam's apple. His hair, ironed to his scalp, matched his slacks.

"Si, senor, gracias," she said, sounding male. She, now he, set his glass next to the pitcher on the dining table. Ash infested his clothes through to his skin, and his own body odor burned his eyes. "Hard work, senor. I'm glad to be done. This environment is no place for children." He smiled nervously.

"You people breed. More useless wetbacks," the thin man growled and glanced at the floor. "I'm sorry, Luis. I've had too much to drink."

"S'okay, Senor Rayfield. We have many obstacles ahead. We'll take our pay and be on our way." He swallowed a boulder. "No more wetbacks to feed."

"You got a big group. There's too many of ya. Where will you go?"

"Texas."

"So you can sneak other wetbacks into the country? Someone will catch you."

"No, senor. No one else is coming. We'll use our money to buy land. We can have goats and grow vegetables."

"Sell lettuce, that's your goal? Figures."

Luis nodded. *"That and a fine school for Miguel. He will be someone respected, a lawyer or doctor."*

Rayfield laughed. *"Tell you what! I'd rather die than have some lowlife spic giving me medical advice or injecting me with needles. Ain't gonna happen."*

Luis nodded again, eager to take his earnings and his family as far from Senor Rayfield and his friends as he could. *"The sun is setting. We should be going."* He turned toward the door. Anchored by fear, he struggled to take a step.

"Got a question for you," Senor Rayfield said from behind him.

Silence.

"If you did get caught," Rayfield said, *"what would you tell the law you been doin' for the past year?"*

Luis had a sick feeling. *"Cleaning house and trimming hedges."*

"Whose hedges?"

"Whoever offered us a decent wage—people I can't remember. We traveled." His knees shook.

"Don't piss your trousers," Rayfield said. *"Go on and gather your tribe or whatever you call yourselves. Stop back and I'll dole out el dinero."*

Luis rushed to the door and grabbed the knob. A ghastly scream echoed from the woods. A scream from someone he could name. He ran across the grass to his beloved. His feet slammed the earth and with every step a gunshot fired, and more screams, horrid, loud, pained. Downhill he ran and froze, rejecting what his brain saw.

The image took shape.

Blood drained from his head.

His son, his baby boy, Miguel, lay slaughtered like livestock under the cold steel sky.

"No!" He gazed at the heavens. *"No, no, no!"* he hollered, unable to see past his tears.

From the tangled forest, coming from the water, demons sang a happy drunken song, slurring and hooting.

Blinded by soul-numbing sorrow, Luis listened, and recognized the murderers. They were coming for him. If he knew with certainty his wife hadn't escaped, he would kill himself. Teardrops fell and cleared his vision. A sparkle between the trees caught his eye. The ax that killed his

son. The evil man who carried the weapon staggered and said to his hell-
raised partner, "Knock, knock..."

Drowning in rage, Luis whispered, "Descansas en paz," and raced
toward the house. There in the shed he would obtain the hammer used to
lay bricks. He would hide and hunt the men one by one—he would crack
their skulls.

Streaks of sapphire blue sliced through the dusk. Senor Rayfield paced
in front of his kitchen window. Luis crouched under the pane and sped
quietly around the garage to the shed. He flung open the door and grabbed
the tool from the worktable, wiped sweat from his brow and tears from
his eyes. Senor Rayfield would be his first revenge. He moved through the
birth of night, he hoped like an illusion, and borrowed traits of a snake to
slither in the side door adjacent to Senor Rayfield's dining room. Hinges
squeaked. Luis paused a moment and turned to glance at the noise. He
returned his sight forward and met with Senor Rayfield, a sly smile, and a
muzzle pressed to his estómago.

Present day, and Zoey stood trembling. At some point she'd released
the barrel, her hand still inches from the weapon. She caressed her swirling
stomach and gasped for air.

"Zoey," Lance said. "Can you hear me?"

She nodded.

"Say something."

"Something," she said in utter shock.

Lance touched his chest. "I said your name about a thousand times.
You were a zombie, completely zoned out. Are you all right?"

She nodded again. Wheezy and speechless, she stormed into the house
and dropped into a chair at the dining room table. Her arms slapped
against the wood top and she automatically examined the furniture,
wanting nothing to do with the items she'd seen in her vision. "Not the
same," she muttered.

Lance followed, and sat in the chair to her left. "Don't shut me out,
Zoey. You can tell me anything, remember, lovers and friends."

"Water, please, get me some water," she said, unable to produce saliva.

Within seconds he'd placed a full glass near her fingers.

She lubricated her throat and slipped right into a confession. "I saw
the ghost, alive. His name was Luis. My uncle shot him in the stomach,
right there." She pointed to the space by the garage door. "There were two
other men I couldn't get a description of, they were blurs. One of them
murdered Luis's son, Miguel. That's the toddler wandering in the woods."
Memories scraped out of her psyche like barbed wire and she paused to

regroup. "I told you about it, what I'd seen. It was disgusting and painful. This vision confirmed everything, and I'm back to square one, wishing I were crazy instead. The man chopped up the boy, a toddler, with an ax."

"Damn," Lance said.

"Would you go to my nightstand and bring me a Valium? I'm jittery. I need to relax."

"You're doing fine. What else did you see?"

"I'd appreciate if you wouldn't tell me how I'm doing. I'd like something to help me relax."

"Then get it yourself," he said.

She slapped the tabletop. "Been chatting with Mitch, or are you smoking crack?"

"Come on." He held her violent hand. "You touched the gun and mentally teleported to the past. Not too long ago you were petting the walls, trying to do what Sterling does. Your wish came true. Why risk tempering your ability with drugs?"

"Why the sudden concern, what's in it for you?"

"Nothing," he said. "I agreed to help you and that's what I'm doing. I've seen the ghost and watched it nearly kill you. Pills, booze, whatever you want, we'll party hardcore when I'm sure this irate spirit won't rage again."

"Irate spirit?" she asked. "Luis. His name was Luis and his son's name was Miguel. I think Luis had a wife too, his beloved, but I don't know her name, and I didn't see her—but I remember hearing the child call for his momma. She must have existed." Zoey's heart ripped in two. "There were more people screaming."

"In the house, outside…"

"Outside, seconds after Luis's wife wailed. She must have seen what happened to her child." A tear tickled Zoey's cheek. "I never thought I'd be grateful for my son's accident. Had he been murdered…" She wiped her eyes unable to imagine Milo in Miguel's place.

Lance kissed the underside of her wrist and rose. "Why'd your uncle shoot Luis?"

"I don't know." She took a deep breath. "Amos and his partners owed Luis and the others money for a year of labor. Luis was getting ready to leave. Amos was worried the workers would tell someone what they'd done. Their dealings remain a secret to me. I didn't see anything. A lot of dirt and sweat—"

"And squeaky-clean murder weapons." Lance strode into the garage and returned with the broom and dustpan. "All three men in the photo are wearing hardhats. Hardhats, picks and dirt, they were definitely mining. Where, though?" He swept the mug he'd shattered earlier and dumped the shards in the trash.

"You heard the drunk at the bar. Big Cat was a mining community. There's probably old mine shafts everywhere. All we have are pictures of unidentified people and the suspicions of a woman diagnosed with complicated bereavement. I think we should concentrate on Evil. One or both of the men in that photo is alive."

"We find the murderers and, what, interrogate them?"

"I don't know, maybe we'll get lucky and evidence will fall in our laps." She rotated her stiff shoulders. "Whatever the outcome, we have to find the sons-of-bitches who massacred this family or the spirit will never rest." She stood and joined Lance in the kitchen. "Luis will get angrier."

"How do you know?"

"Wouldn't you?"

Lance receded in thought for a moment. "Yeah, I would."

Zoey rushed to the garage hoping to get answers from the rifles she hadn't touched. She moved slowly, nervous about witnessing another ruthless act. She drew strength from images of Miguel's quivering bottom lip, and she grasped both barrels.

No vision, voice or hunch. Disappointed, she walked back to the kitchen and turned on the flame under the kettle.

"Where'd you go?" Lance asked, dumping grounds in a coffee filter.

"I touched the other guns." She shook her head and as she reached in the cabinet for a cup, her cellphone rang. She traced the chime to her purse, ingeniously hidden under a chair by the potbelly stove.

"Hello?" she said as she straightened.

"Zoey? It's Kane, Kane Ballentine."

"Oh, hi," she said, still recovering from the landslide of new information. "How are you?"

"Good, thanks. Filing some paperwork and Kendall is reading her book for the tenth time. Beautiful day today, isn't it?"

Zoey glanced out the window and acknowledged the sunshine. "A backpacker's paradise."

"Did I catch you at a bad time?"

"I haven't had caffeine yet."

"I'll take my chances."

"Brave man," she said, heading to the counter to steep a teabag.

Lance wordlessly asked who was on the other end of the receiver, and she cocked her head toward her neighbor's house.

"In my defense," Kane said, "I called the other night. No one answered."

"I probably went to bed early. I know it's been days, but I haven't checked messages. Rest assured, valiant neighbor, I'm drinking Earl Grey as we speak."

Lance mouthed "oh" and flicked on the coffee maker.

"Earl Grey. I'm an espresso guy myself. Last year I bought a Clover— don't ask—the price competes with Kendall's yearly school tuition. Really I've bought bragging rights. I can get the best brew in town, some think in the world, and never leave my home."

"It'll pay for itself with the money you'll save on fuel."

"You're a sound for sore ears. I've been on the phone all morning with business colleagues, butting heads. It's nice talking to a sane person."

"We met in a psychiatrist's office and you think I'm sane?"

"I do." He paused. "How'd you like Dr. Doyle?"

"He's okay," she said in between sips. "Right or wrong, he has good intentions."

"Kendall thinks the world of him. That's all I care about."

"Not to be rude, Kane, but I have company."

"I apologize," he said. "It's my narcissistic tendency taking center stage. Do I tell Dr. Doyle?"

"Your secret is safe with me." Zoey smiled.

"The reason I called was to invite you to dinner tomorrow night. Kendall and I thought it would be an opportunity for us to get better acquainted. It's an open menu. Tell me what you crave and we'll whip it up. Our chef is superb."

"I haven't had much of an appetite lately."

"For about a year?"

Zoey reminded herself that he'd recently buried his wife, and Kendall's mother, otherwise she would have hung up. She didn't respond.

"There must be something I can tempt you with," he persisted. "Almond-crusted salmon with a coconut curry veloute, Mediterranean honey-roasted rack of lamb, filet mignon, lobster or, on the weight-watcher side, Caesar salad with basil-baked rolls and a glass of Pinot Gris, high-quality, from Friuli?"

"You're an impressive salesman."

"Then we'll see you tomorrow night?"

"Sure, why not?" she said. "What time?"

"Six."

"I'll be there."

"Great. We're looking forward to it."

"Okay, well, enjoy the day."

"Will do," he said. "Bye-bye."

Lance held a brown ceramic mug and strolled into the living room. He set his coffee down, sat on the sofa, and put on his boots. "You're going to dinner tomorrow night?" he said, tying his laces.

"Yeah, for an hour or two, right next door. Apparently Kane has a chef he'd like to showcase."

Lance rose and slipped on his leather coat. His onyx hair had dried in sexy ropes, and his blue jeans rounded in all the best places. He appealed to her inner teenager.

"You want to ride?" he asked.

"Ride where?"

"Most of the time whichever way the wind blows, but today I have to outdo your neighbor. Are you willing to skip corn flakes for real food?"

"I shouldn't... I'd feel bad...."

"Have a bowl for dinner. I can't dazzle you with a chef, but there's a secluded diner carved into the side of a mountain that serves the best omelets in Colorado. Local favorite. We'll get fresh air, eat something substantial, and lay out a plan of action."

"I'll get a sweater."

Maybe sunshine would stop her hands from trembling. She rushed upstairs, perspiring and edgy. Withdrawal symptoms, hormones, or too much excitement, whatever the cause, she popped an ibuprofen. Moving to the dresser in front of the mirror, she noticed her hair needed a trim and her eyes weren't green or brown but pigeon gray. Exhaustion came to mind as she grabbed a dirty sock and dabbed her sweaty neck. The camera bag in the corner burned a hole in her heart. She put on a sweatshirt, created a ponytail and swallowed a Valium before going downstairs.

"Nice place," Lance said. "Too bad it's haunted." He strode to the door and waited for Zoey.

"Yeah, it's nice." Zoey stuck the pictures of the alleged rock hounds and *braceros* in her purse and joined Lance.

"Real nice," he repeated.

"What, Lance, spit it out."

"Just looking around," he said. "The house isn't so big you feel swallowed up by it. The yard's fantastic. View is amazing."

They walked across the deck through an earthy-scented breeze and made their way to the Harley.

"What is it?" she asked.

He stopped next to the bike and reached in his coat pocket for the keys. "If in the end the ghost or ghosts are at peace, would you stay?"

"Why do you ask?"

"I don't want you to leave."

"Sorry to disappoint. I couldn't live here, not after what I've seen. There's too much blood, Luis, his son, most likely his wife, no way."

Lance mounted the bike and held it steady while she climbed up behind. They rode in silence against the summer wind under stunning sunlight. She admired the scenic scale, the panoramic landscape blotted with contrasts and bold focal points. Her camera managed to nest in her brain, she hadn't changed completely. Maybe all she needed was that one special shot to reawaken her dormant skill.

A short distance past the Rock Hounds tavern, Lance hung a right on a narrow road she would have missed if she'd blinked. They drove over the bridge, and a paved line that spliced through a patch of forest. The smell reminded her of purity. He turned again at a mountain base and revved forward in a wide upward spiral. When they'd circled the rock a few times, she got dizzy and tugged on his jacket.

"We're almost there," he yelled.

She glued her body to his and closed her eyes. Lance slowed to a stop and shut off the engine. Zoey peeked and smiled.

The local favorite was a biker restaurant atop a mesa. The cook, a brawny mountain-man-type with a squash-shaped nose and cheeks peppered in razor stubble used a spatula to canopy his forehead. He watched hash browns sizzle on a giant flat grill dependent on propane tanks. Thick wooden picnic benches, some beneath umbrellas and others unprotected, studded the grounds and trailed into a gaping cave. Denim, tattoos, bandanas and Harleys consumed most of the space, and a few race bikes and a Mercedes took up a smaller ratio.

She and Lance dismounted the bike. "What do you think?" he asked while shoving keys in his coat pocket. "Badass, right?"

Zoey nodded.

"Wait 'til you taste the food. Come on." He gestured for her to follow him toward the cook. "Ace, hey, what's up?"

"Lance," Ace said, with a touch of surprise in his voice. He and Lance crashed palms in a unique shake. "Haven't seen you in a while."

"Busy, man. Sold a bike and met a lady."

"Speaking of ladies, how's your sister?"

"Marie's on top, man. She's going to law school."

"You're all right, Lance," Ace said.

"It's only money. Can't take it with you."

"I'm taking mine," Ace said.

"It'll burn at sea with you, buddy. I'll make sure of it." Lance patted Ace's back. "Ace, this is Zoey."

"So, you're the infamous lady?" Ace asked, waving his spatula through a cloud of steam. "I know it's hard to believe 'cause he's pretty as they come, but Lance is a great guy."

"I'm sure he is," she said, a little stoned on pills and elevation.

"You don't sound convinced," Ace said.

"We make love. What do you want me to say, he's a great lover?"

Ace looked over Lance. "Using him for sex, huh? I don't blame you."

"Fuck you," Lance snickered. "We're hungry," he added, walking away. "Later."

"Much," Ace yelled.

Zoey and Lance sat near the cave entry. Lanterns lined the walls of the cave and Zoey could see groups of Harley connoisseurs seated at four different tables. A guy with a long black braid poured cream in his girlfriend's coffee. Something about the way he tilted the creamer, considerately, made Zoey miss having someone to rely on. Someone she loved and trusted. A fleeting thought. She shifted, getting comfortable, and then pulled out the photos.

"There's my girl," Lance said, eyeing a sixty-something curvy brunette waitress in Levi's and hiking boots.

She approached the table with two mugs and a pot of coffee.

"Delilah," Lance said. "This is Zoey."

Delilah smiled. "Hey, sugar," she said in a strong southern accent. "How'd you get so lucky?" She cocked her head toward Lance. "He never brings women here."

"He likes the sex, but got sick of corn flakes."

Delilah raised her brows at Lance. "She's a pistol."

"That she is," Lance said.

"Coffee, darling?" Delilah asked.

"Yep, and she'll have tea." Lance chin-pointed at Zoey.

"Anything for you, doll." Delilah poured steamy coffee into Lance's cup and scurried to a stocked counter on wheels near the grill.

"You're testy," he said. "Why?"

"I don't know."

He sipped his coffee and inspected the photo of three men in a mine.

Meanwhile Zoey stared into Miguel's giant glassy eyes and scanned the others. "What happened to the rest of them? In my vision I thought I heard them scream, but I didn't see anyone."

Lance gently tossed the picture next to the condiment container and shrugged. "If so many others were murdered, why do you hear one voice and see the youngest kid? There are five teenagers in that picture."

"More unsolved mysteries," Zoey said.

Delilah returned with a pitcher of hot water. The spunky waitress filled Zoey's cup, opened a Lipton teabag and dunked it twice. "There you go, sweetheart." She placed an unopened bag beside the menu. "In case you want more." Her eyes widened. "I'll be damned," she said, struck by the black and white image of the rock hounds. "Where on earth did you get that picture?"

"Why, do you know them?" Lance asked.

"I know two of them. That's the crazy old rat who hanged himself." She pointed to Zoey's uncle. "Amos Rayfield in the better years of his life. Even then he was a cranky son-of-a-gun. And that one there is Ross Ballentine. Don't repeat this. Back when I was gorgeous and he was charming, we had an affair. He died two years ago of a heart attack. His son is alive. He lives in Big Cat Canyon."

"Kane?" Zoey asked.

"That's him," Delilah said. "He's got a precious little girl too."

"Kendall," Zoey said.

"She's a muffin. What are y'all doing with a picture older than Jesus?"

"The cranky son-of-a-gun who hanged himself was my great uncle," Zoey said, taking a drink of tea.

"Shoot, honey, I'm sorry if I offended—"

"Don't waste your breath on Amos Rayfield," Zoey snapped. "He was a murderer. All three of these men are killers."

Delilah gasped. "What? Who, when?"

Lance interrupted, "Apparently Zoey wants to get sued by Kane Ballentine. Ignore her, Delilah, inheritance BS. You know how it is?"

Delilah smiled. "Sometimes I think family and drama are synonymous. You ready to order?"

"I'll have the Garden Supreme with two buttermilk biscuits," Lance said.

"I'll have the same with wheat toast," Zoey muttered.

"Coming right up." Delilah turned, but stopped midway. She refaced Zoey and Lance. "Wait a minute," she said. "That man with the dimple in his chin, I've seen him—recently."

"No way," Zoey said.

"Yes. That's him."

"Here?" Lance asked.

"Yeah," Delilah said. "Four or five days ago. He's fifty years older, but it's sure hard to forget a man with an ass for a chin. Normally I like dimples, but he was such a jerk, he ruined it for me. Aww, bull-pucky, he acted bothered by air. He wore a brimmed hat, real expensive-looking. He ordered two eggs, tits up—firm, three weenies, and a cup of black coffee. He leafed through an appointment book like he was rearranging dates. As if his ass was on fire, he skedaddled right after he ate, and stiffed me. In this day and age, can you believe it?"

"Do you remember what he drove?" Lance asked.

"I'm drawing a blank. Strange because it's not like we can park many vehicles up here. Plenty of room for bikes, but cars is a whole 'nother story. I suppose I was fussing too much over his crappy attitude to notice. If I think of it, I'll let you know."

"Anything else strike a chord?"

Delilah tapped her pen on the order pad. "Hmm, I don't know if it'll help. He had manicured nails. Any man fixin' to be prettier than a woman needs a reality check. I mean that's just asinine. Anyhow, that's all I can think of. Sorry."

"You've helped a lot," Lance said.

Delilah smiled and hurried to the grill where she handed Ace the order ticket.

"What's wrong with you?" Lance leaned forward. "You can't accuse people of murder. And furthermore you should be dancing on the table. Delilah identified one of the men, and the other is right under our noses. Case closed."

"Really? One killer remains anonymous, but we know what he had for breakfast a few days ago, and the other is my neighbor's father. This isn't over."

"Whatever Kane's father was involved in *is* over. He's dead. We're after one man. Bring the picture with you tomorrow night and see what Kane has to say."

"Why would he tell me anything?"

"Why wouldn't he? He has no idea you've been piecing this thing together. You found a photo of the uncle you never met. You're curious."

"What if this man, this evil, lives here in town?"

"With a manicure?" Lance shook his head. "This may be a wealthy community, but it's still rugged. I doubt local dudes are wearing nail polish."

Zoey exhaled the breath she'd been holding. "I'm waiting to wake up and it's not happening. I'm supposed to solve a fifty-year-old crime and put a raging spirit to rest. That's asking a lot from someone like me. I'm not meant for this kind of shit."

"And you're not meant to inherit millions, or get struck by lightning, or get seduced by the greatest lover on earth, and yet..."

"Don't flatter yourself."

"Am I lying?"

"If you want to talk conquests, I'm game."

"I don't. I want you to get fired up about finding the last scumbag. This guy killed a kid. I'm sure his offenses didn't start or end with Miguel. I don't know how we'll prove it, but for now let's ride this bronco 'til we can't."

"Do you realize if someone had murdered my son, I'd be in prison?"

Lance nodded compassionately.

"I thought my being angry and damaged would carry me through this extrasensory nightmare. I thought because I could empathize with loss and the desire for revenge, I'd be perfect for the job. I realize we're on the heels of a madman and that I should be dancing on the table, but internally I'm falling apart."

"The perils of self-examination."

"Take me home." Zoey stood too quickly and had a dizzy spell. Lance grabbed her forearm. It didn't take much effort to coax her back into her seat.

"Settle down," Lance said. "You're too reactive. You've reached maximum capacity, that's all. You can't mask pain forever. Some people can, but you can't. You're too passionate to sedate your emotions."

"You speak as if you know me."

"I know more than you'll ever give me credit for, and despite your protests, I accept your inability to see past my bone...structure."

Zoey scratched her nose with her middle finger.

Lance snickered. "Let's recap. Over the past few days, we've done a little talking. You told me two things interweaved your soul, your son and photography. You said you wanted to get back to work but every time you picked up your camera, you felt disloyal to Milo. Photography makes you happy, but you can't be too happy because your son will never be able to laugh again."

"I don't know why I'd cut that vein for you."

"Moment of weakness following a life-altering orgasm."

"Of course, why not?"

"Creativity wreaks havoc if it's not expressed. No one argues against the fact that life is a patchwork of unsympathetic contrasts. And no one disputes notions that contrasts draw out the worst and best in people—destruction or creation. It's a matter of perspective. You're a photographer. You probably rely on contrasts. And because you're a professional photographer, I wouldn't think, even if you wanted to, you'd be capable of keeping everything bottled up forever. You observe an image and you give it depth. That's what's happening to you. Depth. You're thawing out."

"Bad timing."

"I'm just saying if you thought you could stay high until your heartache goes away, you can't. Eventually you're going to have to overdose and end it, or clean up and, as Delilah would say, check into reality."

"FYI, before I got sucked into all of this, I planned on killing myself."

"If you were seriously going to commit suicide, you'd have done it after your son's funeral. Pills and alcohol helped, but you're too strong to numb out forever and too stubborn to let anything outside of natural causes kill you."

"Awfully bold interpretation."

"Interpretations are subjective." He sipped his coffee. "Take it or leave it."

"I feel sick."

Lance slimmed his eyelids and gazed into Zoey's pupils. "You're high. You took pain pills, didn't you?"

"So?"

"So I thought you were serious about quitting. You went cold turkey. You did great, and you're willing to throw it all away?"

"I'm not. Just this once."

"I thought you wanted to put this puzzle together."

"I do. I am."

"What if the drugs interfere with incoming information?"

"They don't."

"Maybe not completely, but you were sober when you touched the rifle. That's the most you've seen since I've been involved." He hit the table once with his palm. "You're doing Luis and his family a disservice."

"Kiss my ass, hypocrite."

"Don't get me wrong, I love a good buzz, but there's a time and a place. It's called self-discipline."

"And you, the man who can't keep his dick in his jeans for over an hour, is lecturing me on self-control?"

"I like sex, but I drive my dick, not the other way around."

Zoey slipped off her shoe and, under the table, out of view, put her foot on his crotch. "Let's see…." She rubbed and predictably felt a pulse under her toe. "There it is, less than five seconds and you're horny."

He grabbed her ankle and moved her leg to the side. "It's not sex, it's you. I like sex with you."

"I'm not gullible."

"No, you're bitter." He paused. "Look, I don't want you to die. I'm trying to help you keep your shit together so you can handle this crazy mission."

Zoey glanced at the picture of innocent souls and couldn't suppress the rising guilt. "My hands were shaky. I wanted to put my fist through a wall. I needed something to calm my nerves."

Lance reclined and a tinge of regret washed across his face. "Why don't you funnel all that negative energy into something artistic—self portraits of you and me, naked and sweaty?"

"Oh, and that's practicing self-discipline?"

"No, self-indulgence." He flicked the side of his coffee cup and the noise sounded like the tiny bell on a cat collar.

"Something's different. I'm stoned."

"Wasn't that the objective?"

"Yes and no." She massaged the back of her neck. "Doesn't matter. I don't normally have this strong of a reaction from a couple ibuprofen and a Valium. I'm immune. So I thought."

"Maximum capacity. You'll feel better after you eat."

"Maybe."

"We're almost to the finish line." He flashed a thumb up.

"And I'm bursting out of my skin."

"What're you griping about now, Hawthorne?"

"You, of all people—no boundaries, no ends. Yes, I'm intrigued by the hunt, but this is no ordinary beast. This is something neither of us, and possibly no one on the planet, has ever encountered. One for all and all for one, yippee, let's bring a killer to justice. The whole thing is insane." Zoey crossed her arms over her chest. "We're foolish."

"You need food," Lance said. "Delilah," he hollered. "What's up?"

"I'm coming, sweetface," Delilah yelled. She loaded plates across her arm and, before long, hot omelets occupied space on the table.

Zoey grabbed her fork and shoveled a huge bite of food into her mouth. She added a mouthful of toast and, after a drink of tea, she threw the picture of the rock hounds at Lance like a Frisbee. "We're going to catch this dickhead."

Lance smiled. "We'll have to keep snacks in your car. You like almonds?"

"Why?" she asked, carving out another chunk of omelet.

"You're a fucking downer when your blood sugar drops."

Zoey thought about what he'd said while she ate. It seemed lately everyone had an opinion—pharmaceutical junkie, volatile, complicated bereavement, sex addict, clairaudient. She inhaled her meal. Her energy increased, lightheadedness faded, mood lifted and she admitted she'd been stamped by an astute circle of people. Taking comfort in Lance's discovery, she grinned. At least hypoglycemia had an easy solution. She liked almonds.

Chapter 11

Zoey waited outside the Golden Nugget Hotel where Lance stayed. He ran up to change, and, she assumed, pack his clothes. They'd discussed it, somewhat. He'd asked if he should check out and hang at her place and she'd shrugged.

His musky scent perverted her every thought. She couldn't deny him. And those eyes, those damned glistening eyes, she wanted to drown in them like a hormonal high school girl. She shook her head and kicked a wad of dirt. If possible, she'd make love to him twenty-four hours a day, which was why she'd opted to sit outside. She wanted to hurry home and tell Luis what Delilah had contributed.

Resting on a boulder, Zoey pulled out her cell and dialed Mitch. Fragmented clouds floated softly overhead the way high soaring kites would. She remembered finding images in the clouds with Milo. She gazed at her feet. Circular copper-colored leaves intermixed with pennies would be a deceivingly interesting photo. Yet it didn't move her enough to pick up her camera and break the near impenetrable wall of ice. The shot would come, she hoped.

Mitch's voicemail droned, and she left a message. "It's me. I wanted to give you an update and, if it's not too weird, I'd like to talk to your girlfriend. Call me when you can." Zoey dropped the phone in her purse.

Across the road, a child giggled. The redheaded toddler played in a field of lavender flowers. Two adults stood nearby and laughed. Their joy was photogenic, and the color distinctions brilliant. Zoey's aversion to her camera and the internal tug of war to shoot or not to shoot drove her more insane than the souvenir she'd received from the lightning. She craved tequila and Lance.

"What a joke," she muttered. "What a dry, bleak joke."

Lance poured out of the hotel, followed by twin teenage boys and one older man. The nameless trio shared dark curls and camel-hump noses. The boys knuckle-pushed each other and as they headed round the building to the parking lot, one hollered, "Coldstone, bitches!"

They wore swim trunks and carried backpacks with bottles of water tucked in the side pockets.

Suddenly she recalled the hospital and her first sign of clairaudience.

"Can't be," she said, but intuition told her otherwise. Zoey jumped up, passed Lance, and ran after the strangers. "Hey, yo, guys!"

The oldest man stopped and for obvious reasons looked puzzled.

"Sorry to bother you. I'm wondering…are you going whitewater rafting?"

"Do I know you?"

"No. Coldstone runs behind my house—"

"I thought the war between landowners and paddlers was over."

She smiled. "Nothing like that. Have you heard about the undercurrent?"

"The raft rental place mentioned something about it and I might have read a warning somewhere, why?"

"Why? Because people have died there, and I'd like to think you'd prefer to play it safe and go hiking instead."

He took a step closer to the teens, who sat on the bumper of an apple red Jeep. "I appreciate your concern, but my boys and I make that run every year. We're not tourists. We used to live here. We can handle the current."

"Being a former resident, you should know the death rate from that run is usually low…so I'm told. Recently it's increased enough to gain the attention of city officials, but they can't close the entire river. This is serious. Children have died."

"I understand," he said, disinterested. "We'll be fine. Thanks again for your concern." He proceeded to his vehicle.

"I wish someone would have warned me about faulty equipment before I put my son in danger. He's dead now. I'm giving you an opportunity I didn't have—take advantage of it!"

The man shoved his kids in the car and started the engine.

"Look," she said, "this isn't a game. Someone could die today."

He peeled out to the main road. Beyond the pall of exhaust, he glared at her in the side mirror as if she were spitting up worms.

Zoey pressed loose strands of hair to her scalp and bit her bottom lip. "What a dickhead."

Carrying a duffle bag over his shoulder, Lance approached. "Who the hell was that?"

"An idiot who thinks he's invincible. We have to get to Rayfield." She raced to the Harley and yelled, "Fast."

Lance met her at the bike and fastened the bag to the chrome rear. "All right. We'll get there. What's the hurry?"

"Those people wouldn't listen to me. They're running the river."

"What about it?" He mounted the seat and gripped the handlebars.

She crawled up behind him and clutched his waist. "There's a vicious undercurrent no one seems able to locate. You were there the morning a teenage girl died, and unfortunately she wasn't the first. Prior to that tragedy I've heard a voice say 'woman in the water.' I'm beginning to think someone was trying to tell me something."

"Luis?"

"No. I was at the hospital when I heard it. But it's making sense now. A teenager had just died in Coldstone. The voice came from his room."

"Shit," Lance said. "What can we do?"

"I know it's crazy, but maybe we can stand by the water's edge with rope. Damn it," she said, "We don't have rope."

"Sure we do," Lance said. "There's a bunch in the garage." He prepped the motorcycle. "Your uncle didn't use much."

* * * *

Zoey held Lance tight, his body as much a masterpiece as the terrain they traveled. Miles of feathery trees and storybook hills and a muffler vibrating between her thighs proved a better sedative than those prescribed, though zooming past Rock Hounds, she'd nearly tugged Lance's shirt to stop. It'd be simpler to dodge ghosts and dipshits fated for a death trap, easier to merge with shadows and a bottle of Cuervo. She'd quickly come to terms with the truth, which was that she wanted to push forward and save the dipshits. The burden gave her indigestion.

They wheeled upward onto the reddish road and into her front yard. Lance shut off the motor and they both stumbled to the ground.

"I'll be in the living room attempting to talk to Luis," Zoey said. "You get the rope."

"Come with me and we'll deal with Luis together."

"That's not necessary."

"He's already tried to strangle you and that poses some problems. If you die I'll be accused of murder because who in the hell will believe a ghost did it? Secondly, if you die and I get arrested, who'll rescue the rafters?"

"We don't have time to argue, Lance. I'll do things my way."

He grabbed her wrist and pulled her with him to the front door. "It'll take a minute."

She followed him into the garage, where Lance lifted a snakelike coil of rope buried under the trophies. Then she and Lance rushed to the living room.

Zoey paced a few breaths while sorting her thoughts. She had limited time.

"Luis," she yelled. "Two bad men are already dead. Maybe you can get to them from where you are. Maybe you have friends in low places."

She paused and listened.

"Amos hanged himself right here in this house, but I'm sure you're aware of his passing. You probably drove him to do it. You probably kicked the chair out from under him."

Luis laughed.

Zoey ignored the chills cascading through her flesh. She inhaled, exhaled, and continued. "Most likely Ross Ballentine made your search and siege list too. I found out today he had a heart attack two years ago. Did you know that?"

Luis sighed.

"Not sure what that means. I'll assume it doesn't matter whether you knew or not. He's gone. I have no idea what he did to you and your family—specifically—but if it makes you feel better, he has a beautiful granddaughter he left behind. He won't have the chance to watch her grow up." She waited.

Mi amor?

Zoey appealed to Lance. "*Mi amor?*"

"My love," Lance blurted with game show enthusiasm.

"What about your love? I don't know what you're asking."

Mi amor?

Zoey relied on her intuition. "I don't know what happened to your love. She could have escaped. She ran through the woods when she saw Miguel, she could have gotten away. Maybe not, though."

Luis whimpered.

Zoey's heart throbbed—an intense, achy throb that made it hard to breathe. She swallowed and went on. "The third man, Evil, was at a local restaurant this week. If he still frequents this area fifty years later, he has ties here. Someone will recognize him."

Mi amor.

"I'm sorry. I don't know what happened to her, but as soon as I do, I'll tell you."

Evil is alive.

"Yes, I know. We'll find him."

Mi amor.

Lance scanned the room. He held the rope like an eager rodeo cowboy.

Zoey muttered, "Woman in the water."

"Who is it?" Lance asked.

Acids boiled in her stomach. "We have to go, now! Grab your cell."

"It's in my pocket."

Zoey sped out the door and jumped off the deck onto the lawn. Her heart ticked in her ears, a screaming time bomb reminding her they hadn't a minute to spare.

Mi hijo.

She stopped abruptly. "What?"

Lance banged into her backside. "What—what?"

"Did you say something?'

"No."

"You sure?"

"Yeah, why, what did you hear?"

"I don't know—"

Mi hijo.

"There, that, did you hear it?"

Lance shook his head.

Mi hijo.

"It's not Luis." She glanced at Lance and repeated what she'd heard. "Do you know what it means?"

"My son."

"Damn it," she said. "That's what I thought." She assessed the woods and branches stretching over the path leading to the river. "Let's go!" Without looking back, she darted downhill toward the shaded forest. Her long legs carried her fast, and she sprang from the spongy patch of land to the tree line. She recalled a similar pursuit the night she was struck by lightning. Her scar tingled.

Sticks cracked beneath her feet, and her breath and the rustle of grass had a motivating rhythm—*huh—crinkle—huh—crinkle—huh—crinkle.* She ran hard.

"I'm right behind you," Lance yelled.

She weaved through the trees, down a slope, and scraped her elbow on an evergreen. The woodsy scent overshadowed her state of panic. Approaching a high row of weeds, the air cooled and smelled muddy. She slipped halfway to the water's edge but didn't fall. Panting, she froze in awe of the swooshing white ruffles.

There will be more.

"What?" Zoey asked.

There will be more.

Lance met her, winded and excited. "What do we do?"

"Wait for them, I guess. We're here just in time. That other voice is telling me there will be more. I think she intends to take another life."

"She?"

"Yes."

Lance created a noose around a robust tree stump and held a fairly generous portion loosely, readied to toss. He leaned forward and looked upstream.

Zoey watched too. A dark red rubber raft—an outcast in the palette of muted colors— pushed its way through a tight sieve of rocks.

"There they are." She pointed. "We have to get ready."

"They're moving too fast."

"We can do this," she said. "I feel it."

Spray from the river dappled Lance's face. He wiped his eyes and focused on the rafting enthusiasts stabbing and slicing Coldstone with their oars. The blood-red raft moved swiftly, and the static sound of flowing water made it impossible to communicate. Within seconds the raft came closer, and the bodies inside took shape, shiny helmets, wetsuits and even their arched noses.

Directly across from her and Lance, not too far from shore, the raft began to spin, faster and faster, like debris orbiting a drainage hole.

"What the—" the dad screamed over the noisy water.

"Over here!" Lance threw a long line of rope, which splashed in the river. He pulled in the sopping twine and threw it again. Water weight made it easier to aim and it landed inside the spinning raft.

"Dad, help!"

"Grab the rope, kids. Focus and grab the rope!"

The teens fumbled and flopped but managed to follow orders. They clung to the rope, their screams bouncing off the rocks and echoing into the sky. Dad held on behind. They wobbled to their feet, slanted forward, and in a blink, the raft capsized. All three went under water.

"No!" Zoey jolted.

Lance's muscles tensed as he yanked the meandering tie connecting the family to the tree stump.

Behind Lance, Zoey braced her feet and clutched the rope. She heaved, and heaved, and heaved into a sweat. Freezing water dotted her face. She tugged with all her might, and cussed at her shoulder for hurting. The rope wiggled. Finally, a teen and his dad reemerged, inching up the towrope in counts of two—*one, two, pull, one two, pull, one, two, pull,* until they reached the soil and fell, exhausted, on their backs.

The dad coughed and through purple lips uttered, "My son, Jacob, where is he?" He patted the rescued son lying next to him and checked his chest to see if he was breathing. He exhaled, relieved.

"Crap," Zoey said. She swiped the rope from the waterlogged rafters and knotted it around her waist.

Lance removed his shirt and made a pillow for the trembling teenager. "What do you think you're doing?" he questioned Zoey.

"Ask me when I'm done." She ran into the water and squealed when the numbing temperature soaked through her clothes. The current dragged her under a few times, and she didn't care, over or under, she sensed she was heading in the missing child's direction.

In a placid area, she rose for air, shivering beyond the coldest Chicago winter. Her drenched braid was deadweight on her shoulder, dripping like a gutted boa constrictor. She exhaled and inhaled and held her breath once more. She plunged beneath the crest.

A woman hummed softly, a lullaby. Zoey opened her eyes and let out a muffled scream. Beneath ascending bubbles, a transparent lady embraced the motionless teenager. Black hair fanned like shadows of seaweed. The woman removed the boy's helmet.

For Miguel. There will be more.

Zoey clutched the teen's wrist and tugged, but the woman wouldn't let go. Zoey yanked a second time, and the spirit gripped the boy harder.

Mi hijo!

The river bottom quaked.

Woman In The Water jarred a memory. Zoey swam to a calmer area and raised her head. "Lance!"

He stood at the coast. "You're out of your mind!"

Her teeth chattered and her mouth, completely anesthetized, wouldn't function right. She forced words. "Do you have the antique money clip?"

"Yeah!"

"Throw it to me," she hollered. "Now! And then call an ambulance."

Without hesitation, Lance dug in his front pocket, extracted the sterling silver, and pitched it at Zoey.

The metal plunked behind her and sank.

Zoey held her breath again and followed the glistening ghost hook. Woman in the water noticed the gleaming trinket.

Luis.

She released the boy. Her spectral figure pursued the money clip down to the bottom and blended into the sand.

Luis.

Zoey grasped the boy's forearm with one hand and sliced through the current with the other. Pushed into a monstrous boulder, she had something to lean on. She popped her head out of Coldstone and made sure his nose had access to oxygen. She breathed heavily, and rested. She thanked the universe for the giant stone anchored like an ancient dinosaur bone. The river pressed against her stomach, trying to wash her and the kid downstream. She withstood the pressure.

Jacob's father had revived, and he and Lance inched along the rope, thigh-deep in the river.

"Jake, it's Dad," the father yelled. "I'm coming, son." Despite the current's strength, he rammed forward.

"Ah, shit," Zoey said. She'd better carry the boy onward or she'd have another rescue mission in her immediate future. "Stay there," she hollered. "We'll come to you."

Zoey secured the rope around her waist and cradled the teen in her arms. She lowered all but his face under water, allowing the river to lighten his weight. His lips were blue, and her legs were blistering cold. She focused on the other boy, Jacob's brother, pale and choking up water on the shore. She held the teen tightly and marched forward.

Lance and the boy's father barreled at her with their arms extended. The dad finally reached them and carefully took his son. Lance clung to her wilting side and aided her out of Coldstone.

Land, solid and dry—she collapsed to her knees, hardly coherent. In her peripheral vision, Jacob's father gave him mouth-to-mouth resuscitation, with eyes full of dread and incalculable pain.

Lance freed her from the rope. "I'm here," he said, frazzled. "What do you need? What can I do?"

"The kid," she said. "Is he okay?"

Lance inspected the teen and returned half smiling. "He's okay, Hawthorne."

Zoey rolled on her back, panting, freezing, and thankful.

"His brother?"

"Julian," Lance said. "He's scared, but he'll be all right."

She closed her eyes, wanting nothing more to do with the afterlife or Mother Nature. "Where's the ambulance?"

"On its way," Lance said as he lay on top of her, heating her frostbitten skin with his body.

And despite it all, she loved the feel of his body.

* * * *

Zoey towel-dried her hair in front of the mirror. Steam swelled into the bedroom and fogged the glass. She cleared a circle and dropped the towel. Lance had given her a hooded sweatshirt, and she threw it on over a T-shirt. She had put on jeans and socks too. She'd baffled the EMTs by escaping hypothermia, but couldn't kick her systemic chill.

Paramedics had taken the father, Arvid Loesch, and his sons Julian and Jacob to the hospital. The guys on call assured Zoey that Jacob would be fine and admitted even if the city legally closed a section of Coldstone watercourse, enthusiasts would enter outside city limits and continue to ride the river.

Lance sat on the bed, nursing a bottle of lukewarm Corona he'd brought from the hotel. "Good job, Hawthorne. You left me standing at the shore with my mouth hanging open, but who gives a shit, right? You saved three lives."

"One life. Jacob's. She would have let the others go."

He swigged. "You never did tell me what you saw down there."

Zoey's muscles ached. She entered the bathroom for a wad of toilet paper and wiped her runny nose. "We'll talk about it later."

"You're catching a cold. Let's go downstairs. I started a fire."

"I'm okay." She sniffled.

"Come on." He stood and ushered her into the hall. "Everyone gets sick, Hawthorne. Even badass, supernatural babes."

She smiled and accompanied him to the staircase, pausing a moment to survey the ether for signs of Luis. "We never really get away with anything, do we? One way or another, we pay, or relive a moment we've tried desperately to avoid."

"Don't leave me hanging again."

"Having to tell someone their loved one is dead. After the accident I wouldn't go near Yaphet's parents. I couldn't face Milo's death, let alone comfort them. Mitch had to do it. I've felt guilty ever since, and here I am a year and a half later in the same position—having to..." She elevated her palm toward the ceiling. "You know, deliver bad news."

Lance nodded. "The universe is comprehensive."

"The universe is a bully." Zoey grabbed his beer and swigged.

"The universe is a nurturing but strict mother," Lance said.

"You're full of it." Zoey sneezed.

"Let's get you by the fire."

"Sure, me and my red nose, and the Kick Me, Karma sign I have on my ass."

"If you say so," Lance said as he leaned backward and glanced at her butt. "From where I stand, your back looks mighty fine."

She walked downstairs and neared the potbelly. Fire licked the inner walls of the stove. Lance had moved two seats closer together and left a blanket on one. She set the Corona on the ledge of the potbelly, covered her shoulders, and sat in rippling thermals.

Her lover approached, sexy and quiet, a panther stalking its mate. He made himself comfortable in the chair next to hers. "When do you plan on having your dreaded conversation with Luis?"

"As soon as I figure out what to say." She reclined and pulled the blanket hems together over her chest, then closed her eyes and recalled wearing Luis's skin.

"The woman, Luis's beloved, saw Miguel lying in pieces. She ran through the woods toward the river. Shortly after, two men walked out of the forest, Evil with his ax, and a man holding a shotgun." Zoey opened her eyes. "Now I know how Ross Ballentine participated. Three rifles and three ghosts, each in different locations. Three killers. Evil slaughtered the child near the woods, Amos murdered Luis in the house, and Kane's father shot Luis's wife near or in the river."

"If they're all at fault, who would snitch?" Lance stood and moseyed into the kitchen. The fridge door suctioned open and slammed closed, and he returned holding a fresh beer. "One tormented spirit after the other." He swigged.

Carmen.

Zoey straightened in her chair. "It's Luis. He said the name Carmen."

"Woman in the water is identified," Lance said while scanning the air.

"Luis, Carmen and Miguel," Zoey mumbled.

Carmen.

Zoey rose, slowly, conscious to conceal her fear.

Mi amado, Carmen.

She didn't understand, but assumed he spoke from his heart. "Luis, I'm sorry. I think Ross Ballentine shot Carmen. Her energy is in the river running through Rayfield property. She's killing children on Miguel's behalf."

Heh-heh-heh-heh.

Zoey's heart banged with the force of a sledgehammer.

"It's not funny," she said with stuffy nasal tones. "Those children are innocent."

Nos dicen espaldas mojadas. Cuya espalda está mojada ahora?

"I don't know what you're saying."

Whose back is wet now?

From the kitchen, a stack of dishes broke as if pushed out of the cabinets.

Terror wrenched her stomach. "I'll leave, Luis!"

Lance tried to hold her, but she squirmed out of his embrace.

Evil is alive. Bring him or die.

The empty fruit bowl missed their heads by a fraction and smashed against the entertainment unit. Glass shards rained on the floor. The laptop elevated and crashed against the hardwood.

"Luis! You're right. Evil is alive and I promise we'll get him."

Cupboards banged. The chair next to Lance began to spin like a top, like the raft. Spin. Spin. Spin.

"Luis," she hollered. "Don't you understand? I want to help you! But I will not let another child die in that river. If I have to stand guard, it's time away from finding the man who murdered your child. And believe me, after what I saw, after what that prick did to Miguel, if you don't squeeze the life out of him, I will."

Silence permeated the house. Her quivering breath seemed to echo, and the vibrant fire dwindled.

"Luis?" she whispered, wiping a mustache of perspiration from her upper lip.

A curious noise became audible…a soul-level weeping.

"Luis, I'm sorry. I can relate. Truly I can. I lost my son too. I'll do everything in my power to—"

"Eeeeh!" Lance squealed. He walked a semicircle, hunched over and fell on his side.

She dropped to her knees. "What is it? What's happening?" She patted his frame, senselessly searching for the cause of his condition.

His face grayed and his watery eyes bulged. He winced, unable to speak.

"Lance, shit." Zoey studied his pained expression, his squint and snarl. He might be dying. She stood to call an ambulance but couldn't find a cellphone. She rushed to the end table and picked up the landline. "You're doing this, Luis. I swear, if you hurt him, you'll regret it. I'll come after you. If I can hear you while I'm alive, I'll definitely hear you when I'm dead." She dialed 9—

Lance gurgled.

Zoey tossed the phone and walked through the house. "Luis! Don't let rage consume you. It's irrational. It'll make a fool of you. Trust me. There's no payoff. It made me weak and dependent. A puppet."

Lance gasped.

"You're better than the parasites who murdered you and your family! You are. I felt you in my vision. You're a good, honest man." She peeked at her lover, whose face was red and bloated. A drop of drool sparkled in the corner of his lips. Tears wet her cheeks. "Luis," she said, surrendering to the inevitable, "I'm sorry they've made you a monster. They won."

Lance gasped. He sucked in air and exhaled a few times, then lifted his head and uttered, "Hawthorne?"

Zoey sped to him and knelt as if her knees had given out. "Lance. Hallefuckinlujah! Tell me you're all right."

He breathed again, deep, in and out, and in a weak, sickly voice, said, "What'd he do to me?"

"I don't know." She caressed his forehead and used the tissue she'd been holding to dab saliva from his chin.

He grimaced. "Is that your snot-rag? That's disgusting." He gently pushed her hand away and hoisted himself to a sitting position. "Good one, Luis!" Lance leaned back slightly and massaged his abdomen. "You had me twisted up—professional origami—clever. A windmill, am I right?"

"Lance, stop," Zoey said, terrified he'd refuel Luis.

"No, we're cool," Lance demanded and looked upward. "By the way, I saw God. He said to tell you you're an asshole."

Zoey heard gravelly laughter. Her clenched shoulders lowered.

Lance rubbed his chest and nodded, seeming to mull over the mindboggling event. His caramel coloring had returned, and his skin glowed.

"You should go, Lance." She hated to say it. "The risks are too great."

"I'm not leaving."

"You said you didn't want to die."

He gazed at her with sleepy eyes. "I don't want you to die either."

"Well, if ghosts don't kill me, this damn cold will." She fanned her now-feverish neck.

"As soon as the feeling returns to my legs, I'll ride to town and grab some soup and NyQuil. You have to snap out of this. Tomorrow's a big day. You have a dinner date with a murderer's son."

Chapter 12

Daylight struck her face with the same intrusiveness Milo must have felt when she'd wake him up for school. Zoey rolled on her side and buried her head under her pillow, but quickly came out for air. Plugged ears, crusted nostrils and the added weight of the pillow stirred underwater memories.

She clutched her temples. "I feel like roadkill."

Barely awake, Lance muttered, "Sucks to be you."

"Shut up and make love to me."

"What, and spoil you?"

"Absolutely."

Lance slid his nakedness next to hers, propped up on his left elbow and stared at her face. His beauty frightened her, and the harsh sunlight became a predator hunting for fine lines. She hid in the shadow of his physique.

"Your scar is almost gone," he said, glancing at her shoulder.

"So?"

"So that's badass how fast you've bounced back. I'm beginning to think you're not human."

She grabbed the role of toilet paper from the nightstand, unwound tissue and blew her nose. "I assure you I am."

"Maybe I ate some potent 'shrooms and I'm having a Lance in Wonderland trip. You're the rabbit."

"No such luck. This is your reality."

"You never told me your eyes change color."

He'd noticed and it frightened her. "You never asked."

"That's almost as bizarre as Tank's cat eyes."

"Yeah," she said. "And he doesn't wear contacts?"

Lance snickered. "No. They're real. He can see in the dark too—weird, right?"

"Very."

"I keep telling him if he's not careful the government will make a science project out of him."

"He's the mutant."

"I know, and I'm suspicious of you too."

"The only time my eyes change color is when I'm in agony," she said. "Broken bones, labor, lightning strike, getting pulverized by the river—it's a pain gauge."

"Reminding you to reflect," he said. "Like rainbows after a storm, or bruises following a fistfight."

"What?"

"Hey, I've had many a black eye bring me to states of clarity, from learning what alcoholic beverages don't mix to discovering I have a cousin in Tallahassee who resorts to biting."

"Your thought process continuously surprises me." She coughed. "Unfortunately right now I'm shallow. I have one thing on my mind and that's your cock."

Lance laughed and twirled a piece of hair draping her collarbone. "Wow. I made an impression. You feel like roadkill and yet you can't stop thinking about me."

"About your cock. I'm a sex addict, and I accept it."

"Didn't your bullshit diagnosis counteract anything? Complicated bereavement? Yeah, right. You're complicated, and grieving, but you're also seeing ghosts and talking to the dead. Seriously, don't reduce yourself to a diagnosis. You don't have to be unstable to dig sex." He paused. "When I get home, I'm building a bike in your honor. It'll be sleek emerald green pearl effect with chrome lightning bolts and LED lighting."

She gripped his hard-on. "How about for the next, oh, say, thirty minutes we shut our mouths and communicate physically."

He grinned and nuzzled his face beneath her earlobe, kissed her neck. "The medicine helped?"

His breath caused chills to race along her skin. "Yes. It helped me sleep, but I need another kind of remedy. If I can have an orgasm, it'll take my mind off the fact that I can't breathe and my chest feels like I have a three-hundred-pound person standing on me and why are we talking?"

Lance slinked on top of her, careful not to rest too heavily on her battered body. He pecked her chapped nose and then her lips, and skillfully slid his serpentine tongue in her mouth. Most saliva would be pasty in the morning, but his tasted sweet as watered-down honey. He moved slower than usual. His lips heated hers, and she responded at first desperately and then she relaxed, persuaded by his thoughtful rhythm. He squeezed her hipbone, skimmed her side upward with his fingertips to the round of her breast, and tickled the crevice of her armpit, making his way softly to her wrist.

Her clit throbbed.

Lance pinned both of her hands to the mattress. He gently suckled her nipples.

A sexual torture. She squirmed. "I want you in my throat," she said, focused on the sugary flavor of his semen.

He lifted his head and whispered, "Not today." He bit her good shoulder and gazed back into her eyes. "I'm going to cure your cold one thrust at a time." He rubbed the shaft of his solid dick in between her sacred lips.

Zoey's pulse sped. She threw her legs over his buttocks and tried to muscle him inside, but Lance arched his back. Her limbs fell to the bed.

"Take it easy," he said. "Give up control."

He released her arms, kissed her again, strong and wet, and moved his head down to her enlarged clitoris. His tongue danced and swirled, up and down, in her hole and out. He moaned and sent a mild vibration through her abdomen.

She raised her hips, and again he pressed her to the bed. The visible world faded and shivers skidded across her skin. She moaned and tugged on his thick hair. Oh god, the way he gripped her ass and lapped her spills, she could love him.

Lance raised his flushed face. He moved forward, holding his torso above hers, and inserted the head of his dick. Zoey clawed the sheets. Everything about him, his features, his touch, his scent, drove her wild.

He pushed deep inside of her, juicing her like ripened fruit. His pubes fused with hers, and he gyrated, smooth and knowledgeable, deep in and circular. "You like that?"

"You know I do." Zoey clapped her hands on his shoulder blades and adored the muscles and tendons rolling beneath her palms. Down his backside, she clutched his tight ass. Greedy, she pulled him closer. He hit her G-spot. She sighed and clenched.

He pushed into her, feverish, sweaty, in and out, slick and relentless, in and out, and in and…

"I'm coming." He groaned and swelled.

Warm and tingly, she embraced her crippling orgasm. Eventually she caught her breath, appreciating sex more than she'd ever valued meds.

Lance hit the mattress and closed his eyes.

Lorelei Buckley

Zoey brushed webs of hair off her wet neck and lay calmly facing the ceiling. She peeked over at Lance but he'd drifted asleep. She studied the outline of his lips and the music of his breathing.

The landline rang, and she jolted. Apparently she'd passed out too. Uninterested in answering, she waited for the noise to stop.

Then her cell rang on the nightstand.

Lance opened his eyes and, just above a whisper, said, "What's up?"

"The phone." She stared at the buzzing mobile. "Did you bring my cell up here?"

"Yeah, last night," he said. "You were sleeping and it wouldn't stop ringing. I thought it might be important."

"Not important enough to wake me up?"

"Your home phone rings enough, and you don't answer. I figured you didn't want to talk to anyone. I checked your cell. Mitch called about a hundred times. He finally texted something like, the foot's fine, work is coming together, and Sterling left him. He wanted to cry on your shoulder. I spared you."

"Mitch? He's not the handkerchief type." She thought for a moment. "I'm sorry he lost Sterling. She was good for him. But I know exactly what he'll do to recover. He'll disappear for a week, drink beers, read John Grisham novels, and hang out on the boat." The line separating memories and imagination blurred, and she felt as if she were telling a story. "He'll cruise Lake Michigan under a blanket of blinking stars, hearing nothing but gentle waves slap against the hull. If he gets lonely, he'll head inward and shut off the motor."

Feeling silly, she stopped, but Lance arched an eyebrow, prompting her to go on.

"He'll observe the skyline and admire some of the greatest minds on the planet for their designs. Slowly, he'll regain respect for much of the human race." She took a breath. "Almost ready to reunite with civilization, he'll think a while longer about whatever it was that brought him to the boat in the first place, and ultimately he'll motor closer to the shadows moving about on the Michigan Avenue Bridge. People—mostly drunk—will hoot and holler, and Mitch will laugh, finally reminded that people are both brilliant and stupid and life as a whole is a product of its inhabitants. And in that unassuming experience, he'll return rejuvenated, pick up the phone and call Sterling. He's a dignified griever."

"Well, well, well." Lance got a burst of energy. "This whimsical nostalgic person is not the chick I picked up in Rock Hounds."

"I picked you up."

"I recall a mutual decision but whatever makes you happy. Anyway—you have a sentimental side. You're not just another pretty face either, are you?"

"I don't know what I am." She sat and spat phlegm in her tissue. "I'm sick, and I don't want to go to dinner. But I'm going, so I guess it's fair to say I'm at least determined."

"And at best?"

"I don't know."

"Sure you do."

Drug-free and congested she felt vulnerable. "At best I'm reliable. And even though I have no interest in it, I believe in love, and this family. Luis, Carmen and Miguel adored each other so intensely none of them can move on. That's worth fighting for, isn't it?"

Lance smiled. "At best you're highly principled." He got out of bed and walked into the bathroom, peed, and returned with a towel around his waist. He tilted his head sideways and stared at her curiously. "Why did you divorce Mitch?"

"I didn't. When our son died, I couldn't handle it. I tore our life apart. Milo was Mitch's clone. I avoided my husband because it hurt too much to see the manhood my son would never experience. Mitch divorced me."

"Still love him?"

"Forever," she said softly.

Lance lowered his eyebrows.

"We're not reconciling, if that's what you're wondering."

"I get it. You have me now. Why would you?"

"It's not about you."

"I was kidding. Lighten up. You can't go back because too much has changed."

"You know all of my secrets, and I don't even know your last name."

Lance took measured steps and sat at the foot of the bed. He studied her face as if evaluating the strength of their bond. "Malone."

"Lance Malone." She sat and raised the pillow higher behind her back. She reclined and said, "Tell me about yourself, your past. And be candid. I want grit."

"You're not ready for me."

"Friends and lovers was your idea. 'Fess up."

He exhaled. "Both my parents were diagnosed with schizophrenia and what a fucking nightmare that was, the two of them in and out of mental health wards. Sucked ass. Tail end of it, child welfare placed my younger sister and me with my grandmother on our mother's side. She had a shack in the country with chickens and goats." Lance smiled. "My grandma was a genius in the kitchen. People crossed counties to get her homemade chicken pot pies. By age eleven, I launched Grandma's Grub."

"No shit?"

Lance nodded. "No shit. We sold fresh pies, quiche, goat cheese, doughnuts and homemade pasta to local grocery stores and restaurants. It supplemented her social security checks, and we paid the bills. By sixteen I worked in one of the busiest Harley shops in Denver and made a decent salary. A day after my twenty-first birthday, I opened Performance Authority Custom Bike Shop. A few magazines featured me and, man, they pimped me. Shirtless mechanic posing next to custom hogs—grown men drooled over bikes and women salivated over the biker. Everyone was happy."

Zoey shrugged. "No argument there. You're definitely easy on the eyes...especially naked."

He grinned and affectionately rubbed her leg. "I'm not ham enough for fame. I like building bikes, riding, making love and making money. That's it."

"I understand," she said, mulling over the 'making love' comment. Her stomach cramped. She gasped within a wave of fear. "We haven't used condoms, and I'm not on the pill, what if..."

He gently squeezed her ankle. "No worries, Hawthorne, I'm snipped."

"You don't want kids?"

"Hell no. After what my sister and I went through, my grandmother, shit, my parents? I'm not about to make crazy babies. I'm not that selfish."

"So when I heard voices, and you said you believed me, you weren't lying?"

"You were focusing on what you heard the way people do when they're trying to understand someone with a thick accent—nothing like my folks. When they had episodes, their eyes were vacant as if they were sleepwalking, describing dreams. They didn't recognize me as their son, but as a threat of some kind. Took me a long time to realize they had no power."

"Do you forgive them?"

"It's hard. Mental illness is an elusive handicap. There are no visible markers, no wheelchairs or physical impairments. Schizophrenia is a mean disease, lots of rage and paranoia. I try."

Zoey blew him a kiss.

"Let's change the subject. Are you hungry?" He stood.

"Not really." She coughed up another phlegm ball and spat in the tissue.

"I'll make some toast," he said. "You have to put food in your stomach or the cold medicine will nauseate you."

"What am I, ten? I can handle a teaspoon of decongestant."

"You want butter?" he asked, seeming rattled by his admission. "Dumb question. Who doesn't want butter on toast?" He walked out of the room with the harsh severing qualities of a machete.

Zoey assumed he'd felt uncomfortable with his vulnerability. She understood. She ditched the bed laden with sweat and intoxicating sex odors, and went into the bathroom. The shower sounded like rain hitting pavement. The drain gurgled. Her sinuses burned and she stood under pellets of water, hoping the steam would offer relief. As pointed out by her lover, the mangled flower on her shoulder seemed to shrink more and more every day. She washed lust from her flesh and urges to cancel dinner from her mind. The idea of interrogating her neighbor made her nervous—understatement of the decade—it made her sick.

Dried and dressed, with her hair wrangled into a braid, she opened her nightstand drawer and popped a Valium. As far as curbing her habit, she'd exceeded her own expectations. She refused to guilt herself over one little pill.

Evil is alive. Traedmelo.

"Luis?" She scanned the room.

Silence.

"I'll know more tonight," she said, unsure, and walked downstairs.

Lance had cleaned the kitchen, dining and living rooms. He'd put on his jeans and sat shirtless, sipping hot coffee and staring out the window at the woods.

Zoey took a piece of toast from a saucer centered on the table.

"Don't fuck him, all right?"

"Excuse me?"

"You heard me. Don't fuck Kane."

"What are you talking about?"

"You know exactly what I'm talking about." He rose to his feet. "You think you're a sex addict—define it. What, you're easy? You can't control your sex drive? Just don't sleep with him, okay?" He walked out the door and stopped on the deck, still gazing at the woods as if deciphering a complicated math equation.

Sideswiped by Lance's strange upheaval of insecurity, she remained indoors and drank a cup of tea. The pill calmed her, and she wondered if she'd missed something, if she'd failed to notice their advancement from lovers and friends to—to what? With no space left on her metaphorical heaping plate, she wordlessly joined Lance on the deck and sat on the stair.

He camped next to her and leaned against her arm.

Neither spoke, but she knew he felt what she felt, the unexpected currents within swiftly motioning them into depths they weren't equipped to navigate. Ignore it and it would disappear, unlike Milo's death, her ex-husband, her prescriptions, the four-bedroom shrine, Luis, Carmen and Miguel. Eventually the formula had to work. Ignore it and it would go away.

* * * *

Lance rode to Rock Hounds for drinks, and Zoey trailed his smoke to Kane's house. She drove a narrow road through opened iron gates under an umbrella of swooping trees, and entered an extravagant landscape. A rug of vibrant green lay on both sides of the driveway while soldiers of maple divided the polished manmade home from rustic wilderness.

About twenty feet from the illuminated mansion, she saw Kane's Escalade parked near a small circle of dirt. The patch, skillfully decorated with mismatched boulders, rabbitbrush and a single limber pine harbored a post with a surveillance camera aimed at the front door. She pulled next to his shiny SUV and turned off the ignition. She'd taken an antihistamine, and it dried her runny nose, but her chest hurt. After a session of unhealthy coughing, she made her way to the entrance.

Her finger barely touched the doorbell, and Kane opened the door. His white hair glowed in shocking contrast to his black attire, and his blue metallic necktie matched areas of sky. Like Mitch, he had unambiguous strength that came from somewhere unseen, an unwavering presence.

"You're just in time," he said.

"For?" she asked nasally.

He opened the door further and revealed young Kendall standing in the foyer with a tray of chocolate chip cookies. She wore a pale pink T-shirt and purple pants with a line of embedded rhinestones along the mouth of the front pockets.

"Wish I could smell them," Zoey said.

"Oh, you're sick?" Kane asked.

She wouldn't scare a ten-year-old with tales of drowning teenagers. Besides, she didn't owe Kane an explanation. "I'm afraid I am. I'm willing to reschedule, or wear a mask."

"Kendall has the immune system of a shark. She doesn't get sick. And me, well, I can use a cold. Time off would be marvelous."

"Are you sure?" Zoey asked, feeling germy.

"Yes, please stay."

If not for the photo and new information, she wouldn't have gotten out of bed.

"Kendall made the cookies from scratch, for you," he said while gesturing Zoey indoors.

"I know we shouldn't have dessert before dinner," Kendall said, "but they're good when they're warm. You do like chocolate chip, don't you?" She pursed her lips.

"Uh, yeah," Zoey said. "They're my favorite."

Kendall sighed in relief and moseyed ahead toward a luxurious lounge area with recessed lighting and double-wide furniture. "Come on," she said before veering right into what Zoey assumed was the dining room.

"You'll have to excuse her," Kane said softly. "We haven't had a woman here since her mother died. She's excited."

Zoey cleared her throat. She hadn't time to be a mommy figure. She was a poor example, and still mourning her son. She had a killer to find.

"Oh, I'm sorry," Kane said empathetically. "There's nothing expected of you."

"Am I that transparent?"

"As long as you don't take up gambling, you'll be fine." He raised an eyebrow. "Kendall misses her mother. She might be a tad clingy, pay her no mind. She's a child. She's emotionally clumsy."

"Aren't we all?"

Kane didn't seem to agree. "I don't know about you, but I'm famished."

Zoey smiled.

"Shall we?" Kane gave gentle direction with his arm to follow Kendall.

From where Zoey stood, straight ahead and to the left were huge closed arched doors. A whole section of the house appeared to be behind those doors. To the right, the rooms were massive and airy, differentiated only by furniture.

Zoey proceeded through the spacious sitting area and entered the generously windowed dining room. The personal chef Kane had mentioned stood behind a granite countertop not far from the table in a quaint built-in kitchen. Plumes of steam curled around him.

"You have a lovely home," she said.

"Tess designed it," Kane said. "I'd like to introduce you to Chef Bouvier." He ushered her to the cook.

Chef Bouvier stirred sauce in a pan. He bowed his head. "How do you do?" he said in a heavy French accent.

"And this," Kane presented, "is Madame Hawthorne. Tonight we'll disregard formalities. Zoey, meet Martin. His golf swing needs work, but his food is superb."

"Monsieur Ballentine, you are too kind."

"A well-deserved intro, my friend. Be a sport," Kane said. "Announce the menu."

"Of course," Martin said. "We start with a spring green salad premixed in homemade portabella mushroom dressing, and freshly baked basil rolls. The entrée—poached wild salmon smothered in dill caper cream sauce. Over there—" He waved his wooden spoon at Kendall. "Madame Ballentine has prepared a savory dessert."

Kendall beamed.

"You've succeeded in making me very hungry," Zoey said, half serious.

"Excellent. Now I'll attempt to whet your whistle." Kane walked to the opposite end of the chef's station and lifted a bottle. "As promised, Pinot Gris, the good stuff. Can I pour you a glass?"

"Please," she said, thankful for the liquid sedative.

"When can I try some, Daddy?" Kendall spouted with a mouthful of cookie.

Kane eyed his daughter. "You can have a sip at your sweet sixteenth, and a glass with dinner when you turn nineteen. I advise you to enjoy those opportunities fully because on your twenty-first birthday, I'm locking the liquor cabinet and sending you to a convent."

"What's a convent?" she asked.

"It's where fathers send their beautiful daughters to protect them."

"Protect them from what?"

"From stinky boys." Kane handed Zoey a glass of wine.

"You're a boy and you don't stink."

"Fathers who plan on sending their daughters to a convent don't stink. We smell like petunias. We'll talk about this again when you hit puberty. Until then, let's pick a topic our dinner guest can participate in."

Kendall looked at Zoey and patted the seat next to hers. "If you sit here, you'll see the owl." She pointed at the window and an ancient tree on the other side of the glass. "He lives there and when the sun sets, he triggers the security lights. He's really big. Dad says he's the size of a poodle. Do you like owls?"

"I've never known one personally, but I don't have reason not to like owls."

"My grandpa used to say they were flying rats. He tried to shoot one before and I cried and he stopped."

Zoey glanced at her drink, unsure how to respond.

Kane approached Zoey and clanked his glass to hers. "To new friendships, and a meal with happier stories." He peeked at Kendall, who appeared regretful of her rant. He sipped and added, "It's no secret my father had a contentious streak. Are you aware he and your uncle were buddies?"

Too soon for particulars, Zoey nodded reluctantly. "I found an old photo of them." She took a gulp of her wine, which was undeniably delicious. "I didn't know Great Uncle Amos. Or his friends."

Kane chuckled. "Consider yourself lucky. They were a grumpy bunch who'd have traded their wives and children for more money and quieter shotguns." He sipped and evened his glass with his belt. "Amos didn't have children. He never left his house long enough to court a woman. Not sure it would have made a difference. I find it hard to believe there's a woman on earth interested in gutting raccoons and squirrels for the rest of her days. Dream man, eh?"

Zoey finished her wine. "Amos was my mother's uncle, her father's brother. She'd stopped speaking to him before I came along. We were all surprised when Amos left everything he owned to my son. Too bad. Milo would have done some good in the world."

"More wine?"

"Yes." She extended her glass and Kane poured.

Kane blurted, "My mother told me she stayed with my father to keep an honest eye on him. She swore he'd be too destructive otherwise."

"Your mother sounds like a wise woman."

"Uh, what she sacrificed to keep the planet safe from Dad astounds me. No one else could have put up with him. She didn't really have patience for him. She just figured out how to outsmart him."

Kendall interrupted. "How about picking a story your daughter can participate in, Dad?"

"Kendall, Kendall, Kendall," he said. "My precious victim of adolescence."

"Whatever, Dad. Will you guys sit with me, pleeeease?"

Zoey read Kane's signals and they joined Kendall at the dining table.

"Over here, by me, Zoey—if you want to see the owl."

Appeasing her young hostess, Zoey sat in her allocated chair and rubbed her palms together. "Bring it, owl. I'm ready."

Kendall snickered.

Lorelei Buckley

Kane stood in the soft gold lighting. His black attire and dazzling tie suited his personality—distinguished and unafraid. His eyes were intriguingly unstable.

"I like your hair. Your braid," Kendall said. "My mom had long hair too. She used to wear it like that. Mostly she wore it down. It was brown, though."

Zoey took a sip, thinking how to reply. "Brown like chocolate, or brown like autumn leaves, or brown like dark coffee?"

Kendall popped up in her seat. "Brown like almonds."

"Ooh," Zoey said. "Pretty."

Kendall nodded sadly.

Kane sat across from Zoey and Kendall. "This is supposed to be a happy occasion. We're meeting our new neighbor. How about a smile?"

Kendall did what her dad asked. "I had a moment, but I'm fine now."

"Dr. Doyle's advice." Kane addressed Zoey. "If we fight grief, it fights back, but if we give ourselves permission to have moments of sadness, it subsides on its own and we can move on. That is, until the next moment."

Despite her buzz, a welling discomfort crept inside. Sitting with Kendall and Kane made Zoey miss family dinners. Milo challenging her and Mitch with mobster trivia: What are the five principles of the initiation oath? What year did Al Capone go to prison? Which prison? They never understood his fascination but had fun playing. She missed hearing Mitch's renovation ideas, and grew especially queasy at the thought of her dusty portfolio. Conceivably, she was having a moment.

Chef Martin wheeled a cart over and the racket shattered her memories. He served salad and placed individual baskets of rolls near each setting, then lifted a tall crystal grinder. "Pepper?"

All heads shook no.

He pushed the cart back to his station and raised a pan lid. Stainless steel clanked, and dishes thumped on the counter.

Kane leaned back in his chair. "Kendall loves the Jonas Brothers. And I can listen to Sarah McLachlan for hours, or the Cocteau Twins with their buoyant bass and diaphanous vocals. Great stress relief. How about you? What are some of your favorites?"

Zoey hadn't cared about music for, well, for over a year. "I don't know. I've been so busy."

Kane and Kendall sat, hungry for Zoey to elaborate.

She straightened in her chair. "I really don't have a favorite musical artist and I'll tell you why. Before I moved to Colorado, I worked insanely long hours. I was a professional photographer. Most of my clients, especially fashion models, would bring their own music, whatever helped them feel confident. I enjoyed the variety, but the noise never ended. Even at home I dealt with editors and galleries and contracts, and family stuff with phones, television and YouTube videos blaring in the background. I've come to appreciate quiet."

"Interesting," Kane said. "What do you think, Kendall?"

Kendall stared at her water glass. "When Mommy died I couldn't stand music. Everything reminded me of her and made me cry. Mommy watches me. Sometimes at night before bed I can smell her."

"You can?" Zoey asked.

Kendall nodded.

Jasmine.

"Jasmine?" Zoey repeated.

"How did you know?" Kendall asked with eyelashes nearly touching her brows.

Zoey shook her head. "Lucky guess." She concocted a story. "I remember a very beautiful model telling me the most gorgeous women in the world smell like jasmine."

"My mommy was beautiful."

Zoey nonchalantly wiped her sweaty palms on her slacks. "Jasmine and what else?" She secretly probed the ether by questioning Kendall.

Kendall thought hard.

A whisper penetrated Zoey's ears. *Protect my baby.*

"From what?" Zoey asked.

"Pardon?" Kane asked.

"Crap, nothing. I'm thinking aloud. Must be the wine reacting with cold meds."

Confusion washed over Kendall's face.

"Sorry I said crap. I shouldn't have come."

"Why?" Kendall asked. "Crap isn't a bad word. Aren't you having a good time?"

"It's not my best day. I'm a little lightheaded, that's all."

Kane exhaled. "It's the chipper conversation. Death and dinner are as compatible as fire and ice. Give it a rest, kiddo. I know you miss Mom, but our guest suffered a loss too, and maybe just this once we can keep the discussion light. We're all in a fragile place. We can use a break from mourning. Let's talk movies," he added with impressive composure.

Kendall yelled, "*Tangled*—hey, look!" She pointed at something behind Zoey. "The owl."

Zoey spun and the large bird, whitish and feathery, flapped through the woods like a ghost. "It's breathtaking, Kendall."

"I think so too," Kendall said.

"My daughter doesn't understand the concept of wildlife. Everything's a pet."

"She has compassion," Zoey said.

Chef Martin exchanged the salad dishes for dinner plates.

"This is going to be delicious," Kendall said, eyeing the steamy salmon. "I've been smelling it cook."

And it was fantastic—all but Zoey having to blow her nose throughout the night, and conceal sneaky muscle aches. Morbid conversation ended up rather fun. Zoey laughed a few times, hard, at Kane's travel disasters, his way of describing things, like the man of many tongues. A fellow had asked Kane directions in ten different languages before realizing Kane was lost too. Or the time he and Tess had their first huge argument and she, to be a weasel, cleaned out his wallet, no driver's license, credit cards, cash—zilch. That same day Officer Pain in the Butt—which really got a rise out of Kendall—stopped him for speeding. Kane unknowingly handed over his empty wallet and the officer, upon hearing Kane's domestic woes, returned his wallet and said, "You got your hands full, pal."

Kendall shared animal stories, raccoons stealing sodas and birds yelling at her to fill the birdbath.

Zoey talked about life as a young photographer—learning to position limbs in group photos to avoid one person looking as if they had three arms or four legs. About wedding pictures and countless snarling bridesmaids caught on film, and working with time hoarders, inflated egos, whiny prima donnas and fly-attracting food. Eventually she'd refused to work with flies, and opened her own studio.

At about ten-thirty, Kendall rubbed her eyes. "I have to go to bed."

Kane joked, "Sleep is for senior citizens."

"And kids, Dad."

"Yeah, yeah," he said, standing. "Excuse me," he addressed Zoey, "while I escort my angel to her room."

"Of course," Zoey said. "It was so nice to meet you, Kendall."

"You too," the child said. "Maybe you can come next weekend and we'll barbecue and swim."

"Swim?" Zoey tried not to flinch. "That would mean I'd have to wear a bathing suit and reveal my bony legs."

"You don't have to swim," Kendall said in a motherly way. "Wear a long skirt and read in a lawn chair."

Kane nudged his daughter. "Like Grandma used to do."

"Yeah." Kendall bopped her head.

Zoey smiled. "A dress, now there's an idea. I can hide without sweating to death."

"We'll work on it." Kendall mimicked her father's comedic tone. "Have your people call my people. I'm going to bed. Good night."

"Good night."

"I'll be right back," Kane said before vanishing around the corner.

The chef had cleaned his kitchen and retired with a slight bow of the head, as if she were royalty.

Zoey gulped the last of her wine and fought dizziness. Cold medicine, a Valium and too much alcohol took her for one hell of a spin. She should have been more careful. Unable to handle her usual intake of chemicals, her defenses were melting.

But her gift thrived.

Zoey closed her eyes and listened for the voice she presumed to be Tess Ballentine's. "What happened to you? Why are you here?"

Bright headlights. Protect my baby.

Zoey's eyes popped open. She recalled Kane saying his wife had died in a car accident. Accidents happened. So protect the child from what?

Kane walked in and casually resituated in his dining chair. "Have to tuck her in at night and aim a shotgun in the closet and under the bed. Apparently even monsters are afraid of bullets. Unbeknownst to Kendall, the gun isn't loaded."

"Smart," she said, conscious of guns and the men she called monsters. Her head cleared a bit. "Oh, hey." She reached in her purse and extracted the photos, revealing the men in miner's hats first. "I found this in an old trunk at Amos's."

Kane held the image. "I'll be damned. My dad, Amos and Simon in a mine shaft. One of their short-lived get-rich-quick stints, I'm sure. No dollar amount was ever too big or too small."

Zoey's heart raced. She rose and hurried to Kane's side. She crouched and with a trembling finger pointed to the person who up until now had born the name Evil. "You know this man?"

"Sure, that's Simon Rickert, a true blue son-of-a-bitch."

Visions of Simon slaughtering Miguel webbed her mind. She suppressed her rage. "A son-of-a-bitch?" she asked quietly. "Why?"

Blackness lay on the windows like a cloaked eavesdropper.

Kane remained poised. He gazed at the photo with fury in his eyes and gritted his teeth. "Simon Rickert killed my father."

Chapter 13

She stalled, regretful she wasn't sober. If she were, she'd probably listen to her internal alarm warning her to leave Colorado and never look back. Without the soft veil of her narcotic and the invincible sensation of alcohol, she'd comprehend the nature of this game she never meant to play. Do or die. Like a fading dream, she'd have let the saddest eyes on the planet—those of the child in the woods—dissipate in daylight, and she'd have jumped in her car and driven—fast.

The same things that frightened her drew her closer, a moth to fire, and she couldn't turn away. "What happened?"

Kane tossed the photo on the table and walked to the bar. He poured himself a drink and guzzled it gone. "Most of this is ancient history, but as you can see, my hatchet isn't buried." He moved slowly, and stood in front of a window. "Dad, Simon and Amos were in business together for ten years before Amos's drinking created a rift. He'd get belligerent and accuse my father and Simon of clandestine transactions."

"Was there truth to his accusations?"

"Sure. When you surround yourself with rattlesnakes, sooner or later you'll get bit." He returned to the bar and poured another drink. "Amos withdrew from his business dealings, and from society, and became Big Cat's surly old recluse. Dad used to tell me Amos Rayfield claimed to hear voices. Dad and Simon were cunning. They planned to swindle Amos. Even before the alcohol ruined him—how should I put this? Well, Amos wasn't too bright. Ruthless but dumb as a rock." Kane took a large swallow from his glass. "In previous years, using small print and big words, they'd tricked Amos into signing an unfair but binding contract. Two of the wealthiest men in town and they pinched pennies like a single mother of ten."

"Okay," Zoey said, completely enthralled.

"Certain Amos would eventually kill himself, they refused to buy his shares. Unfortunately, Dad's health deteriorated first. Why he expected Simon to buy him out baffles me, but if I were to make an assumption, Dad considered himself a friend of Simon's. Simon felt differently."

"Simon recently stiffed a local waitress. Doesn't sound like a friendly guy."

"He's a cheap sadist. He riled my father on purpose. Eventually Dad hired an attorney. Simon hired a better one. My father didn't last three months. Two years later, your uncle hanged himself. His property and money went to you, and because Dad had passed, Simon absorbed everything else. Mr. Rickert plays hardball."

Zoey stood, feeling anemic. She braced herself against the chair, blew her nose and clenched the used tissue. "Your father trusted the devil and got scorched," she said, trying to disguise her disdain for the entire trio.

Kane's lips quivered. "My father was the devil. Simon is something else, lower than Satan. Is that possible?"

"He's proven it is," she said. "Were you close to your father?"

"No, but I'm aware that it's because of him my daughter is afforded opportunities most people can't even imagine, and I'm grateful."

Zoey nodded while picking up the photo. "Do you have any idea where this picture was taken?"

Kane approached Zoey, piercing her with anger disproportionate for a man who resented his father. He stared into her eyes. "Could have been anywhere. They were young and greedy with overinflated dreams of mining gold across the globe. The only one who succeeded in that arena is Simon. Rickert Gold. Google it."

Zoey took two steps backward. "I will." Her chest tickled, and she grabbed a fresh tissue from her purse, smothered a cough and then showed Kane the picture of the migrant workers. She raised her voice a notch in hopes of shifting the darkening mood. "By chance, would you know who these people are?"

He gazed at the image and shook his head. "No. Where did you find this?"

"Stashed with the photo of Amos, Simon and your father."

Kane walked to the mini kitchen and poured a glass of ice water from a sweating pitcher. He guzzled and set the glass down. "God only knows. Show Simon the picture. He should have answers for you."

Tipsier than she wanted to be, Zoey sat and coughed again into her tissue. "What's the best way to get hold of him?" She attempted to rub the spinning sensation from her forehead. Hot and achy, she wondered if pneumonia was setting in.

"You don't look too good," Kane said, rushing to her side. "Let me drive you home. You can pick up your car in the morning."

"No, thanks, I don't think I can move. I'm nauseated, and, uh, do you think I can lie down?"

"Certainly," Kane said. He helped her to the lounge area and brought her to the sofa equipped with loose pillows and an afghan.

"I'm so embarrassed." She lowered herself onto the cushion. "I just need to sleep a while. I don't want to be a burden."

"I apologize that I insisted you stay." He covered her and either she'd shut her eyelids or he'd flicked off the light. His voice traveled from somewhere in the blackened room. "I'll arrange a meeting for you with Simon later this week. I recommend you work on getting healthy. You'll need your strength."

Her muscles soft and hot as fresh-mixed pudding, she lay like a human splotch, useless and misshapen.

It was impossible to know what time the woman came, but the walls glowed with blue moonlight. She hummed something unfamiliar but hypnotic.

The woman slipped her arms under Zoey's back and knees and lifted her effortlessly. They traveled through the woods, and Kendall's white owl flew from tree to tree, guiding their path through the arctic night. Zoey trembled. Suddenly heat radiated from the being and warmed her chill. Far behind Kane's house, Coldstone River sliced through the earth, spitting droplets as it pushed forward. They neared the edge, and Zoey hovered above the shoreline in the visitor's embrace.

The being lowered Zoey into the water, and Zoey kicked and screamed as her nose submerged. Incapable of holding oxygen in her sickly lungs, she panicked. Her heart thudded in her ears. Her throat crackled with trapped screams. Before she surrendered completely, a mild pressure clung to her biceps. She opened her eyes and two sets of ghostly hands pulled her from the current.

Both vaporous women had long strands of blinding energy flowing about like windblown hair. They removed the rubber band from Zoey's sopping braid and let the length drape her pale arms. She should've been cold. The women unbuttoned her blouse and slacks, and undressed her. She stood naked and dripping wet.

The ladies dipped their arms in the river and scooped from the bottom. Their hands became visible again, and they slopped gritty globs of sand on her flesh. Zoey jerked as clumps of clay covered her body.

The women rubbed her down, their fingers sensuously medicinal. Every pore, scar, bend and wrinkle craved their strokes. They scrubbed circularly, exfoliating her skin. Minutes, hours, she didn't know. They positioned her on her back and set her in the flow, cupping water and rinsing the mess. Her body cooled too.

Starlight smeared across the river.

What had crawled inside her lungs and ate at the lining? So much pain, every breath had been a struggle.

The women placed their fingertips in the crevices of Zoey's collarbone and tapped with the passion of plump raindrops—tap—tap—tap. They did the same under her arms, and left and right groin.

Aches and pains faded.

Their magical fingers trimmed the sides of her nose and fanned outward toward her stimulated collarbone. They repeated the method from her navel to her armpits, and then from her navel to her groin as if the tapping had convinced some interior network to purify toxins.

Zoey inhaled painlessly and color infused her muted surroundings. Something sparkled and she looked at the woman on her left, at the silver pendant attached to a thread of seaweed—Luis's money clip.

She gasped, reigniting her sense of smell. She questioned how her brain could compute the message sent from her nose. Stunned by the overwhelming odor, she turned to the woman on her right, awed by the scent of jasmine.

Zoey hollered and opened her eyes to find herself on Kane's sofa.

Dressed for a new day and seeming refreshed, Kane knelt next to the couch. He dropped a wet cloth in a bowl of water. "You were burning up," he said quietly. "I washed your face and neck."

Her hair covered her arms. "Did you undo my braid?"

"No. You were too hot; you needed a cold bath. I left for a minute to run the tub in the guest bathroom and when I returned, your hair was down. So was your temperature."

She briefly massaged her itchy scalp and withdrew her hand momentarily, rolling tiny granules within her fingertips. "Sand?" She barreled over insurmountable confusion. "Did you see anyone or smell anything?"

"Pardon?"

"Never mind." She shook her head, hoping to clear a narrow passage back to logic. "What time is it?"

"Almost six." He stood. "Let me get the Escalade. I'll run you to the emergency room."

"No, no, I'm fine." She straightened her back and inhaled, then coughed pain-free. She could breathe, and the smell of coffee filled the room. "I've got to go," she said, stumbling to her feet.

Kane graciously helped her balance. "You should see a doctor."

"Maybe two or three hours ago. I'm fine now. I need to get out of here, though, before Kendall wakes up. I don't want her to misunderstand us."

Kane nodded. "Can I get you some coffee or water?"

"No thanks," she said. "I'm done with water for a while." Apparently Kane had placed her purse by the sofa. She leaned over and grabbed the stiff strap. "The pictures?"

"They're inside your bag. I hope you don't mind. I didn't rummage. I just set them in."

"That's fine." Zoey checked. Miguel's eyes jarred her memory. "Did you say you'd arrange a meeting for me with Simon?"

"Yes. I'll phone him this morning."

"What makes you think he'll see me?" She sniffled.

"Nothing would make him happier than chatting with Amos Rayfield's niece while Amos rots in a hole."

"Should I bring a weapon?" Zoey asked as she turned and headed to the door.

"Precautionary measures aren't a bad idea."

"Seriously?"

"Depends on where your conversation leads. I'm not sure what your intentions are, or why you want to see Simon, but be mindful. He's a demon, and if he feels threatened in any way, he will strike."

"Good to know."

"I'll call you later with details." Kane ushered her out of the house. He stopped and took in the sights. "It's going to be a beautiful day today. You should sit on that deck you have and bask in the sun."

Zoey smiled. "Maybe." She paused. "I appreciate the TLC, but if you don't stop saving my life, I'm going to have to think of ways to repay you. I'm not that creative."

"Don't ever believe you owe me. I'm happy to help. You survived a lightning strike and what I'd predict was a damaging if not lethal fever. It'll be interesting to see where life takes you next."

"I'm a bug in your microscope?"

Kane belted out a laugh. "No, not at all. More like a shooting star in my telescope."

She felt whimsical and special until she got a whiff of herself—nothing like the odorous aftermath of a feverish sweat…and river bottom.

"Anyway," she said, cutting the blithe conversation short. "Thank you for a lovely evening." She extended her hand to shake.

More than cordially, Kane took her hand, bent forward and kissed her cheek. "My pleasure. We'll have to do it again soon, I hope."

The slowness of his kiss and the gentle way he held her hand made her edgy, but she wouldn't bother with minnows when she had Moby Dick in her sights. She'd taken notes on affability from a cheerful ten-year-old. "Have your people call my people." Zoey turned and walked to her car, wondering if he was watching.

Her BMW offered a comfort similar to her silky robe, kind, fitted, familiar.

Less than ten minutes later, she pulled up the driveway of Rayfield Ranch and disengaged the ignition. She pressed the clicker and raised the garage door. No iguana green Harley.

Through the garage, Zoey cautiously entered the house, cognizant of Luis's supernatural reach. "Lance!"

She set her purse on the dining table and spotted his business card with a handwritten note under the print. *Keep in touch.*

"What?" Zoey yanked out a chair and her fatigued body fell onto it. She grabbed his card. "Keep in touch? You cocksucker!" She started to dial Lance's number when an incoming call interrupted. "Damn," she said and answered. "Hello?"

"Zoey?"

"Mitch," she said, relieved to hear a trusted voice.

"Where the hell have you been? I've left messages and texts. Do you ever check your phone?" He lowered the volume on his TV.

"Not lately."

"You have a cold?"

"Yes, Mitch, I have a cold." She held a particular piece of tissue so long she was hesitant to ruin it.

"Why, what's going on?"

Zoey blew her nose. "People get sick."

"I got your message. Tried to call, but it's hit or miss with you. You said you had to talk to me."

"Where to start? Are you sitting?"

"I am now."

"Let's see. I saved a boy from drowning in Coldstone. Carmen didn't want to let him go. Creepy Carmen turned into a saint, though. She and Tess, Kane's deceased wife, carried me to the river and cleansed my fever."

"You're joking."

"I'm not. I'll spare you the details." Zoey removed the picture of Luis and his family from her purse and stared at their faces. She suspected Luis and Carmen were the people standing closest to Miguel. "Best news of all, I know who the maggots are that murdered the family haunting this property. I'm meeting with the only surviving killer sometime this week." She set the picture down. "And finally, this morning, I came home to find a note from my lover and supposed friend that reads: Keep in touch. How about you, what's new?"

A deafening quiet pulsed in her ears.

"You have nothing to say?"

"Where did you come home from?"

"Kane's house. I spent the night. And no, I didn't fuck him."

"I didn't ask."

She kicked off her shoes and wiggled her stiff toes. "Beating you to the punch."

"Who's Carmen?"

"Luis's wife. She was shot by Kane's father."

"What?"

"Don't try and wrap your brain around this one, Mitch. It's unexplainable. I'm having trouble with it too." Zoey gathered her hair and draped it over her shoulder. She examined her split ends.

"There was a time when we were both pretty rational."

"Yeah, back when a person could take their kid to a carnival and leave with cramped cheeks, a stomach ache and the same number of people."

Silence.

"I'm sorry," she said. "When all this began, I wondered why I saw and heard strangers on the other side and not my son. I felt like I'd purchased a new home excited about a great new life only to watch it burn to the ground on moving day. I resented it. And then after seeing the tragic lives and deaths of these so-called strangers, I realized Milo didn't visit because he wasn't stuck. He came in my nightmares, but that had nothing to do with him. That was my refusal to let go. Wherever he is, Mitch, he's in peace and I am beyond grateful."

"Me too," he said with a crackle in his throat.

"Where's Sterling?"

"What?"

"She left you. Why?"

"I don't want to talk about it."

"Would you rather discuss Lance?" Her leg bounced with nervous energy.

"Your boy toy, no thank you."

"I'm sitting too." She stood and walked to the kitchen for something to munch on.

"She wasn't who I thought. I met a high-powered real estate agent with money on the brain. How to make it, how to increase it, how to hold on to it? I liked that about her."

"She was predictable.

"Yeah—no—she was safe."

"Mitch," Zoey said, surprised by his honesty. "Safe?"

"Don't lecture me. I know it's silly."

"It's not. But don't you think it's weird that both your ex-wife and ex-girlfriend have similar esoteric gifts?" She searched the cupboards and refrigerator, but nothing looked appetizing.

"What are you implying? I'm some sort of Martian magnet?"

"I'm offended."

"Me too. I don't want to live in the past with ghosts and their problems. I want someone who can confront what's coming at us right here, right now, in the real world."

She stopped and set her hand on her waist. "Ghosts and their atmosphere are real. It's merely an alternate dimension."

"When did you become a paranormal specialist?"

"When did you become so unadventurous?"

Quiet, but she sensed, if only by experience, he'd realized he wasn't completely happy with who he'd become. Milo's accident had scared Mitch straight.

"Consider yourself lucky," Zoey said, tapping the counter with her index finger. "Sterling is gorgeous, and she can bring home the bacon, fry it up in a pan and channel the pig to apologize. What more do you want?"

Mitch laughed.

"Trust me, she can't help what she sees and hears, but it makes her better than the rest. It does. She uses her power for good and that should mean something to you."

Mitch chuckled again.

"It can't be healthy for her to keep her sensitive side boxed. Gifts are supposed to be unwrapped. I'm glad she's stretching out," Zoey rambled, feeling oddly paralleled with Sterling. "Seems you're too narrow-minded to accept her for who she is, but you have to know at least this—she's a trustworthy woman, and she loves you. The way you're behaving, I don't blame her for walking out. And I wouldn't blame her if she never wants to see you again."

"I must have dialed the Sterling Fisk fan club by accident."

"There are no accidents, Mitch." The words numbed her bones.

"Okay, you're right. I'm an ass. I'll call her. Which reminds me," he said abruptly, "she's been trying to contact you. I assumed you two had talked. Have you?"

"No."

"Call her, and if you wouldn't mind, set the stage for me. I'll need a beer or six to admit I screwed up."

"You're not the Lone Ranger. I've done plenty of that this past year."

"Are you ready to clean out the house?"

"We almost had a genuine conversation. I have to go. I have to take a shower and make some calls."

Zoey closed her cellphone and stomped to the dining room. Her scalp itched from sand, and she smelled. A shower and change of clothes took precedence over updating Luis and Sterling and calling her Houdini lover to rip into him.

She went upstairs and on her way, thumbed through her text messages. One from Sterling read: *Get out Zoey. You're going to die. I see it clear as glass. Leave now!*

Zoey muttered, "Everything dies." She noticed the single bar on her cell. "Including phones."

She entered the bedroom and tossed her near-dead cell on the bed. She undressed, sauntered into the bathroom and started the shower. Steam loosened phlegm and she coughed. Disenchanted with water, she stepped into the cubicle, slowly. The greatest shower she'd ever taken was with Lance. She slammed her palm against the marble. "Dickhead!"

Wrapping her torso in a towel was the last thing she remembered when she opened her eyes. Her limbs pressed deep into the mattress, and her mouth tasted gummy, as if she hadn't moved in days. She glanced at the sunrays folded against the wall. They flickered like lightning and she jerked, remembering the night her life had drastically changed. She hadn't thought about it, not seriously or with a sober mind, since it'd happened. In a dark place on spongy grass, a red bolt had torched her arm. "Not now," she scolded the memories flooding forward. "I just woke up."

She sat, boggled as to when she had plugged in her cellphone or hung the towel on the doorknob or set her cold medicine on the nightstand.

"Hello?" she yelled and put on her robe. "Anyone here?" She walked the hallway and hollered down the staircase. "Hello?"

An eerie emptiness upset her stomach, and she headed back to her room, got dressed and combed her sleep-messy hair. She looked again at the towel, phone cord and cold medicine, certain she had nothing to do with their whereabouts, and whispered, "Luis?"

Gentle thudding came from downstairs, lightweight but loud enough for her to hear.

She stood and inhaled, then let the air loose. She followed the noise.

Her purse lay on the dining table, vacant and saggy, and its contents dumped next to it. On the wall near the kitchen counter, the picture of Amos, Ross and Simon dangled by the point of a steak knife, and the photo of Luis, Carmen, Miguel and the other workers rested on the wall beneath the knife, held by something invisible. Familiar thudding, this time because she'd patted her speedy heart.

"Luis, I didn't get a chance to talk to you. I don't know why. I must have been exhausted." She paused and removed the knife and pictures from the wall, and set them on the counter. "The man who killed Miguel is named Simon Rickert. I'm meeting him sometime this week. Damn. I don't know what day it is. Anyway, I'm going to show him the photos and question him, see what he has to say."

Traedmelo.

"I don't understand."

Bring him.

"I'll do my best. But that may not be possible."

Bring him. Bring him. Bring him.

The demand reverberated within, somehow, and she clapped her palms to her ears.

Bring him. Bring him. Bring him.

"Yes, yes, Luis, okay. I'll bring him," she said, hoping for silence.

Quiet until her cellphone chimed again.

"I can't take much more of this, Luis. Keep that in mind," she bitched while running upstairs to answer. "Hello?"

"Zoey, hey, did I catch you at a bad time?" Kane said, fast and sharp, as if he'd had too much caffeine.

"Not really, no."

"Good, good. Are you feeling any better?"

"Oh yeah. I've been resting. In fact, this may sound like a ridiculous question, but what day is it?"

Kane chuckled, "Are you sure you're all right?"

"Sleep does wonders. I just don't know how long I've been out."

"It's Tuesday."

"What?" She sat on the bed. "I slept four days?"

"You tell me."

"Yes. I did. That's fucking crazy. Oh, shit, sorry. Oops. Damn. Doubly sorry."

"You're an adult, Zoey. You can use any language you'd like."

"Of course," she said, irritated. "I'm trying to be considerate. Trust me, it's a chore."

"Then I graciously accept your apology."

The deer-antler lamp had collected a lot of dust. She wiped it clean with her sleeve. "I slept four days."

"I do recall you saying something to that effect."

"Have you ever slept four days without being drugged or injured?"

"No. But you had a doozy of a cold, and a dangerous temperature. You must have needed the rest. You said you're feeling better?"

"Yes. Like a new person." She rose and stepped in front of the mirror, envisioning her features with short hair.

"Then the timing is appropriate. I contacted our friend Simon. He'll see you this evening if you're up for it."

She'd almost pushed for an earlier appointment, but bit her tongue. "I'm up for it. When and where?"

"Six. He has an office outside of Telluride. I'll text you his address."

"Great. I can't tell you how much this means to me."

"I hear the elevation in your voice. You're happy."

"Very. Speaking of happy, how's Kendall?" Zoey lifted a framed picture of Milo, kissed it, and relocated it to the nightstand.

"I put her on a plane yesterday. She's attending summer camp in Europe."

"You hadn't mentioned anything about camp the other night. So far away?"

"It'll be difficult for us both, but in time, she'll enjoy it."

"She's a lucky girl."

"Yes, she is," he said. "She had a moment, not too bad. Besides, it's for her own good." A lengthy pause and Kane blurted, "I hope your meeting goes well."

"So do I." She crossed her fingers, unsure how to define success when dealing with an alleged sociopath.

"I'm playing golf tonight with Rupert Walrath. He's older than the Egyptian tombs, and he cheats. If I catch him, he clutches his heart and threatens to drop dead. I can't win, but I need the exercise."

"You're kind."

"And you're captivating. I look forward to getting to know you better."

"Take care."

"You as well."

Zoey closed her phone, leery of Kane's desire to know her better but loaded with adrenaline over Simon—the child-slayer. Her heart picked up speed and suddenly she worried she'd go ballistic and hurt him. She'd feel great afterward, but the outcome would be unproductive. Perhaps she'd take a Valium and stop at Rock Hounds for a shot. If she was there, she could ask about Lance, nonchalantly, or flirt with another horny biker, blatantly, to send a message.

"Lance is consuming space in my head!" Zoey said as she sprang to her feet and walked downstairs for his card. She dialed his number. "What am I doing?"

Amor.

"I know that word, Luis, and no, it's not love."

Venganza!

"What?"

Revenge.

"Not that either. I can't be responsible for my actions. I'm on autopilot," she mumbled as the phone rang. "I must thrive on humiliation."

Amor.

"Stop it. It's not love. I don't want to argue."

Estupido.

"Says the guy who's trapped between dimensions."

From out of nowhere, she remembered one of the last things Lance had said.

Voicemail: "Yo! This is Lance Malone. Say it."

BEEP.

"Hey, uh, Lance, it's Zoey," she said gently. "I, um, shit. I didn't sleep with Kane. I was too sick to drive or sit or call. I passed out on his sofa. In case you're estupido, this is me sober and rested, admitting I miss you. And I can't believe you took off like this—you're a prick, and I want to be glad you're gone, but I'm not. Don't get me wrong. I'm no fool. I don't know what I am."

Obstinado.

Zoey set her phone down. "Shut up, Luis. This doesn't concern you." She went in the kitchen and turned on the flame for tea water. "What does concern you is Simon Rickert. I'm meeting him tonight at six."

Here?

"Not likely. Kane will text me the address."

Bring him.

"We've been through this. I will." She leaned against the counter. "Lance has mentioned this before and now I'm facing the same scenario. If you kill Simon, I'll go to prison for murder."

Lo hice.

"Come on, my Spanish obviously blows."

I did it.

"You don't exist."

I do.

"Immortal, invisible, dead, doesn't count on this plane."

Zoey picked up the whistling tea kettle and poured hot water into a cup, then dipped a bag of Earl Grey. Her cell jingled in the dining room. Her heart swelled. Lance must have received her message. She rushed and viewed the text. Kane had sent Simon's phone number and address, and said Simon's prior engagements had cancelled—pop in any time.

Another text followed from Sterling: *Are you still there? Get out! And call me!!*

In response to Sterling, Zoey typed: *Still here, but fine. Luis and I have everything handled. We'll talk later. BTW Mitch is sorry. Call him.*

Lance had become grease on a blouse right before a job interview. It bothered her, the messiness of it, but she didn't have time to track him down. She had to move quickly with Simon. She sensed Luis's rage building, or perhaps she was projecting. In her mind's eye the image of Miguel's demise emerged and she wanted to staple Simon's eyes closed before slathering him in honey and burying him neck deep in the woods.

"Good news, Luis. Simon will see me any time today."

Bring him to Carmen.

The idea sent chills through her soul. "Love it. But how?"

Lie.

"About?"

The mine.

"What mine?"

Lie.

Chapter 14

Lately everything hit with the fast flooding traits of a tidal wave, including the face and name of Evil. She'd hoped retribution would surface equally quick and unsparing. In the parking lot of Rock Hounds, Zoey turned off the ignition and held the cellphone against her ear, practicing introduction calls to Simon.

"Hello, scumbag. I'm your worst nightmare." She closed the cell, reopened it and made another attempt. "Simon Rickert? Hi, I'm Zoey Hawthorne, Amos Rayfield's niece. Yeah, that's right, you and he and Ross Ballentine murdered an innocent family. Err." She closed the phone but quickly tried again. "Hi there, Simon, you sick fuck. How can you do what you did? He was a child. I hate you and can't wait to watch you die." Unworthy of an Academy Award, she banged on the steering wheel. If she wanted answers, she'd better take Luis's advice and lie.

Outside, birds effortlessly soared the clouds. She studied their grace. A few seconds of relaxed breathing and she repeated the process. "Simon Rickert? I'm Zoey Hawthorne, Amos Rayfield's great niece. I appreciate your hectic schedule, but I'd like to ask you about a photo I found. Is there a convenient time for me to stop by?"

Satisfied, she dialed.

He answered.

She'd never knowingly spoken to absolute wickedness. Her hands shook. She zeroed in on the birds and inhaled their elegance. "Simon Rickert?"

"Yes."

"This is Zoey Hawthorne, Amos Ray—"

"I know who you are. What do you want?"

She tapped the steering wheel with her forefinger. "I found a couple old pictures in my uncle's house and wondered if I can swing by and ask you about them?"

"Why?"

"I've never met my uncle." She adjusted the review mirror. "He's family. Maybe you can tell me a little bit about him."

"He was tall. What else do you want to know?"

"Okay, well." She recalled Luis's distant words. "I want to know about the mine."

"What mine? I have about fifty of them."

"You know what mine." Looking at the picture of three men in a shaft, she gambled and added, "The mine you, Ross Ballentine and Amos spent time in between 1955 and 1960. Or, if you'd like, maybe you can come by the house, we can talk there."

"Do you have my address?" he asked.

"Yes." Anxiety welled and she chewed her pinky nail.

"From the main highway, you'll pass Rock Hounds and hang a right on the third road. You'll drive through a mile of field until you see a small business center. Turn in there. Look for Rickert's Financial Planning."

"Okay. See you shortly."

"I'll be waiting."

Her gut did somersaults, yet she had to continue the polite charade. Without drugs, alcohol or sedating orgasms, bullshit made her queasy. She thought about running in for a drink and then said, "Screw it," and peeled out of the barren driveway. She arrived at the old-fashioned village of offices, spotted his sign and parked. All along he'd been twenty minutes away.

She got out of her car and hoofed to the startling yellow door. She knocked, thinking about professionalism, subtlety and patience.

He opened and briefly inspected her with perceptive eyes. Despite wrinkled skin, cottony hair and an average old-man physique, he stood firm and broad, wordlessly asserting his supremacy. His gray suit shined, and if Zoey were to photograph him, she'd capture his merciless glare. At about five-eight, he raised his dented chin and appeared to note her height. He grinned.

"The bigger they are, the harder they fall," he said before receding into the partially lit office.

"That's not very nice," she countered, mentally burning ties to professionalism, subtlety, and patience. She marched in and closed the door. "But then again, according to Kane Ballentine and a disgruntled waitress, you're not a very nice man." She stopped in the middle of his domain, riveted by the life-size cardboard images of Simon attempting to trick potential clients into believing he was human. From left to right, he held a fluffy orange kitten, patted the head of a blond toddler, cheerfully licked a strawberry ice cream cone and, lastly, gripped the stick of a miniature American flag. She pointed to the cutouts. "Now that's just sweet."

"Not sweet, smart. It's a moneymaking persona. Something foreign to you." He stepped on the other side of his metal desk, face motionless as stone and body armored in impenetrable arrogance. "What do you know about the mine?"

"Plenty," she said, waving the picture of the men in a mine shaft.

"So what?" he laughed. "A snapshot of the gang posing in a mine."

"You're denying the three of you mined together?"

"Yes, I'm denying it. We tried and failed. Not something I'm accustomed to. Mining was one of a zillion ideas. We settled on easier and more profitable ventures."

Zoey bent forward and looked into his callous eyes. "And I'm the Pope."

"I'm extremely busy. What is it you want, Ms. Hawthorne?"

She reached into her purse and withdrew the picture of sixteen migrant workers, and again showed him but would not release it. A grand rage surged inside. "I know what you did to this child. I know what you all did, and guess what, you will pay."

He didn't flinch. "What is it you think I've done? Because before now, I've never seen those people."

"You hacked this baby boy into pieces while he was alive." She pointed to Miguel. "He wailed in pain and you licked a spot of his blood off your bottom lip and kept hacking, didn't you?"

"You're crazy."

"And you're a murderer. You killed the boy, Amos shot his father and Ross killed his mother, Carmen, near Coldstone River."

"That's absurd."

For a moment she believed him, and then his eyelid twitched and his neck reddened.

"What did you do with the rest of the bodies? You obviously murdered them too. Where are they?"

"You don't know anything, do you?"

"I found the rifles."

"And you dusted for prints and discovered what?"

Zoey straightened her spine and raised her voice. "You will not get away with this, do you hear me? I'll make sure of it!"

Unruffled, he said, "Let's say this twisted story is true. You have no proof. You see, in a court of law you would need to present facts and evidence. A picture of three friends in their youth and a picture of a bunch of Mexicans doesn't prove anything." He chuckled and opened the top drawer of his desk, pulled out a cigar, cut the end and lit it. Amidst a puff of smoke, he added, "Another thing, Ms. Hawthorne. You'd have to be credible to sway a jury. I happen to know you have a fondness for alcohol and men half your age."

"What?"

"I was at Rock Hounds the night you stumbled in with your shirt on inside out. I sat in the back at a table with Kane. We saw you drink more than our local wino and leave with a bottom-feeding biker. Thing is, much of Big Cat was there. Much of Big Cat saw you behave like a juvenile delinquent. Would you consider yourself credible?"

She wouldn't give him the satisfaction of knowing he'd jumbled the rhythmic pattern of her heartbeat. "I was grieving the loss of my son. The jury would understand."

"Why not grieve in the arms of church and family? Don't you see? My attorney would insist you are a drunken whore, and Big Cat and the jury would believe him."

"And I care what people think of me?"

"Not one bit. But if you're trying to drag me to hell, you'd better be in top shape, because I fight filthy."

"I saw you brutally murder a helpless child. And I have the rifles you, Amos and Ross used to kill the others."

"You saw me? This gets better and better. And whoopdeedoo! You found a few rifles. This is Colorado. Everyone has rifles. And everyone in this town knows Amos had enough ammunition to equip an army. While this is all very entertaining, I'm here on a business trip, and I'm going home in the morning. So if you don't mind, show yourself out."

Zoey stormed to the door and swung it open. She faced him and said, "I'm not done with you. I know what happened, and I will find the proof I need to put you on death row."

"Blah, blah, blah, Ms. Hawthorne, you're bored since your son died. Go home and knit some socks. Better yet, you like telling tales, write a novel."

"Say anything about my son again and I will cut your tongue out and feed it to you."

"Now, have you actually done that? I have and it's not pretty. I'd have to burn them—my clothes, not the mutes, though I doused a few of them in gasoline. You're wasting my time. Be a good girl and remove yourself from my property."

If he could have felt her anger, he'd have understood a different degree of fire. Fueled by rage, Zoey blazed to her car. She took her keys from her purse and scratched a long line in a white Cadillac she believed to be Simon's. She paused, wondering what she could use to bust the windshield and saw nothing readily available. A drop of rain hit her nose. She stood, debilitated by fury. When her cheeks were wet enough to hide her tears, she jumped in her car.

Feeling powerless wasn't sitting well. On her way home, she pulled to the side of the road and vomited. After Milo's wake she'd done the same thing, only her puking fit had lasted a month. Mitch had picked up her slack, though. These days she had only herself to rely on. Life made her dizzy. Or her damned blood sugar.

"Get a grip, Zoey," she mumbled as she lifted the hem of her shirt and wiped her mouth. "You'll think of something."

She passed Kane's home, fighting the urge to drive through his foyer. A smooth liar like him, she wanted to punch him or spit in his face. She fumed and it hurt. Why had he deceived her?

Small puddles formed in the maroon road leading to her house and by the time she'd parked in the driveway, the sound of the windshield wipers had lulled her nerves. Her cellphone rang nonstop. Not Lance. She didn't answer.

"What next?" she muttered as she walked through the drizzle and opened the front door. She set her purse on the table, rinsed her mouth in the kitchen sink, and decided to phone Sterling. Perhaps between the two of them they'd tune in on a missing link that would corner Simon.

Evil.

"I spoke to him," Zoey said. "It didn't go well."

Why not here?

Zoey scrunched off her shoes. "I invited him, but he didn't budge. I have nothing he wants. He said the rifles had been wiped clean and mentioning the mine didn't faze him."

Why not here?

"I tried, Luis. He has no reason to come. We have nothing on him. No evidence."

Lie.

"I did, and he wasn't convinced."

Dark gray smeared across the sky and shadows began to eat the room. Zoey clicked on a lamp and stood still, sensing danger. A crash of thunder caused her to jump, and bouts of lightning had her cowering. She remembered feeling cooked alive.

Her muscles contracted with every flicker. She sat on the floor between the coffee table and sofa, insulated from the voltage. Rain fell heavily, whipping the windows and hitting the house with the strength of stones. Blackness spread across the horizon like a plague and contaminated her home.

Lightning.

"Yes, I know. It's frightening me."

You're not alone.

"What?"

You're not alone.

Zoey strained to see through the darkness. Corners, curves, straight lines, silhouettes of lifeless objects dominated her eyes.

"I am alone, Luis. You're dead." A tear trickled down her cheek. "So is Milo. So is everyone, in one way or another. I've run Mitch off, Lance left me, my family and friends stopped calling months ago. I am alone. I'm so fucking alone, and it's killing me."

Flashes of lightning spat at the walls. She recoiled, resentful of her weakening state. The storm had completely snuffed out daylight, and elongated raindrops caused a near whiteout—perfect graphic contrast against the ashen sky. She gazed at the quills of rain. If she were to shoot a photo, she'd set the shutter speed at 1/2000 of a second and freeze every drop.

Get out.

"What? Why?"

Get out.

"You sound like Sterling. Are you threatening me?"

You are not alone.

A flash of red lightning shook her nerves.

"Lightning is outside. I'm inside."

Wood creaked from under the stairs.

"Hello?" Zoey stood. "Luis?"

"Who's Luis?" a man asked, enveloped in obscurity.

That ominous feeling she'd had earlier returned. "Who's there?" Zoey asked sternly. "Don't come any closer. I have a gun."

"Then we're on level playing ground." Kane stepped forward, aiming a handgun at her stomach. He wore black leather gloves, a dripping wet black hooded raincoat, and a nylon mask over his face.

"You!" she said. "You're a lowlife."

"I'm not," he said as he rolled the nylon up to his hairline with his vacant hand.

"You are! Simon told me the two of you were together the night I had drinks at Rock Hounds."

"You and I exchanged a smile."

"Silver fox?

"What?"

"You asshole!"

"I'm sorry, Zoey."

"And then you invited me to dinner? Why? Who are you? Never mind. I see clearly who you are. You're here modeling your true colors, aiming a gun at your new neighbor. What are you going to do with that, shoot me?"

"Yes," he said, visibly pained by his response.

"Why, Kane? What have I done?" She clenched her fists.

"The pictures, Zoey. Simon doesn't want to take a chance. He'd planned to offer you an incredible amount of money for the ranch, but changed his mind after we saw you in the bar. He's a cheap SOB. He said you'd get bored and sell the place. He'd still buy it, but he wouldn't risk raising red flags. You showed me the pictures, Zoey. I had to tell him. And then you went gangbusters, accusing him of murder. What were you thinking?"

"He is a murderer."

"How do you know?"

"I can't explain it, but I know."

"Simon had one of his guys watching your house. When your biker friend left, Simon called me. You put me in this position. I have no choice," he said with a steady hand.

"Sure you do. This is crazy."

"My father kept a journal of everything he did with Simon and Amos. Everything. When my father passed, I found his book hidden in his closet wall. I wish I hadn't. The picture of the Mexicans—they were *braceros*. The timing, as my father wrote, was divine. Simon was just outside Houston on his brother's farm when he got the call. Amos had discovered a gold mine. Literally. The three of them were too greedy to mine legally. They didn't want to be regulated, taxed or sued for polluting the environment—it takes seventy-nine tons of waste to extract one ounce of gold. And they certainly didn't want to pay fair wages. Simon said he had a solution. He smuggled his brother's *braceros*, promising them a decent income to work the mine with bonus money to keep their mouths shut."

"Ten adults, five teenagers and one toddler—hardly a workforce."

"I agree. After reading what they'd done to those people, how they worked them until their fingers and feet blistered, until they coughed blood and lost weight, how my father and his buddies disposed of human beings when they'd made their fortune. You're right, Simon butchered a boy, my father shot innocent people—and a woman—the boy's mother." He grimaced.

Luis sobbed.

Kane went on, "I couldn't sleep for two months and finally I confronted Simon. The next night, Tess was run off the road. Her killer escaped. The following morning I received a call from Simon telling me if I didn't hand over my father's book, he'd kill Kendall too. My word against his. There was no proof he or his goons had anything to do with my wife's death. No one will harm my daughter. I caved. I brought him my father's journal. He thinks I made a copy. He said if the topic arose in the future, he'd make sure Kendall rested next to her momma."

"Kane, I'm so—"

"And then you came along and told Simon he hacked up a boy and licked a drop of blood from his lips. You need to tell me how you knew that, because he believes I told you. And now, my dear, they have my daughter."

"What?" A cyclone spun in Zoey's stomach. "She's in Europe."

"She wasn't. Not yet. I hid her in a cabin in Virginia. Sons-of-bitches found her. Do you see what's happening? We're playing a game. Maybe you've heard of it—Simon Says. And Simon says if I kill you they'll return my daughter unharmed." His lips quivered.

Thunder banged, and she jumped.

Kane cocked the gun.

"Cool it, okay? I won't run. How can you trust him, though? What if you kill me and Simon doesn't keep his word?"

"She's worth the gamble."

"You have money. Lots of it. You can fight him."

"I'd rather be penniless and have Kendall home than visit my daughter's gravesite after court. Do you see my dilemma? Simon has been making lives miserable for a long time. In fact, resistance to Simon or Rickert Gold Mining Industry often leads to death. He has mines all over the world and a list of violations from employee abuse, mercury and cyanide contamination, to murder. This is not a man with thin skin."

"Where do you plan on killing me?"

"Hell. I don't know." He tilted his head and cracked his neck. "I'll shoot you near the water and let your body wash downstream. That's it. I'll put a bullet in your head and come back. I'll stage a robbery."

"I don't have a lot of cash on hand, and there isn't anything of value in the house."

"You have enough for some punk to buy drugs."

"Kane, listen, please. There has to be another way."

Kane motioned the gun for Zoey to walk. Three steps later she felt the barrel press against her back. She opened the door and rain sprayed her face. She shivered.

"How about a little help, Luis?"

I could not protect my family. He wept. *I am weak.*

"Who else is here?" Kane asked.

"No one."

"Who are you talking to?"

"My imaginary friend."

Kane pushed her forward onto the deck. He stood next to her, gun still a threat, and lowered his nylon mask. "Let's get this over with. Move, hurry." He shoved her down the stair.

Her sock-clad feet landed in the soggy grass. "If you didn't have a gun, I'd kick your ass, Kane!"

He shoved her again and she fell. "I'm sorry. They're watching. Get up!" He pulled her hair skyward, forcing her to stand.

"Luis!"

No reply.

The clouds ceaselessly dumped rain. She and her assailant were soaked. Kane dragged her through the cold wet lawn toward the river, and suddenly she believed him. He'd shoot her and feed her to Carmen.

"Kane, you don't have to do this." She blinked rainwater from her vision. "Stop. Please."

He halted and threw her down again. "I'll shoot you right here if I have to and carry you the rest of the way." His eyes looked hard as hail. "Now get up and be quiet. Your death will save the life of a child."

Zoey stood, the rain beating against her cold skin like torture. "Go ahead, then, kill me."

"Drop it, jackass."

Zoey spun, relieved at the sight of Lance standing about ten feet away, pointing a gun at Kane. "Lance. How…"

"I caught some ogre motherfucker watching the house." Lance wiped his face. "That's why I left. To see what shook out. I couldn't let you know or you'd interfere." He looked to Kane. "What the hell are you doing, man?"

Kane turned and raised his gun. Lance fired.

Kane hit the ground.

"No!" She clapped her hands over her mouth. "They have his daughter." Her saturated hair stuck to her arms. "They'll kill her now."

"Don't worry. We've got everything under control."

"We?"

Lance nodded.

The rain lightened to a drizzle, and a familiar red lightning bolt speared nearby soil. Zoey and Lance sped uphill toward the house. She froze at the feel of drunken dragonflies zigzagging in her stomach.

"Don't freak out yet, Hawthorne. I can see the finish line."

Zoey stared into his eyes, and then beyond his shoulder. An inferno ignited in her chest. Within spitting distance, Simon stood in a trench coat, pointing a gun at Lance.

"Behind you," she said.

Lance turned. Simon fired. Lance clutched his chest and fell.

Zoey gasped.

Simon raised his gun and aimed at her head. Without hesitation, she turned and ran downhill, expecting a bullet to split her spine in half. Not too far away, lightning zapped the lawn. She could have sworn that's where she'd stood when she was struck.

Unreasonably, she rushed toward the repetitious voltage. She reached the spongy soil and thought, *yes*—as the ground sprung gently up and down beneath her—*lightning favors this spot*. She stood, panting and jittery.

"Now what?" she whispered. Her jumbled instincts had her wait.

Simon neared. For an old man, he moved as sturdily as a bull. The desire to obliterate glowed like lanterns in his eyes. Her heart battered her ribs. She'd die of cardiac arrest.

"You whore! We have the girl. If I don't return, my employee has instructions to slice her throat."

Without knowing why, she waited.

"Is that what you want?" he yelled.

About fifteen feet away, he quit running and raised his gun.

Turtle.

"What?" Zoey said before she recognized the voice. "Miguel?"

Turtle.

"Okay." She walked backward…slowly.

Simon mirrored her unhurried pace, but moved forward.

She stepped backward. He stepped forward.

"You're going to die," he muttered between his teeth. "So is Kendall, damn brat, screaming and yelling. Lord knows I hate kids."

She took two steps backward. He took three steps forward.

Nature was waterlogged. Zoey reached the edge of the forest, where Miguel stood next to her, fearfully eyeing Simon's reptilian grin.

Simon's final footstep landed on lightning's striking zone. "Godforsaken biker gang robbed and killed you and your friends. Damn shame." He shook his head, elevated his gun, and with a long, echoing shriek, he disappeared.

Chapter 15

The earth had belched up a dozen bats. They flapped and squeaked as they faded into the gray horizon. Zoey stood at the edge of a gaping hole, looking down into pitch-black.

"Get me out of here," Simon said.

"Out of where?" Zoey asked, rubbing her arms for warmth.

"Out of this hellhole."

From below she heard a scraping noise and some rustling. A light flickered.

Zoey blinked and focused. Simon held a lighter and the tiny flame illuminated a tunnel of terror. Zoey wheezed. Skeletons peered out from underneath collapsed debris. Larger- and smaller-framed bones. If her eyes were truthful, some of their jaws were agape as if they'd died screaming. Distant voices overlapped—sobbing, wailing.

Zoey plugged her ears. The shrills and moans grew louder—children, women, men, begging and pleading. *No, senors, not my baby. Not the children.*

Momma, ahhh!

Not in front of my daughter.

Have mercy, senors, please have mercy.

Boom. Boom. Boom. Boom.

Oh no, my dear God.

Why?

Boom. Boom. Boom. Boom.

They're children, only babies.

Boom. Boom. Boom. Boom.

BOOM—

Zoey felt feeble. She wiped tears from her eyes. The distant cries evaporated. "You piece of shit. What happened down there?"

"I can't change the past. Now help me out of here before I file a negligence complaint."

"You, sir, are lying in a pit of evidence. Not to mention you shot an innocent man and kidnapped a child with no intention of letting her go. The devil will make love to you nightly, Simon."

He grumbled and winced, and tried to lift his head, but failed.

Zoey scanned the scene, the skeletons and rotted wooden beams, rusted shovels, picks and dusty hardhats. The fictitious mine was a reality, the men and their crimes unburied, a forgotten family, their labors and vulnerability, their children and raped dreams made relevant.

Simon gurgled. "Please, help me. My head, my leg." A splintered board had speared his abdomen near his hip and the wound gushed blood.

"What did you do with Miguel's remains?" she asked.

"Who?"

"The child you chopped into pieces, what did you do with him?"

"Miguel? How do you know his name?"

"I'm asking the questions. Where is he?"

"What stories are you concocting now? I don't know anything."

"If you don't spill your guts, Simon, I'll climb down there and spill them for you."

"I seem to remember a young boy, a spic, getting attacked by a bobcat."

"Bullshit!"

"That's how I remember it. He smelled bad, made us gag. We buried him in the woods. Now, please help me. I have a car nearby. Go and get my bodyguard."

"Never."

Zoey turned and, due to a sore ankle, hobbled up the hill. Two decent men lay unconscious in the wake of a monster. She stood next to Lance, whose pale skin and dehydrated lips warned her his time was short. She collapsed near his arm and nudged his body. "Hey, get up," she said. "We got him. Evil is alive and he's suffering and it's fantastic. Wake up."

A red blotch bloomed on his chest.

"Lance? Shit, you're bleeding." She hit his arm. "You're an asshole. Coming and going, coming and going! Why are you screwing with my mind?" She rose to her feet and cried in her palms, and then heard something slosh through the mushy grass. She lifted her head.

Lance's friend, Tank, towered over Zoey. He seemed from another planet. His slivered pupils dilated so often they seemed to breathe. With one arm, he held Kendall, who'd wept on his shoulder. He crouched and set the shaken girl on the ground.

"She's fine," he said, rising. "Some squirrely dipshit had her in a Lexus. He's hogtied in the trunk."

Kendall noticed her motionless father. "Daddy!" She ran to him, but Zoey grabbed her midway.

"We can't touch him, Kendall," Zoey said gently. "It's called tampering with evidence. Do you understand?"

She nodded.

"I'm sorry, honey."

"The police are on their way," Tank said.

"See, there," Zoey said, caressing Kendall's cheek. "An ambulance will be here any minute. Your father's going to be okay." She'd say anything to comfort the kid as she would have her own.

"Take her inside," Tank advised. "I'll look after Lance."

"If you get bored, the mastermind of this destruction is lying injured in an old mine." She pointed to the hole. "Feel free to piss on him."

Tank smiled.

Zoey took Kendall to the house and wrapped her in a blanket.

"I'm going upstairs to put on some dry clothes," she said to Kendall. "Will you be all right by yourself, or do you want to come with me?"

"I want to be alone. But hurry back, okay?" Kendall sniffled.

"Of course."

Zoey raced up to her bedroom, to the dresser. Sirens blared. She peeled off her wet garments and quickly opened a drawer. "Where were you, Luis? Why didn't you help me?"

No outside.

"You can't go outside?"

No.

"Why not?" she asked while slipping into a cotton blouse.

Silence.

"Miguel helped me."

My Miguel?

"Yes, Luis, he said turtle, and I knew to walk slowly. That's how I found the mine. We lured Simon onto the mine shaft and he fell through. He's still there, hopefully suffering."

Family.

"I'm sorry, Luis. Amos, Ross and Simon shot the others in the mine and then sealed the shaft. I saw their skeletons." She put on clean jeans. "I was standing on the mine when I was struck. My perspective is different. I don't feel targeted by the universe anymore. The mine attracted lightning.

I was in the right place at the right time, and now we have all the proof we need to convict Simon Rickert."

Where is my son?

Zoey took a deep breath and exhaled. "He's buried in the woods." She ponytailed her hair and put on shoes. "It's over, Luis. Maybe you all can find peace now."

You too.

"Yes, me too."

A multitude of car doors slammed outside.

"I've got to run, Luis." She paused and sneezed and sighed. "No rest for the…" She sneezed again. "Shit."

Zoey blew her nose and merged into the pandemonium outdoors. Police officers spread over the property like overgrown dandelions, and paramedics rushed to Kane and Lance. She reported the incident as best she could, omitting ghosts and clairaudience. Everyone had heard of her, the woman struck by lightning, and they listened closely, intrigued by how lightning had periodically hit the mine.

"Probably veins of metal," an officer said. "Iron or copper."

She agreed and continued with her statement. She mentioned the photos she'd discovered in her uncle's trunk, and how she'd questioned Kane and Simon. She'd had no idea Simon considered the pictures incriminating enough to hold a child hostage and commit murder. On Luis's behalf, she also lied, and said Simon had confessed to axing a child to death. She said amidst a heated argument Simon had slipped and told her he'd buried the boy's body in the woods.

At some point, Tank, who'd apparently checked on Simon, passed Zoey on his way to a patrol vehicle and muttered two facts that would alter the course of Zoey's life yet again.

"Simon was DOA. Roof caved in." He shrugged suspiciously, advanced a step and paused. "Oh, and your boyfriend's breathing. They're taking him to Monroe Memorial." His huge frame vanished in the chaos.

Yellow tape festooned the premises, and police confiscated the pictures and rifles while a forensic team investigated the mine. Later, Officer Honeycutt drove Zoey and Kendall to the police station, where she filled in as many blanks as she could remember.

"Kane Ballentine tried to kill me because he had no choice. Simon Rickert kidnapped his daughter as collateral in exchange for my death. Kane was desperate."

"Kane Ballentine is recovering," Detective Grady said. "I encourage you to press charges."

Kendall sat in a room to Zoey's right. She saw her through a window, swinging her legs and sniffling, waiting for a relative to pick her up and take her to see her dad.

"I would have done the same thing, and don't kid yourself, so would you," Zoey said. "I'm not pressing charges."

"You're a Good Samaritan, but I'm pretty sure Big Cat will have the final say on what happens to Mr. Ballentine."

"Kane has friends and money, and he'll get in the ring. As long as his daughter is safe and happy, he'll hire a high-dollar attorney and move on, which is exactly what I need to do. Are we finished?" She stood.

"For now," he said. "Just don't leave town." He reclined in his chair. "I'm sure I'll have more questions."

"I've been living a tourist's dream here, why would I leave?" She walked over to where Kendall waited and opened the door.

Kendall's eyes were vacant.

"You want company?"

Kendall nodded.

"Listen to me, Kendall, this is very important."

She stared at Zoey.

"Don't believe all the bull—nonsense you're hearing about your father. Everything he did, no matter how dumb, how dangerous, how weird, he did it for you. You understand?"

Kendall repeated her robotic nod.

"And don't be afraid." Zoey neared Kendall and stroked her head. "You and your dad will overcome this, and everything will be fine. You'll see, okay? Trust me."

"Are you mad at him?"

"No." Zoey coughed. "But I am sick, and I'd hate for you to catch it, so I'm going home and going to bed. If you have trouble sleeping, you can call me." Zoey took a pen from her purse and jotted down her cell number. "Would you like me to stay?"

"That won't be necessary," Detective Grady said from behind her. "Kane's cousin Helen is here."

Zoey offered a delicate goodbye and exited the station, escorted by an officer assigned to drive her home. She'd stepped onto the sidewalk, humid air wrapping around her like a damp shawl and stopped when Tank pulled up in a black GMC pickup.

He lowered the window. "They released me."

"Me too, but I can't leave town."

"Me either," he said. "Law enforcement is all over the place, but they'll fly straight soon as tomorrow. Forensics found bullet casings, hair, clothing fibers, and fingerprints. Those amateurs left everything down there."

"Bodies too."

"Bodies too, with teeth. Maybe the victims will be identified. Jump in. I'll drive you home."

Zoey let the officer know she'd be fine and hopped in the passenger side of Tank's truck. She slammed the door. The vehicle had a spacious cab, but Tank had made it roomier by removing the rear seats to suit his extraordinary size.

"I've been here all night. I couldn't get to the hospital."

"Lance's sister is with him. He's in ICU, and she said he's going to pull through."

"Were you able to obtain any information?"

"Some," he said. "Simon put a nine-millimeter bullet in Lance's chest, left side. I'm sure he meant to hit his heart. Lance would have been fine, but he was a bleeder. He went into shock."

"What about Kane?"

"Lance never intended to kill Kane. Dumb-nuts will be fit for trial."

In an exhausted state of quiet, they returned to Rayfield Ranch, and the ongoing commotion—uniforms, machinery, reporters, lights and police dogs—had them both groaning.

"Hotel?" Tank asked.

"That'd be great. Let me grab a few things."

A policeman blocked the news cameras and ushered her indoors. He waited for her outside on the deck, posing for the cameras.

"Luis?" she said, walking softly through the house. "It's truly over, my friend. By morning they'll have gathered enough evidence to close this case."

Miguel.

"I saw lights and machines in the woods. They'll find him."

Carmen.

"I don't know if they'll find her, Luis. She died in the river. Her spirit's there, but most likely her body washed away a long time ago."

Peace for Carmen.

"I think so. I wasn't at the river the first time she spoke to me. She wanders within a larger vicinity. Maybe a piece of her died with her son when she saw him getting murdered. She must know what's going on."

Silence.

"This is awful. I'm sorry for you and your family. If there were some way to change the past, I would. Fuck. You know I would."

I believe you.

"I'm going to a hotel tonight, but I'll be back when things settle down."

Silence.

"Luis?"

She strained to connect to the mystifying place where all spirits that'd once traveled the earth had a voice and a message. Inner tranquility—was it hers or his?

Zoey packed a duffle bag and made sure to include that one item she'd relied on for years to convey her depiction of the world. She smiled, and hurried out to the truck. She considered Tank a sight for sore everything. Kind and stable, she thought him a gigantic angel or compassionate extraterrestrial. Guys like him were rare. There was another man, though, genuinely unique. Her chest pained for his well-being.

* * * *

Monroe Memorial brought back memories of anger and darkness. As she walked stiffly toward the information desk, she bumped into Dr. Selden. After a brief chat about her session with Dr. Doyle and her frank refusal to see him again, she gladly showed Dr. Selden her healed shoulder.

"Amazing," he said. "When I was a boy, oh say, maybe ten or eleven, I heard a kitten crying in a tree. By golly, I went door to door asking for a ladder, and—"

"Dr. Selden," she interrupted, "no offense, but I'm here to see someone."

"I was going to tell you about how fast a knee injury healed. I was getting to it."

"Another time?"

"Right, sure. You had quite a circus at your place last night. Kane Ballentine?" He shook his head. "Not his nature to hurt anyone. Now, his father was another story."

"Yes. I know." She paused. "I'm here to check on a patient. Any chance you could pull strings and let me at least peek in on someone in ICU?"

"Who?" He squinted.

"Lance Malone. He was shot saving my life."

"He's a friend of yours?"

"A very good friend."

"I don't see why not," he said. "Sure, it's prohibited, but I've been a doctor for five decades, and if there's one thing I've learned about medicine, it's that it's not enough. There are several components to healing. Perhaps if he sees or hears you and learns you're okay, it'll give him incentive. Let's take a look." Dr. Selden brought her to floor seven, and reached behind the nurses' station. "Put this on." He handed her a white mask for her nose and mouth.

She followed his instructions, and traced his steps to Lance's room.

Dr. Selden patted her forearm. "Don't stay long. He needs his rest."

"Okay."

Dr. Selden glided back to the nurses' station with the mojo of a gossipy old woman. He knew an insider related to the juiciest secrets ever revealed in Big Cat. She eavesdropped a moment and heard, "That's Zoey Hawthorne, the woman who was struck by lightning. Remember, The Bride?"

She hardly remembered that part of herself. Zoey cracked open the door and slid into the room, devastated by the tubes and wires sprouting from his body. His black hair lay feathery against his pillow, and at least he wasn't corpselike. His caramel coloring had returned, and his exquisiteness remained radiant.

She stared at him, admitting something had happened as brilliant and unexplainable as the Milky Way, and for that matter, her confrontation with lightning. When he recovered she'd tell him she wanted to let their relationship get messy—dangerously messy, friends and lovers and whatever else, freefall. Definitely she would tell him. She looked forward to purchasing a motorcycle too, and learning to ride.

Her cellphone rang. She observed the name and answered. "Sterling?"

"Don't 'Sterling' me. I haven't slept a wink. I had dreams you were shot and added to a pile of bones."

"FYI, I didn't get shot, but eye-candy did. And so did my neighbor, Kane Ballentine. And Simon, the man who killed the boy wandering in the woods, is dead."

"What? And why do you sound muzzled? You'd better start talking, Zoey, or I'm hopping a plane."

"Chill out. I'm visiting Lance. I have a mask on. And don't bother coming here, I'm coming home. Clear your calendar because I have so much to ask you about clairaudience and psychic phenomena in general."

"That's wonderful. I'm glad you've come to terms with your gift."

"I wouldn't say that. I'm curious."

"Fabulous."

"Are you and Mitch communicating?"

"Yes," Sterling sighed. "We're ironing out some kinks, and I think we'll eventually come to an understanding."

"You think, or you know?" Zoey shifted her weight.

"I'm afraid I'm as blind as everyone else when it comes to love."

"Stop worrying about me and focus on your man. I'm safe, and the ghosts of Rayfield Ranch are at peace. I'll explain everything in detail when I get there."

"When are you coming?"

"As soon as the police allow me to leave town."

"What?"

"It's all right, Sterling. Really. I'll fill you in later." She lifted the mask slightly, took a breath and let it snap back in place.

"I'll be pacing until I hear from you again."

"We'll talk soon, okay?"

"Your soon could be weeks."

"Sooner than that, I promise." Zoey hung up and dialed Mitch.

"Zoey?" he answered. "I'm watching CNN. I'm on my way."

"No, no, I'm fine. In fact, I'm coming to Chicago."

"When?"

"As soon as the police let me go."

"I'm on my way."

"No, Mitch, I can handle this. It's okay. It's just, people died and were injured and a little girl was kidnapped and rescued and we discovered an old gold mine, but I have it under control."

Mitch laughed. "I see. Remind me to take cover the next time you're in control."

"I'll explain everything. Anyway, I'm ready to clean out the house. If you don't oppose, I'd like to donate all of Milo's toys and clothes to charity. I'm ready to sell the place and move on." Despite the grasshoppers with spiked legs jumping in her stomach, she knew Milo would be pleased with her decision.

"Are you high?"

"No. I'm exhausted but sober."

"I'm proud of you."

She talked softly, so as not to disturb Lance. "Don't give me too much credit. I'm edgy, and angry. I'm hoping it'll get easier."

"It will. You moving forward is the best thing you've done for yourself in a long time. You're brave."

"No, I'm terrified, but it's time. I'm thinking of coming back to Colorado, though."

"To the ranch?"

"No. That place is unlivable. It's a cemetery. I'm having the house leveled and converting the land into a wildlife sanctuary." She nodded.

"Nice."

"Yeah, it's something my ex-husband would have done."

"I'm blushing," he said. "What about the truck?"

"Tell you what?" She stared at Lance's perfect eyebrows. "Anything belonging to Amos is tainted. He was a sick individual. I'd like to scrap his truck, and since I've got a few bucks to spare, I'll buy your employee a car."

"Who are you?"

"I don't know. I'm still experimenting."

"Okay, well, if you're demolishing the ranch, where will you live?"

She scrunched her nose, uneasy about telling him. "I'm thinking Denver, for a while at least."

Dr. Selden popped his head in and pointed to his watch.

Zoey covered the mouthpiece. "I'll be out in a minute."

The thoughtful doctor left.

"Listen, Mitch. I have to go. I'll call you later."

"Be careful."

"I'll try." She hung up, reached in her bag and extracted her 35mm. Her blood seemed to thicken and her imagination outlined angles, lighting and composition. She looked through the viewfinder and instinctively waited.

Afternoon sun bounced off a silver water pitcher and reflected onto her lover's closed eyelids.

Slowly, his eyes opened and a small bright square sparkled within the grain of his indigo irises. Vitality! She snapped the photo, and knew that click would be the beginning of many more.

Satisfied, she hung her camera around her neck and approached his bedside. "You are badass. I don't even think you're human."

He held his thumb up.

She leaned over. "I'd kiss you, but I'm ill." She softly touched his swollen lips. "Thank you. I am so going to fuck your brains out when you're well."

He held two thumbs up.

"I have to go, but I'll be back, and Tank is nearby too. So is your sister."

Lance closed his obviously tired eyes, and Zoey tiptoed out of the room. She bumped into a gorgeous younger woman with short black hair and indigo eyes. Zoey lowered her mask.

The young woman said, "Zoey?"

"Yes." Zoey thought for a moment and it dawned on her. "Lance's sister…"

"Marie." She smiled and they shook.

"I'm sorry about your brother. If I had known he was going to play Rambo, I would have stopped him."

Marie rolled her eyes. "Good luck with that. Lance does what he wants."

"Still, I'm sorry."

"It's no secret," she said. "He would have died for you. You must mean a lot to him or he'd have been on his bike heading home."

"I'm not sure that's the case," Zoey said, high as the moon. "He's a good man. He would have done the same thing for anyone."

"Not my brother. He'd have only put his life on the line for someone he loved. And I can promise you, if you're in Lance's heart, you're in excellent company. Tank and I are there too," Marie said with a demure smile. "I better get back inside. Maybe we can meet for coffee later?"

"I'd like that."

Marie added Zoey's number to her directory. "I'll call you in a few hours."

"Great. I look forward to it. Hey," Zoey added. "He opened his eyes. Only a few seconds but I saw a lust for life. He's going to be okay. I feel it."

Marie leaned forward and hugged Zoey. "I'm glad you came. He needed to see you." She let go and hurried into Lance's room.

Zoey reflected on what Marie had said. Could it be possible? Lance loved her too. What an adventure ahead, new discoveries to be made, especially within herself. She smiled and walked down the hall toward the elevator, quietly making plans for lunch. Maybe she'd drive up the mountain and touch base with Ace and Delilah, and have one of those amazing omelets. She had to admit, as much contentment as helping Luis and his family had brought her, she was happy to get on with normal, silent days.

Right before that thought streamed into another, she passed a room riddled with doctors and nurses frantically needling in and out. Someone yelled, "Flatline!"

Zoey shook her head, understanding the depth of loss.

He killed me.

Zoey froze.

He will kill again.

She inspected the commotion, and within the madness spotted a male nurse furtively leering at the bustling doctors.

She had a sense the murderous nurse wanted to show the world his definition of power. Her stomach flipped. She stuck her hand in her purse and dug around for her cellphone. She removed it and stared at the gadget, doubting her initial idea. Fuck it. She pressed a familiar contact.

"Hello?"

"Sterling, it's me again."

"Yes."

Zoey moved from the center of the corridor and backed against the wall. "I'm wondering if you can take vacation time."

"I'm self-employed. I decide. Why?"

"Something came up, and I think I'm going to need your help."

Doctors and staff zoomed back and forth.

"*Something?* What is it, Zoey?"

"I'm at Monroe Memorial hospital visiting Lance." She bent her knee, resting the bottom of her shoe on the wall.

"That's right. And…"

"And as I'm on my way to the elevator, a patient dies."

"Why is my skin crawling?"

She straightened her leg and started walking. "Because I'm being told the murderer will kill again."

"Murderer? So you're hearing the victim?"

"Yes, and I believe the killer is an employee. A psychopathic nurse."

"What on earth would we do?"

"We'll follow him. He's bound to screw up. We have an advantage. We're psychic. We'll be a step in front or crowding him from behind."

The lens cap dangled from Zoey's camera, and she stopped to twist it back on.

"Mitch and I are just beginning to repair our relationship."

"Mitch isn't going anywhere. He's not a nitwit. Not always. He knows how lucky he is to have you."

"He'll hate me." Sterling's feline mewed in the background.

"He won't. Come on, it's for a noble cause."

"Why am I contemplating this?"

"Why wouldn't you? You have a gift, and it could save lives."

"We're not detectives, Zoey."

"No, we're badass supernatural females. Do you really think we should waste this shit on guessing colors and cheating in Vegas?" She paused. "Are you coming?"

"I'll call the cat-sitter."

"Is that a yes?" Zoey held her breath.

"Yes. I'll catch a flight out tomorrow."

"See you soon, then." Zoey shut her phone and exhaled. "What an idiot." She gently smacked her forehead. "What the hell am I doing?"

Thank you.

As she continued through the hall toward the elevator, she smiled, knowing exactly what she was doing. For the first time in a long time, she felt whole again. She loved deeply, and intended to live fully. She wanted to listen, truly listen, not just to the voices across the veil, but to her lover, family and friends, to her inner self. This time around she'd take better care of her health. No drugs, less booze—well, maybe not, but for sure she'd keep her blood sugar regulated. Almonds were tasty. At least they used to be.

The elevator opened and a woman stinking of inexpensive perfume knocked into Zoey's shoulder when she exited. She glanced at Zoey as if she expected an apology.

"I'm giving you a count of five to do one of two things," Zoey said. "Say you're sorry, or run."

The woman jerked her head back. "What are you, crazy? I'm sorry."

"You're forgiven." Zoey turned abruptly and entered the elevator. She giggled and pressed the Lobby button and got smacked with a wave of guilt. "Shit. I could have handled that differently. What can I say?" She looked up at the ceiling appealing to principled spirits. "I'm not perfect."

Truer words have never been spoken.

"Seriously? Countless ghosts and I get a smartass?"

What shall I do? Run?

As the elevator doors closed, she wondered if every floor of the hospital heard her laughing.

She waltzed to her car, renewed. She had everything she needed—her health, her heart, a purpose and a vigorous funny bone. Bring it, world, bring it!

Meet the Author

Lorelei Buckley is best known for writing romance novels, but she's penned works in almost every genre. When she's not glued to her laptop, she's assisting a stray animal or helping injured wildlife. To date she's a full-time writer residing in Texas with her husband, two dogs, and six handfuls otherwise known as cats.

Lorelei's Website:
www.loreleibuckley.com
Reader eMail:
lbhhp@aol.com

www.ingramcontent.com/pod-product-compliance
Lightning Source LLC
Chambersburg PA
CBHW031422250626
47155CB00004B/1591